THE MOON TURNS TO BLOOD

LEONA FOXX SUSPENSE THRILLER #3

TED PETERS

APOCRYPHILE
PRESS

Apocryphile Press
1700 Shattuck Ave. #81
Berkeley, CA 94709

THANX

In our California home I live with Leona, a black cat that looks like Midnight; Angie, a Norfolk Terrier mix whose daily delight is a walk around the lagoon; and Karen, who reminds me of Leona's mother in this series of espionage thrillers. All three are inspirations. But Karen deserves special thanks. She reads, scrutinizes, edits, and enhances every chapter. Such freely offered grace in this life is neither earned nor deserved. One can only respond with gratitude.

The Sun shall be turned into darkness,
and the Moon into blood,
before the great and the terrible day of the LORD comes.
— Joel 2:31

CHAPTER 1

THE SUN in the eastern morning sky glistened off the Queen Ann's Lace, Black-Eyed Susans, and Tiger Lilies beyond the drainage ditch beside the Diamond Point Road. Leona's light green sweat band was darkened with dampness. So also, sweat marked her well-worn and now-faded Michigan State T-shirt with a long narrow triangle between her shoulders. Her auburn ponytail rhythmically swayed back and forth with each stride. The stately jogger had reached the Northway, I-87, and was now returning from what would be an eight-plus mile jog.

Leona's strides lengthened as she launched into the final and downhill leg of her Monday morning run. Leona passed the decrepit house where Gretchen Schmidt once lived. Frau Schmidt had been a teenage immigrant from Germany prior to the outbreak of the Second World War and spoke with an exotic continental accent. For decades her garden furnished flowers for weekly worship at the Saint John's Community Church. Gretchen died at the age of a hundred and one. It appeared to Leona that her surviving family let the house go to ruin. Even so, there was something nostalgic and comforting about passing it on her morning run.

As Leona jogged downhill for the final stretch of her run, she passed the U.S. Post Office on her left. Her heart rate jumped as her eyes caught site of gyrating lights. Red. Blue. Rapid. Bright. A posse of cars from the State Police and the Warren County Sheriff's Office were randomly parked, doors wide open, covering the church lawn.

The church rested at the bottom of the hill where Diamond Point Road ends at Lake Shore Drive, identified on the typical GPS as Route 9N. Lake Shore Drive parallels the west coast of Lake George, a thirty-mile ribbon of deep pure water lying between Albany and Montreal. Built of local gray and tan sandstone and roofed with Vermont slate in 1876, the quaint Saint John's chapel was now sitting in the eye of a hurricane of human activity.

Bypassing the parsonage, Leona's pace turned from a jog to a full run. She headed straight for the sacristy door and entered through the rear of the church. Uniformed police and a fire rescue team were huddled and conferring in the front section of the sanctuary. They looked up when the shapely jogger presumptuously approached the conference. "May I ask what's going on here?" she asked in a demanding tone.

"And who might you be?" responded a scrawny highway patrolman, somewhat too small for the size of his uniform.

"I'm the pastor of this church," she said, exuding a sense of proprietorship. Leona moved her sunglasses from her eyes to the top of her head.

"You?! The pastor?!" gasped a fireman. The public servant spoke while eyeing the clergywoman's shapely legs.

"Yes. And I'd like to know why you are here and what you're doing."

The fireman nodded toward the chancel. Leona turned her gaze. The scene on the altar assaulted her eyes with an uncanny and gruesome sight. Beneath a blood-spattered brass cross and red splotched open Bible laid the partially dismembered corpse of a young child. Perhaps two years old. Leona was suddenly viewing a diorama of horror.

CHAPTER 2

"PLEASE DON'T DISTURB or even touch any evidence, Reverend," the highway patrolman ordered.

Leona approached the altar slowly and deliberately, as if it hosted the sacrament itself. Despite the inner revulsion and temptation to turn away, Leona silently forced herself to scan the altar and its surroundings. The brass cross rested in its usual place, now upside down. The altar Bible had been opened. Leona closely examined the Bible and noticed it was opened to a passage in the ancient Hebrew portion. The visible pages included a smudge, a finger smudge in blood next to a text not unfamiliar to this worship leader. The prophet Joel was announcing that "the moon will turn to blood."

Leona's gaze shifted to the small child lying nearby, scrutinizing every inch of the tiny, innocent body. The child's eyes were wide open. The frozen facial expression preserved the terror and pain of its last breathing moment. Despite the admonition not to touch, the pastor tenderly wiped her hand across the child's brow, closing the two eyes with her fingers. The milky white skin was soft, tepid. Rigor mortise was just beginning. The untimely death could have been only a few hours previous.

One arm hung listlessly over the front edge of the altar. The chest had been sliced open by two knife swipes, one horizontal and the other vertical, issuing immediately in a surge of blood shaped like that of a cross. The now empty chest cavity revealed something missing. Something essential to the being of the innocent child. Something without which none of us can be who we are in life.

Leona studied the revolting remainder of a once living and precious human being. She could see that blood drowned the genital region. A closer looked proved what she had suspected. The child was female.

For what appeared to the watching fireman to be only a second, yet to Leona felt like eternity, she froze. Leona's mind was suddenly in another time and another place. In her thought theater she watched a repeat performance: the death of another innocent young woman many years prior, in what often seemed another lifetime. That prior atrocity had occurred in an Iranian prison. It was political. Not religious. But political torture and ritual murder produce the same result: death to the innocent. Such gruesome acts live forever in her memory. Leona thawed. She warmed to the present moment.

The pastor's eyes fixed on the stained-glass window rising above the altar and behind it. She re-read words she'd seen many times. "Peace through the blood of the cross in hope of eternal life." Leona lifted up a silent prayer. "Father, into your hands I commend the spirit of this innocent child."

Before she could whisper amen, a sheriff's deputy interrupted her. "What can you tell us about this, Pastor?"

Leona turned to face her interlocutor. "Nothing. Nothing at all." She turned back to look at the altar, and then back once again at the officer.

"This is your church, isn't it?"

"Why, yes," she responded slowly.

"Now, I didn't get your name. You're Pastor...?"

"Pastor Leona Foxx. Lee Foxx. I live in the parsonage across the lawn in back of the church. When did this all happen? I slept here all night. I heard nothing."

"That's just what I was going to ask you," said the deputy. "Are you certain you saw or heard nothing unusual?"

"Yes. I just said that."

"Did you schedule any meetings here in the church for last evening? Church council meeting? Altar guild? Boy Scouts? Or, maybe the youth fellowship?"

"No. Nothing was scheduled." Leona then addressed the group. "How did you discover this macabre scene?"

"We received a call," said the state policeman.

Leona slowly walked past the circle of uniforms and sat in the front pew. It would be a long discussion. She would begin by answering questions put to her. But, she could anticipate that she would eventually be the one with the most questions. Among other things, she would want to know whose finger print left the blood smudge on Joel 2:31-32?

CHAPTER 3

"AND JUST WHO MIGHT YOU BE?" The Highway Patrolman was asking a stately woman who had just entered the church from the front door. The new arrival, perhaps sixty, blond hair woven with slim streaks of gray, had shock written all over her face. "My name is Brenda Beale, Officer. I'm the president of this congregation. Pastor Lee just texted me about an emergency and I came rushing over here."

Leona stood and hugged Brenda without saying a word. Leona then sat down in the front pew while the patrolman guided Brenda to the gruesome scene in the chancel. Brenda's shock turned to revulsion, to disbelief.

After studying the horror for a few minutes, Brenda turned and walked toward her pastor. Without words her face spoke: what is this all about?

Brenda sat down to Leona's right and the two women interlocked their fingers. The patrolman, with cell phone in hand for note taking, restarted the interrogation.

CHAPTER 4

AFTER AN EXHAUSTING DAY OF INTERROGATIONS, investigations, and irritations, Brenda departed for home. Leona then left the little stone church through the back door. Evening had fallen and the bubble tops were no longer flashing. The sirens had long stopped screaming. *Thank God,* she muttered, relieved. She was sure that the police investigative unit would loiter in the sanctuary for longer than she could bear. Leona thought to herself, *there is something about gruesome events that capture morbid attention. I just need to get away.*

The pastor took large strides across the back yard towards the parsonage, toward her haven of peace and refuge. This manse was the one place where Leona could retreat from the world of pressures and problems and find solace. But on this day, as she unlocked the side door and stepped into the fireplace room, she felt a curious chill, as if the warmth and energy had been sucked from the floorboards and walls.

For an ominous moment, Leona stood silent and stiff, as if in doing so she could detect something out of the ordinary. Could that fearsome event just yards away contaminate her own home and personal sanctuary? Can evil travel like an oil spill, profaning and polluting as it radiates from its source?

She heard nothing. Scanning the room, she saw nothing out of place. It looked just as she had left it. Or so she thought. As is her frequent habit, Leona spoke silently to God in prayer. *Oh, God...please stand with me. Please help me see what is real and not let my fear run away with me. I have been through so much, and you have always led me to where I needed to go. Don't desert me. Please. Amen.*

Leona, frightened yet alert, took two deep intentional breaths that filled her lungs all the way down to her gut. She slowly exhaled while repeating *stand with me. Stand with me.* This exercise had always centered her, clarifying her thoughts. It almost worked this time, but the fear lingered in the pit of her stomach, lessened somewhat by two more deep breaths.

Taking short, quiet steps, Leona moved cautiously into the kitchen to find Midnight on the table nestled against a ripening cantaloupe. Any other day, Leona would have scolded her black cat for bedding down on the tabletop and abruptly shooed her away. This evening Midnight's calm demeanor indicated that everything must be okay. Like a canary in a coal mine, Midnight's calm demeanor signaled safety. Leona gently rubbed the top of the cat's head while Midnight partially stretched and returned immediately to her nap.

"Oh, no! Buck! Buck, where are you?" Leona was so consumed by the moment, she hadn't realized that Buck, her fully mature Siberian husky, had not run up to greet her. "Buck! Buck!" she shouted with increasing volume and anxiety in her voice. Leona rushed to the rear laundry room to discover the screen door slightly ajar.

"Oh, Buck, for the sake of Carbondale, where are you? What frightened you?"

She opened the door and surveyed the side yard. The dimming light made it difficult to make out any detail. There was no rustle of leaves or any indication that Buck was attempting to camouflage himself in the deep foliage at the ridge overlooking Smith Creek. All was dead silent.

Leona returned to the house puzzled, worried, distraught, and anxious. She sat down at the table feeling as if lead was pulling down her every limb. She knew that sometimes Buck would take off on his own adventures, chasing a squirrel or a neighbor's cat, and returning when he was good and ready. But this had to be different. Buck's keen ability to sense danger was his protection. And her protection as well. She knew driving around to try to find him would be fruitless, so she said another prayer for his safety and return.

THE LAST THING that Leona could think about was eating, even though the day was moving through the stages of twilight. *I wonder if I will ever be able to eat again?* Leona grabbed a half-consumed bottle of Alexander Valley Redemption Zin left over from a previous evening, and poured herself a glass. The same winery also offered Sin Zin, but the Redemption Zin not only tasted better, it also fit her sense of vocation.

She sipped carefully, took another couple of deep breaths, and knew she had to examine the entire house to assure herself there was no one or nothing lingering.

With glass in hand, Leona reached under the old 1950's aluminum-framed kitchen table where she had taped her Glock 19. The habit of keeping a gun close was in one way repugnant to her as a pastor who was striving to make the world more peaceful and loving. At the same time, she had to steward the reality that her life as a former CIA operative would never be totally erased, and what she knew and carried in her memory could at any time be the bargaining chip with her now distant Uncle Sam. Though she'd never consider taking out membership in the N.R.A., Leona was grateful for firearm protection.

Leona anxiously loosened the gun from its lodging, setting the wine glass aside only long enough to load her Glock 19. She sipped again and began to navigate her way through the house, turning on every light as she slid against the walls, her Glock tucked tightly behind her back.

CHAPTER 5

THE CORNERSTONE of the manse was placed not on the corner but rather above the front door. It memorialized its construction: "Erected in A.D. 1894 in Memory of John C. Cramer by his Sister, Mrs. J.K. Porter." Living in the parsonage was like living in the nineteenth century, the century of Edgar Allen Poe.

Every turn through the old Victorian, from the deep closet next to the kitchen, to the living room, to the long steep stairway triggered in Leona a startling charge of fear that was quickly followed by assessment and a repeatable phrase: *Oh, it's nothing*.

By the time Leona reached the top of the landing on the second floor, she was surprisingly calm and convinced there was no one hiding in the shadows. She quickly moved through bedrooms and closets to find everything in order.

Having persuaded herself that neither prowlers nor ghosts were hiding on the second story, Leona prepared to end her evening. Her concentration was broken by the shrill sound of the upstairs parsonage phone ringing. "Saint John's Community Church," she answered.

"Pastor Leona Foxx, please," said the male voice.

"This is Pastor Lee."

"This is Father Stephen Korsky at St. Cyprian's Orthodox Church in Saratoga. I've heard what happened today at your church. I'm simply aghast. If there's anything I can do, please let me know."

"Oh for the sake of Capernaum!" Leona exclaimed. "News certainly travels fast. Thank you so much for your concern. I'm so bewildered right now, I just don't know yet how to think. I'll let you know."

"I could come by your parish Wednesday, Pastor Lee. I know something about these things. Afternoon okay?"

"Yes, afternoon will be okay."

Leona accepted the offer of a visit with a voice that was weak and tired, as if confirming an appointment previously scheduled. She gave no thought to either accepting or rejecting the offer. She was simply tired.

After the phone conversation had ended, Leona forced herself to call up the last of her reserve energy to send herself an email with notes regarding the day, facts she might like to retrieve at a later date.

BETTER CALL ANGIE, she said to herself. Leona hit speed dial on her mobile, and in a moment her high school BFF living in Michigan was on the phone listening to a report of the incomprehensible events taking place in Diamond Point.

"Oh, I can't even imagine such a thing! How are you holding up? I know you are one tough cookie, but this is over the top. Are you alone? Do you really think you are safe?" Angie shot off questions like a repeating rifle.

"And what about the animals? I know you love those critters. How are the animals reacting?" Anxiety was building in Angie's voice.

Leona responded. "Midnight seems oblivious. She's a cat, after all, and a black cat. You'd think she'd show more interest, but no. All she is interested in is her nap and her food. I do think if she sensed danger she would act differently. So that assures me a little bit, anyway."

"Well, dear friend, you seem to have a different barometer for measuring danger than the rest of us. I hope the cat understands that. I hope you are not underestimating the danger you could be in." Angie replied with a gentle admonition. Angie knew that Leona could not be talked into doing or not doing what she didn't want to do or not do.

"Buck has disappeared, Leona added. "I'm dreadfully worried about him. It is not like him. He sleeps with me and I see him as my protector."

"I don't think you should be alone, Lee."

"I'm not alone. I've got Midnight and Buck. Well, at least Midnight."

"You know what I mean. Why don't you ask that hot guy, Graham, to come to Diamond Point and cradle you sympathetically in his strong arms? Appeal to his instinct to protect a damsel in distress. Be a damsel in distress for a change."

"I knew I could count on you for saying just the right thing," Leona exclaimed. "It's easy for me to neglect the residuals of primordial feminity still within me."

Angie and Leona laughed in unison, with the kind of familiarity and understanding only two long-time friends could have.

Angie's last thoughts on the conversation were a hope that she might have provided Leona with some good girlfriend advice.

"Bye," the two said in unison. "Talk soon."

These two had known each other since grade school and had been through so much together. It was Angie who was by her bedside when she returned from the Iranian prison. Along with Leona's mother, Karen, they kept vigil through her long recovery. It was these women who were there through her PTSD, through her therapy, and through her ultimate decision to go to seminary. Leona is godmother to Angie's first-born daughter, and the one who baptized her into God's kingdom.

Bonds like ours are hard to come by.

After finishing the call, Leona's appetite returned. Talking to Angie always helped her ground herself and make her feel more normal. She ferried a second glass of Zin along with the leftover half of a tuna-on-rye sandwich up to the master bedroom.

Leona rearranged her night stand so that the food would be handy while reading in bed. Then she moved her loaded Glock to the dresser. Her eyes fixed on the pinkish label fronting her *eau de toilette spray-vaporisateur*. One fragrant squirt was applied to each wrist. As was her habit, she read aloud the brand label: "Amazing Grace." She also read the fine print aloud: "Philosophy: In the end, it all comes down to one word—grace." She sighed.

Once in bed, the comfort food along with a couple chapters from a J.R. Mabry urban fantasy novel helped her wind down.

Forest crickets provided natural mood music. The gentle circadian rhythms were disrupted every quarter hour or so by a motorcycle downshifting on Lake Shore Drive, turning the corner, and revving up as it sped west on Diamond Point Road. The abruptness of the noise prevented Leona from dozing off.

By the time she'd finished nibbling, reading, and involuntarily counting motorcycles, it was nearing midnight. The Sand Man finished closing Leona's eyes as well as those of Midnight, now curled and sleeping at the bed's foot.

Leona's last thoughts were of Buck and where he might be and why he was gone. She fell asleep with a tear slowly running down her cheek.

CHAPTER 6

SHORTLY AFTER TWO AM, Leona was jolted from a deep, headaching sleep. She bolted upright, her heart pounding and her mouth dry. Her breathing, short and deep, made her dizzy and confused. The wine and terror of the previous night left her groggy. *What was that noise? Was it a noise at all? Yes, that was a noise!*

Leona dropped her chin, sucked in as much air as her lungs might hold, and leaped from the bed, grabbing the Kimber Super Match II .45 with a sound suppressor that she had tucked under her pillow. She left the Glock sitting on the dresser, where she'd placed it earlier.

Maybe the evil ones are here to finish what they started, she thought. Midnight, still curled up at the end of the bed, seemed unconcerned. *Some canary in a coal mine you'd make!*

Leona slowly made her way down the steep set of creaking wooden stairs, holding on to the rail with her right hand to keep herself steady, stopping every two or three steps to listen. Her left hand held the Kimber upright at shoulder height and close to her body, ready to aim when necessary. The same muffled sounds. *Kitchen? Backdoor?* She made her way to the bottom, turned down the hallway, through the well-lit kitchen, and peered out the back-door window.

"Buckie! Oh, thank God! Buck!"

Leona rushed to let her beloved husky in. He jumped up with one paw on each of Leona's shoulders and gave her a full-tongue lick on the cheek, letting her know he was as happy to see her as she was to see him. He returned to all fours as Leona scratched his back, his head, and his ear.

"Where have you been, you great watchdog? I have been so worried about you? Do you have any idea how empty this house is without you?"

Almost as if Buck knew what she said, he nervously whimpered and darted into the dining room, stopped suddenly, and took a few short steps backwards, continuing to whimper.

"What is it, boy?"

Buck's usual confident, canine bearing seemed to have left him. Leona knew he was trying to tell her something. Everything looked fine to her, just as it had when she first arrived back at the parsonage last evening. *So what is Buck trying to say to me?*

Then, she noticed. Three sacramental artifacts—a communion cup, a wine flagon, and a bread paten— were sitting just where she had carefully placed them on the antique curio shelf. Except, something was not in order. They were upside down.

CHAPTER 7

"J. Holmes Chapman" was written on the sign above an office door near Lincoln Center. A well-attired man nearing forty, wearing a single-breasted black suit, Armani white shirt, and paisley necktie, entered.

"May I help you?" asked the receptionist with unusual friendliness. A slender young woman, perhaps in her early twenties, brown hair in a bun, with brown-rimmed glasses, sat up alertly to greet the office guest.

"Do you plan on singing Mimi in La Boheme some day?" he asked.

Like melting candle wax, her taut body immediately turned supple. "Yes, I want to sing on stage someday. But today, it's earn-the-rent-money day by sitting behind the computer and answering the phone."

"Mr. Chapman has a one-fifteen appointment. I'm here a bit early. I hope this quarter hour won't make a difference," said the visitor apologetically.

"Oh, no. Mr. Chapman is expecting you. Please feel welcome."

The aspiring soprano stood, opened the inner office door, and spoke. "He's here, Mr. Chapman."

J. Holmes Chapman stood from behind his desk to receive his guest, whom he immediately bade sit down. "I'm so glad you could come."

"Well, I am a tad early."

"Oh, that's okay. No problem. I'm simply grateful you could come on such short notice. It was only yesterday that I phoned St. Peter's Church."

He reached across the desk and the two shook hands.

"Well, Pastor," Chapman began. "My matter is quite serious. It's spiritual, but it's also legal, political, and dangerous. I desperately need counsel. It's such a relief to have you here."

"Because of the message you left at St. Peter's Church," said the visitor, "I've taken the liberty to investigate options in advance. What I would like to do is recommend that you visit someone who is particularly well prepared to deal with your type of concern."

With this, the visitor laid a small piece of paper on Chapman's desk. The written message was brief: "Wishing Tree. Lake George Village."

Chapman picked it up and looked inquiringly at his guest.

"I believe this is all I have to say for the moment," said the visitor. "I'm confident you will get what you most deeply want in Lake George Village." He paused, then asked, "Is there a back way out of this building?"

"Yes, of course," said Chapman, while staring at this mysterious note. "I'll walk you down the stairs. I've got a couple more questions. We'll exit by this door, not the one you came in." In a moment, the inner office was empty.

In the outer office, however, the receptionist was welcoming another guest.

"I'm here for our one-fifteen appointment," said a well-dressed man of about forty. He wore a black suit with a black shirt and clerical collar. "I'm Pastor Leonard Hicks from St. Peter's Church in the CitiCorp Building, 54th at Lexington. I believe Mr. Chapman is expecting me."

CHAPTER 8

THE PARSONAGE PHONE rang in a phone closet adjacent to the
dining room. For some reason never explained, some resident in a
previous generation converted a closet to a telephone booth complete
with a door to ensure privacy.

"Saint John's Community Church, Pastor Leona Foxx speaking."

"Lee, this is Daren Richardson. Perhaps you know me. I'm the
priest at St. Cuthbert's Episcopal Church in Bolton Landing. So
sorry to hear about this sacrilege of your altar. You must be
distressed!"

"I really am, Daren. Thanks so much for your concern. As of this
point, I am not even able to grasp what's going on."

"If there's any way...."

"Yes, of course..."

Immediately upon hanging up the parsonage phone, Leona's cell
phone sounded. Brenda spoke hurriedly. "Oh, Pastor Lee, I just don't
know what to think. I couldn't sleep at all last night."

"Well, Brenda, it was a bad night for me too. But Buck, who had
been missing, returned. Thank God. But Buck was traumatized by
something that happened."

Leona had seated herself comfortably on the divan in the living room to continue the conversation. Midnight spotted the open lap and made a move to settle there, oblivious that time and eternity had just become linked by uncanny malevolence.

"Pastor, I just don't understand all this," Brenda went on. "Not only is the death of that poor little girl unsettling and unnecessary, I find it so confusing. Why in our church? Just what does all this mean?"

"I don't know yet. But, believe me, Brenda, I will find out. Please know that you can call me any time. You can come over any time. We're going to get through this, I'm confident." Leona's hand trembled as she hit the off button.

Moments later, while Midnight the black cat was lying peacefully on Leona's lap, the pastor hit the speed dial on her cell phone. Waiting for the connection, her eyes surveyed the very familiar parlor. The parsonage had been fully decorated and furnished when she accepted this parish call. Fully furnished was fine with her. One less thing to worry about.

The patriotic wallpaper reminded her of World War One: three inch wide ribbons from ceiling to floor enclosing a series of one inch Liberty Bells alternating with the American eagle, wings spread, with a red, white, and blue shield covering the eagle's tummy. In the northwest corner a flat black wrought iron fireplace was topped with a dog-legged stove pipe for venting smoke. In the center of the north wall hung a faded tapestry of the nativity scene complete with Baby Jesus, Mary and Joseph, along with one cow and one horse. *What happened to the sheep? Every manger scene has sheep.* She smiled to herself.

Leona's eyes returned to the cell phone when she heard a "hello."

"Grammy? Is that you?" she hollered.

"Lee! How delightful!" exclaimed Graham Washington. "How are Midnight and Buck?"

"Oh, Graham, thanks so much for picking up. Never mind about cats and dogs. Something horrifying and inexplicable has happened here at the church. I need you to help me think this through."

"Yes, of course," he offered.

Leona proceeded to tell Graham about the body of the sacrificed child with most of the gruesome details. Leona needed to tell the story, as if by sharing it, she would not have to hold it all inside where it festered and gnawed at her psyche.

They both remained silent for a few seconds.

"It happened again, Graham. The flashback. While I was examining the body of that ravished little girl, I could not keep from returning to prison in Iran. There I was again. The body of the innocent Ariana with her severed head at her feet. I could see it in every bloody detail. It's as if I live in two times and two places at once. It terrifies me. In fact, life terrifies me. No. It's death—actually, innocent death—that terrifies me."

Graham said nothing. Leona paused. Silence. Then, Leona re-engaged. "I think I'd like to name that little girl. Without a name she lacks dignity. I will nickname her Sarai. That's pronounced like 'sorry'. It means *Princess*. That was Sarah's name in Genesis before God commissioned her to become a blessing to nations. That's it! I want to think of her as God's princess. This little girl will be Sarai until I learn her real name."

Graham did not respond. He paused to allow Leona to contemplate. His pause lasted longer than necessary.

"For the sake of Chicago, what do you think, Graham?" she pleaded.

"Obviously, the death of the child is a symbolic act," he said. He paused again. "I believe you're in danger, Lee. This is part of something bigger. I don't know what, but it's much bigger than this particular event. I don't want to see you on that altar like that poor little girl. I mean, Sarai."

"I'm not frightened for myself," she said. "But..."

"But I'm frightened for you, Lee!" he interrupted with anguish. "Don't fall into denial. Get it? I'm frightened for you."

After her own pause, Lee spoke haltingly. "Thanks, Grammy."

"I'm coming," he said with emphasis. Have you got a spare bedroom in that big ol' parsonage?"

"Lots of space. "

"Should I bring Hillar?"

"Why?"

"Well, he's off school this time of year. He misses Buck and Midnight. Maybe even misses you. And, this trip might perk him up. He's not been performing well in school; and he's generally discouraged. He just stays in his garage working on his computers, drones, and other electrical gadgets. Hillar's turning into a real geek."

"We certainly have enough room. Bring 'm. You can take a non-stop flight from O'Hare to Albany. Either rent a car or I can pick you up and bring you to Diamond Point."

"I'll rent a car and find you."

"I can't wait for you to get here, Grammy. Hurry."

CHAPTER 9

THE PARSONAGE DOORBELL RANG. It was the front door. Nobody uses the front door.

"Are you the pastor?" asked a bedraggled woman toting a rather large straw bag that seemed to be carrying her life's possessions.

"I'm the pastor," said Leona, "Pastor Lee. What can I do for you?"

"My name is Susan. I'm here today for the disabled program. I'm what they call cognitively disabled. We come twice a week. We gather in the church basement. I just thought I'd like to meet you."

"Well, Susan, please come in. I'd like to meet you too!"

The guest entered through the front door and sat herself in the parsonage living room next to the wrought iron fire place. It became clear that Leona would have to take the initiative in the conversation.

"Susan, tell me about yourself," said Leona in interview fashion. Susan looked puzzled.

"I like coming to your church two times each week," said Susan.

"I'm so glad you do," responded the pastor.

"I think I should get back to the program now," said Susan. "Today we are making ceramic ash trays."

"Do you smoke, Susan?"

"No. We make these ash trays as gifts for those who smoke," she announced.

"Do you have any family members or friends who smoke?" asked Leona.

"No. But, when I get a friend who smokes, I'll have a gift ready. I need to leave now. Good bye."

Susan departed the way she came in.

———

LEONA'S CELL PHONE SOUNDED. She glanced at the return name and number. "Angie. Oh no, not now." She clicked "decline."

CHAPTER 10

Leona walked hurriedly through the house to the east porch. She let the screen door slam behind her as she walked out onto the east veranda of the parsonage. Before the door could close completely, Buck followed her through the portal, adding a second bang. Both pastor and dog situated themselves on the porch.

Leona and Buck watched expectantly as the Warren County Sheriff's car drove slowly across her expansive lawn and came to a stop in front of the white birch tree. Two men got out. The one in the sheriff's uniform asked loudly, "Are you Reverend Foxx?"

"Yes," she returned. "Do you take your coffee black?"

"Yes," each of the two responded with new grins.

"Find a chair here on the veranda. I've got a freshly brewed pot waiting for you. I'll be out in a minute. While I'm gone, meet Buck."

At that, Leona disappeared through the screen door. With wagging tail, the husky sniffed the visitors. The two found chairs among the forest green wicker furniture. In a moment, the hostess had returned with three steaming and filled-to-the-brim coffee mugs.

"Thank you for agreeing to see us. Let me introduce myself," said the uniform with an extended right hand, which Leona gripped without shaking. "I'm Sheriff Arthur Bolton." With a wide face and white short cropped hair, the sheriff looked like he'd worked his way up the ranks many years prior. "We met briefly the day of the crime."

"Welcome, Sheriff," Leona responded, though not actually remembering the previous introduction.

"My colleague here is from the NYPD," Bolton continued, nodding toward a much younger man with black hair cut into a standard Mohawk, high cheek bones, deep complexion, dressed in a khaki sport coat with open shirt collar. Where the collar was open Leona spotted a portion of a tattoo, perhaps a necklace.

"I'm Sherman Evans. In the department I'm known as Mohawk. Pleased to meet you, Reverend," said the second policeman without offering a handshake. "I'm a detective with the New York Police Department."

"Thank you again for your willingness to talk with us, Pastor," said the sheriff, making empathetic eye contact. "We know this has been difficult for you. And you must think law enforcement questions will never stop. But, unfortunately, this questioning is unavoidable in such an investigation. I hope you understand."

"Please don't worry about me, Sheriff," she responded. "I need to get to the bottom of this just like you do. I am shaken to the core. But I'm also resilient and not without my own resources for pursuing this matter. Have you identified the little girl, yet?"

"I regret to say no, not yet," said the sheriff.

"I'm calling her Sarai until we find out her real name."

Each in turn sipped their respective coffees.

"But," said Leona, turning to the Khaki coat, "why is the NYPD here. Who are you, Mr. Evans?"

"I'm here to ask the questions, Reverend," said Mohawk with a combination of nervousness and uneasy authority. "Would you mind if I record our conversation on my cell phone?" He pushed some buttons and set the phone on the wicker coffee table top. Leona said nothing.

"Would you please tell me about your professional training?

Where did you do your undergraduate degree? Where did you attend seminary?"

"I should think that if you're some hotshot NYPD detective you would've done your homework! You should know all of this already. Why ask me now? Take a look at my web site, for the sake of Crimea."

"I just want to establish a baseline, Reverend."

"A baseline for what!?"

Astutely, the sheriff interrupted. He regained control of the conversation with a dissertation directed toward Leona. "When this situation here in Diamond Point became known to other law enforcement agencies, Reverend, some in the NYPD thought that perhaps there's a connection with certain events happening in The City. Mohawk contacted me and asked if he could join in the investigation. We are now working together to solve this cruel and horrific crime." After a pause he continued. "Please tell us again, Pastor, where you were on that tragic night. I gather that you were home here. Where do you sleep?"

Leona pointed upwards. "My bedroom is upstairs in the southeastern corner. As I've already told the other investigators, I heard nothing that night. I only became aware of what happened after the authorities had arrived."

"Do you sleep alone?" asked Mohawk.

"What kind of question is that?" Leona responded indignantly. "Yes. I'm the only person in this house. Except for Buck, whom you've met, and Midnight, the cat who hides when strangers come by."

The sheriff took over the questioning. "What about Buck? Did he register any disturbance?"

"No. And this is curious, Sheriff. Neither Buck nor I were awakened by anything suspicious that night. The next day, the day of the investigation, however, Buck did disappear for a period. I still don't know why."

The sheriff started down a different path. "Do you have any young couples in your congregation in the process of divorce?"

"We have young couples," said Leona pensively. "But if they're contemplating a divorce, I might not be the first person they tell. What might you be thinking, Sheriff?"

"Maybe, just maybe, someone losing a custody battle might decide to go ahead and lose everything. Out of spite and for insult, to blame the church in some distorted or even perverted way. Just speculating. Could this little girl have been a part of such a family?"

"Not that I can think of. I know all our members quite well. To mention again, I call this little girl Sarai." Leona paused. "Can't think of any members who are struggling with their marriage and have a female toddler about that age. But, of course, I'd be glad to have you review our membership records. It's all computerized. Easy to arrange."

"May I see the crime scene?" asked Mohawk during a pause. "The Sheriff's had the opportunity. I have not."

"Yes, of course," said Leona. "Let me get the keys."

CHAPTER 11

ONCE LEONA HAD keys in hand, the three humans plus one large, energetic canine walked down the porch steps, passed the parked cars, and proceeded sixty feet to the sacristy door.

Once unlocked, the entourage entered the rear of the church. Buck led the way, inspecting the sanctuary's interior with greater vigor than the three more sedate humans. But once he sniffed the edges of altar area, he whimpered and took small steps backward as he had done in the parsonage the Monday before. Buck returned to Leona's side, leaning against her calf.

All three watched Buck, while exchanging intense glances, knowing that the dog sensed more about the sinister nature of the crime scene than any of them were able to articulate. Though the first phase of forensics and cleaning were done, the deeper removal of stains and odors was yet to be completed. Leona reached down to pat Buck on his head, feeling that the connection she had with him helped to ease the deep level of pain at seeing this sacred space defiled.

Mohawk Evans turned pensive. Trudging methodically, he circumambulated the entire worship space, studying each stained-glass window in turn. He slowly and softly read aloud the Latin

words on a scroll—"*Fides, Spes, Caritas*"—as if he might have under-
stood their deeper meaning. Mohawk mumbled into his phone, obviously recording some observation he thought significant. The sheriff
offered Leona a series of inane compliments about the red carpet, the
restored dark oak pews with red cushions, and the beauty of the
chancel and altar. Leona accepted them with a gracious thank you,
knowing that even as a seasoned officer, the sheriff was feeling an
unexpressed discomfort and a high level of lingering revulsion.

"What do you think, Mohawk?" Leona decided to break the
silence and tension with an open-ended question.

The detective continued to study his surroundings. "I'm thinking
about the missing heart."

"Me too," she added, her brow furrowed with concern at the very
necessity of acknowledging the dreadful act.

"You know," Mohawk continued, "three centuries ago this was
Indian territory. Once in a great while, there are rumors about a few
—very few—who today want to keep the ancient ways, traditions that
are both good and evil. They hold on to an enduring anger against the
Europeans that took their lands, brought disease, and destroyed their
culture. "

"So, what are you saying?" asked the sheriff.

"Well, the Huron were a violent people who sacrificed their
enemies. Priests would remove the heart while still beating and eat it.
They thought this would give them the strength of the defeated
warrior. It was a kind of spiritual delusion—to us today, anyway."

"So, Detective, how is this relevant?" asked the sheriff. "My
ancestors lived here too. I have spent my whole life here on the shores
of Lake George."

"My ancestry goes back to when Lake George was known as
Horicon," declared the detective.

Sheriff Bolton paused. "I never heard stories like that. In school,
we learned that the shoreline of Lake George was dotted with
villages belonging to the Huron and Mohawk tribes. Not far from
here is where they hunted, fished, and raised their families. The

French and Indian War was fought underneath our feet, that's true. But Hurons eating hearts? I don't think so."

At this, Leona broke into the conversation with thinly veiled disgust. "Now, wait just a minute, *Mister* Mohawk! Like Sheriff Bolton, I too think your history might be flawed."

"Flawed? How would you know? I didn't say it was all true, just that rumors do abound, you know!"

"Flawed because you have 'the rumors' mixed up with facts— which is, of course, why rumors take off, I guess."

The detective turned to look directly at the pastor and the sheriff.

Leona could feel frustration building up in her, piled on top of the pain and fear. "I know we live in a post-truth political climate," she said. "Still, if you are going to do some speculation, start with getting your facts right. Since I moved to the shore of Lake George, I studied and studied a lot about this area. I believe I am obligated to know the history of where I am ministering."

Bolton and Mohawk realized in that instant that they had better defer to this woman. At least for the moment...

Leona continued. "I find this history fascinating, the whole progression of what happened here in the eighteenth century. I read Cooper's *The Last of the Mohicans*. And his critics. I've even read some of Father Isaac Jacques' journals. You got the Huron *ALL* wrong. They scalped their enemies. They burned their captured warriors and even captive missionaries alive in the campfire. It was gruesome. But, they did not remove human hearts or eat them. I think you've got matters confused."

Mohawk had not expected such a direct confrontation. His face registered surprise that his historical pontifications were failing to impress this audience as it apparently had his NYPD fellow police officers.

Leona continued. "What you seem to overlook is that all the Amerindians in this region practiced scalping, but never heart exci- sion. Your tribe, the Mohawks, even cut their hair to fit warfare. Warriors shaved their heads, leaving a circle of long hair. They dared their enemies to take their scalps. That's the history, Mister Mohawk."

Mohawk, feeling a need to re-enter the verbal foray and defend himself, spoke. "Okay, maybe I don't have every detail right, but, all those tribes fighting for survival in past centuries engaged in some level of violence. And had some strange customs. The French and the British tribes were as violent, if not more violent."

Like a pit bull, Leona would not let go. "You are right. They were all violent, including our European ancestors. But here is your confusion, *Mister* Mohawk. Some early Americans did in fact eat beating human hearts. They were the Mexica Indians who lived *four thousand miles away* from here, for Chiapas sake! Just before the Spanish arrived in the New World, the Aztec leader proclaimed that the Mexica were destined by the Sun god to rule the world. But the Sun god, he said, drew upon a mystical energy, *chalchihuatl,* the life force of the cosmos. The way to feed the Sun god this purported elixir of the universe was through ritual sacrifice. Aztecs would compel conquered warriors up the stairs on their pyramids, cut out their bleeding hearts so the priests could eat them, and then throw the still writhing corpses down the side. Both the Sun and the rulers became powerful by devouring the power of their defeated victims. Now please get this point: this is Aztec, not Huron sacrifice, Mister Mohawk."

Stunned at being confronted with such an unexpected level of erudition, Mohawk, attempting to recover, asked, "How do you know so much history? You're only a pastor."

"And, you're only a detective," Leona said with a snide bit of sarcasm. "I notice also that your nickname is Mohawk. I bet you heard disparaging stories about the Huron while growing up in a Mohawk family?"

The detective fidgeted and stared briefly at his shoes. "We need to find some sort of connection between what happened here in this church with other events."

"You have not yet told me what these other events in New York City are," she drilled.

"Just events," he said.

"Certainly you don't think we're on the verge of a Huron uprising, do you? If anything, you should be concerned about the Aztecs, because many of today's Mexican drug cartels have adopted *chalchihuatl* spirituality. They even perform versions of human sacrifice to gain power. If you're looking for a connection, look to Big Apple drug trafficking, not at the long-forgotten Amerindians of Lake Horicon."

"For goodness sake, stop this!" interrupted the sheriff. "Is this debate getting us anywhere in our investigation?"

CHAPTER 12

As THE SHERIFF's car was departing via the rear driveway that knifes through the hedge onto Diamond Point Road, Leona heard the crush of gravel under the tires of a car entering the turnaround in front of the church. The incoming car paused, as if the driver might be lost. Leona walked across the expansive lawn toward the visiting vehicle, a white Lexus SUV. She made herself conspicuous so the car's inhabitants could see her.

Once parked, both front doors opened. On the passenger side, a petite woman with short cropped black hair emerged. Below her "Lake George" T-shirt she wore jeans and sneakers. From the driver's side a rather corpulent man in a black suit with clerical collar stepped out. He introduced himself as Father Stephen Korsky. He was accompanied by his wife, Sophia.

"Welcome to Saint John's Church! That is, welcome to Saint John's desecrated church." Leona greeted them. They exchanged names and shook hands.

"We were so shocked to hear what has happened," said Sophia with plaintive eyes.

"Oh, thank you. May I call you Sophia?"

"Yes, indeed."

"I'd like to take a look around," grunted the priest. Leona obliged by walking the visitors up the front steps of Saint John's and unlocking the large wooden door. Through the open door walked Reverend Korsky, expecting the other two to follow him. As he walked, he raised his two hands almost as high as a referee signaling a successful field goal.

Just as the Orthodox priest approached the threshold to the sanctuary he stopped. He waved his two hands very slowly. He expected his two followers to halt as well. All three stood motionless for a moment.

"A malefic cloud shrouds this sanctuary," announced the priest. "I can sense the evil. Satan has been here. A Black Mass has been performed here. The house of God has been profaned by blood sacrifice. I know this without you telling me."

Neither Leona nor Sophia spoke.

"I don't want to enter this nave now that it has become a Mephisthophelean asylum. Let us depart immediately. Back through the front portal, through which we just came." The three took their leave, single file.

The trio walked slowly and quietly back to the parsonage. Leona broke the solemn mood with a soft-voiced invitation to join her for a cup of coffee in the dining room. They all sat down without speaking.

Conversation began with an awkward opener from Leona. "So now what?"

"Just let it be for now," said Korsky. "I don't quite know how to process this. It is one thing to be knowledgeable about such things, another to experience them, to feel them viscerally."

After a short pause, the conversation shifted to small talk, touching on how long each had been in the Adirondack region and career milestones. Leona learned that Stephen Korsky had been appointed by Bishop Tikhon five years previous as senior priest at St. Cyprian's. She further sensed that he was an ambitious though frustrated man.

"Stephen would like to become bishop some day," announced

Sophia. "But, of course, he can't. That's because of me. In our church, priests can be married but bishops must be single. And male!" She laughed.

Father Korsky sat with a stern look on his face. He said nothing. When Leona pointed to the upside-down sacramental vessels, Korsky recoiled with a jolt.

"Did you place them upside down?" he asked Leona.

"No, of course not. I found them this way following the desecration of the church. It's evidence that someone had entered my parsonage as well as the church."

"Satan's demons love the Christian tradition, because they can so easily terrify us by violating our symbols. The upside-down cross is their favorite sacrilege. Iblis uses different forms of blasphemy to horrify Muslims or other religious believers. Here's the key: you know Satan is present if the religious symbols no longer convey God's grace. Pastor Lee, if you right-wise these communion vessels, that alone will re-sanctify the house."

CHAPTER 13

LAKE GEORGE VILLAGE lay on the southern end of Lake George. In the seventeenth century, the French Jesuits under the leadership of Father Isaac Jacques had explored the thirty-two-mile-long sea of glass flanked by Indian villages in the neighboring forests. The Jesuits renamed what the natives had previously called Horicon with a name meaningful to the Christians: *Lac du Saint Sacrament*. Only after the French and Indian War of the late 1750s could the British rename it after their own monarch, King George.

Walking west from the reconstructed Fort William and Henry, J. Holmes Chapman passed the Lake George Steamboat Company and headed for the town center. Of the three steamships actively sailing the waters of the lake, the *Mohican,* the *Mini-Ha-Ha,* and the *Lac du Saint Sacrament,* only the *Mohican* was tied at the dock as the New York City visitor walked by.

After turning north on Canada Street, he walked passed shops: Lake George Olive Oil, the Adirondack Winery, and the as-conspicu-ous-as-obnoxious Frankenstein Wax Museum. One restaurant caught his eye: the Moose Tooth Grill, with its inviting motto, "Food You Can Sink Your Teeth Into."

Fifteen percent of the region is Irish, so Molly Malone's Irish

Gifts finds enough customers to sustain a going business. Its motto: "Hide Your Sausage."

Chapman was looking for a specific address. He found it on the west side of Canada Street. Just a door with a small sign, "Wishing Tree." He opened it and walked in.

Immediately his eyes were challenged to adjust to the darkness. In the center of the darkened hall Chapman saw a tree, like a Christmas tree lit from below. To his right on the north wall stood a ten thousand-gallon aquarium lit from behind. He was astonished to see a six-foot-long Great White Shark looking directly at him. Their eyes locked. Chapman walked slowly toward the giant tank, maintaining eye contact with the sea monster. *Does this shark already know something about me?* he asked himself silently.

Then, Chapman's ears picked up the sound of a voice addressed to him. "Welcome to the Wishing Tree!" said a sixtyish woman with bleached blond hair, thick lipstick, excessive make-up, and glasses draping from a librarian chain. She stood just beyond the tree. "My name is Zuphlas."

Chapman nodded a greeting while turning to walk toward her. "I'm just looking." His nose picked up an aroma of pine, coming perhaps from the scented candles or, more likely, the pine tree. A living pine a tad larger than a living room Christmas tree grew up from the middle of an artificial pond with gurgling water. Coins carpeted the pond's bottom. A hand-made sign painted in multiple colors asked, "What Do You Wish For?" Beneath this question appeared a list with words: FAME? POWER? ROMANCE? FAMILY SUCCESS? FINANCIAL SECURITY? GOOD HEALTH? REVENGE?

"How do I make my wishes come true?" he asked as a customer would ask.

Zuphlas smiled, exhibiting her many experiences with just this question. "You fertilize the Wishing Tree," she replied without changing the smile.

Now smiling in kind, he continued. "And, just what do I use for fertilizer?"

"Why, money of course. This tree grows on money. You've heard of money growing on trees? Well, the Wishing Tree does just the opposite."

"What I see in the pond is a bunch of coins," he chided. "No bills. No checks. Must be a cheap tree."

"Those coins are silver dollars. The Wishing Tree just loves dollars. If you give me some paper dollars, I'll provide you with silver dollars to throw into the pond. Some time ago the U.S. Mint stopped making these coins, but we have quite a supply just in case you'd like some."

"How much does a fulfilled wish cost? Are they all the same price?"

"Some are more expensive than others, of course. But the price is determined more by your level of commitment. The more you commit, the more the Wishing Tree is able to fulfill your wish. If you drop just one silver dollar into the pond and wish for romance, there is a small chance you might meet a future someone on your way out the front door. But, the chances are much better if you drop a thousand dollars into the water. And still better...well, I think you see how it works."

Chapman nodded with the smile of shared understanding. "I think I get the picture."

"Now, Mister Chapman, just what on our list do you wish for?"

How did she know my name? "Well, I'm not sure what I want is on your list."

"Tell me what that is."

"Justice. I want justice."

"Oh, you mean REVENGE."

"No, no! I want justice. This has nothing to do with revenge," he insisted.

Zuphlas silently watched Chapman for a moment. Then, with

her face registering a knowing expression, she inquired, "Now, just how big of a commitment might you be willing to make?"

"Pretty big," he answered. "It means a lot to me."

"Just how big? Are we talking thousands? Hundreds of thousands? Millions? More?"

"Whatever it takes."

"'Whatever it takes,' you say. Might you be willing to make, shall we say, an ultimate commitment? Perhaps even *the ultimate* commitment?"

Chapman looked at Zuphlas quizzically, recognizing she was making an important point but not understanding just what she might mean. "I'm not getting what you're saying," he answered.

"Follow me," she said with a wink and a nod. She walked slowly but deliberately around the Wishing Tree toward a closed door near the back of the shop. She pointed to the door. "Beyond the door you'll find a stairway. Follow this stairway up one flight. Shake the pull chain. When someone comes, recite these words: 'when the Moon turns to blood.'"

CHAPTER 14

THE DOOR ZUPHLAS had pointed to opened on its own. Out walked a man dressed in an Indian costume, bare-chested, a single feather in his folded hair. He looked like he was ready to scalp someone. Chapman waited for the foot traffic to clear before re-opening the door.

Once the door had closed behind him, Chapman found himself at the foot of a spiral stairway. The stairway was totally enclosed in a silo, a vertical pipe of some sort. The walls were painted black. A red light from some unknown source permitted wispy visibility. He ascended carefully, one cautious step at a time.

After making numerous circles on his upward climb, Chapman found himself on a landing. Where one would expect a door, there hung from ceiling to floor numerous chains of black plastic baubles. The crowd of hanging chains was so dense that he could not see beyond them. To his right he found a thick yellow rope with a white tassel on the end. He yanked it once.

No sound. At least at first. "What do you have to say?" a melodious female voice asked.

"When the Moon turns to blood." He spoke with a slightly raised voice, attempting to be clear on each syllable.

"Enter!" commanded the same intriguing voice. Chapman blazed a path through the black jungle. On the other side he found himself in a small lounge, again with black walls and red lighting.

Sitting atop a bar stool with one leg on top of the other was a woman. Her long black hair draped over her shoulders, cascading down the front of a low-cut red blouse. Her black shorts yielded to fish net stockings, one black and the other red. A red high-heeled shoe ended the black stocking, and a matching black shoe terminated the other. Her elbow was cocked and rested on the top of her knee. In her right hand, she seductively held a burning cigarette.

"You may be seated in that comfortable chair, Mister Chapman," she offered, pointing with the cigarette to an overstuffed chair just across from her.

"How did you know my name?" he asked with composure while placing himself in the armchair as instructed.

The mysterious woman re-crossed her legs and took a long draught of her cigarette. "Did you come to the Wishing Tree by accident? Or were you sent?"

"Sent."

"Sent by whom?"

"Well, actually," Chapman meandered on. "A friend suggested that the Wishing Tree might have what I'm looking for."

"You mean the gentleman in the black suit, right?"

"Yes."

"Well, he is our friend too."

"Just what do you mean by 'our' in 'our friend'?"

"You will soon learn the answer to that question. And many others." Her red lips cupped the cigarette erotically as she slowly drew smoke into her lungs, showing no signs of hurry or schedule.

"You know my name. So, what's yours?"

"Eudaimonia."

"Eudaimonia? What kind of a name is that?"

"Actually, it's my office, not my name. You can call me 'Mona' for short. Care for a drink?"

"What've you got, Mona?" he asked, trying to mimic her relaxed yet flirtatious disposition.

"A single malt Scotch in a tumbler with only one cube of ice. Just the way you like it." She poured his glass and then leaned over to hand it to him. His eyes could not avoid staring down her cleavage toward the imagined delights hidden below. Chapman's facial expression turned quizzical. Then, he settled in to what he now recognized as a set-up.

"Do you know what our greatest pleasures are, Mister Chapman?" she said softly while straightening up again atop the bar stool.

Chapman sipped and savored his Scotch. "Well," he stammered purposely, "I suppose getting one's wishes met. That's the definition of pleasure, isn't it? Fulfilled desire?"

"But the fulfillment of some desires elicits greater pleasure than others. Don't you agree, Mister Chapman?

"Well, I suppose so."

"What would you put on top of your list of the most pleasurable?" she asked in a throaty voice, leaning forward and again exposing her cleavage.

"I suppose fine liquor and great sex," he answered in a feigned pensive posture. Then, with a smirk, "I've already got the first in my hand." He followed this with an inviting look in his eyes.

Unmoved, she moved. She leaned backwards. Inhaled and exhaled smoke. "There's one more you've not mentioned. It sits on top of the list. It's the pleasure that gives complete satisfaction. It is humanity's deepest wish, and its fulfillment can be matched by no other."

"Yes. Go on. Name it."

"Revenge."

"Now, I think there may be a misunderstanding," he responded with a tone of impatience. "The woman downstairs thought I had come here for revenge. I told her this is not the case. But she seemed not to hear me. She sent me up here to you. Now you mention revenge as well. What's going on here? What's all this charade with the black and red colors, with the mystique of evil? I can do much better with my stage sets."

Eudaimonia simply sat silently, tapping cigarette ashes onto the floor and surrounding herself with a halo of exhaled smoke. "What did you come here for? What wish are you willing to pay for to get fulfilled?"

"I want justice," he emphasized. "I don't want to see someone get away with murder. I don't want a certain individual to bask in his own success at the expense—at the destruction!—of others. It's unfair. I want to put the situation right. That's my wish."

Mona smiled, indicating she was hearing what she had expected to hear. "So, you don't want to get mad; you want to get even!"

"When Lady Justice behind her blindfold holds up her balance, the trays are even."

"By 'even' you mean an eye for an eye and a tooth for a tooth, right?"

Chapman simply looked at Mona, somewhat acknowledging what had just been said while maintaining an expression that asked, *what comes next?*

Eudaimonia looked away. She snuffed out her cigarette into an ashtray full of previous such snuffings. Still looking away, she addressed Chapman. "Mister Maletesto is here this evening. In fact, he's expecting you. If you'll take your drink back through the doorway and up the stairs one more flight, he will greet you. Good evening, Mister Chapman."

With that Mona walked behind a black curtain and disappeared from view.

CHAPTER 15

CHAPMAN FOLLOWED Mona's directions and found himself upstairs in a rather small dimly lit lounge with only two overstuffed chairs. One was empty. In the other sat a distinguished looking gentleman with silver hair in a gray suit with tie. The host signaled for the newly arrived guest to take a seat.

As Chapman moved toward the empty chair he noticed a large portrait on the wall. It was Baphomet, the version of the Devil who looks chimeric: half human and half goat. As he turned twisted to sit he noted one other piece of furniture, a small desk-high table. Sitting on the table was a legal size piece of paper. A single ball point pen seemed to be calling for a signature on that paper. Behind the paper on the table stood a Christian cross. It shocked Chapman to realize that the cross was upside down.

"So you want revenge, Mister Chapman, is that right?" asked the refined gentleman.

"No, I distinctly said I want justice," replied Chapman.

"Yes, justice of course," were the words accompanied by a knowing smile. "We here can deliver the kind of justice you're looking for. I'm Renard Maletesto. I'm pleased to meet you."

"How do you know so much about me?"

"We do our homework, shall we say. Now, just who is it you wish to exact justice against?"

"If you've done your homework, as you say, then you'd know the answer to that question."

"It's important for you to state what you wish to see happen. After all, you're at the Wishing Tree. And, of course, despite our homework, I'm not omniscient. Please start from the beginning."

"You probably know that the Manhattan Opera Company is doing better now than it ever has. This is due to my ingenuity and leadership. When I bought out the previous owner, it was on the skids. Now it's the premier opera company in the world, I might say. Our young singers become stars overnight. Our audition lists are maxed out. We have sellouts sometimes a year in advance. We're the envy of everyone in the fine arts."

"So, what's the problem?"

"My wife, Helen, plans to file for divorce. She demands half of the family assets. She's found a new lover and plans to run off with him and take my money with her. When she files, all our assets will be frozen until settlement. Then, most likely, the court will require that we liquidate the opera company by selling it. I'll lose everything I've worked for."

"So, why do you call this a justice problem? In the state of New York, it's simply taken for granted that a spouse receives half the assets in a divorce. That's justice."

"But *I'm* the one who built the Manhattan Opera from nothing to its billion-dollar value! I'm the one who invested the blood, sweat, and tears to make it a success! I'm the one who had the genius! All Helen did was dress pretty for the openings."

Maletesto's facial expression conveyed that he was listening intently. Chapman went on. "What I suspect is that Helen plans somehow to buy me out and turn operations over to the guy who'll become her new husband. She'll end up with the spoils of marriage without having earned them. No matter what, Helen will take away what I've built."

"Like Helen who left Menelaus to run off with Paris to Troy, your Helen will run off with her Paris and take your hard-earned profits with her. And you want to take revenge against Helen."

"Not revenge. Justice."

"I certainly agree that you are being treated unjustly. And, I suspect, exacting justice against Helen will, shall we say, give you pleasure. Am I right?"

"I don't think of it as pleasure. But it will give me satisfaction."

"Isn't satisfaction a form of pleasure? Well, that's beside the point. No doubt you'd like to see Helen dead before she files for divorce, right?"

"Well, yes. And no, too. I'm conflicted. There would be an advantage if she would die sooner rather than later. Immediately, actually. How can you help me, Mister Maletesto?

CHAPTER 16

MALETESTO ROSE FROM HIS CHAIR. He walked deliberately around his chair and stood before the near life-sized portrait of Baphomet. A lampada hung on three slender chains going from the ceiling to the bottom of the portrait's frame. Otherwise known as the Sabbatic Goat of the Knights Templar, Baphomet combines binary opposites: goat and human, Sun and Moon, male and female, light and dark. Maletesto lit the virgin olive oil in the lampada and illuminated the Satanic icon.

"I light this lampada," Maletesto said over his shoulder, "for our enlightenment. The name Lucifer means god of light, as you probably know. Before God created the world, there was nothing. The first thing God said was *let there be light*. After that there still was nothing. But, with light God could see it better."

Chapman sat without changing his facial expression.

"That's an old joke, Mister Chapman. To be enlightened means to know that nothing is what's primary. Non-being will always trump being. Non-existence will destroy what exists. That's what Lucifer sheds light on. What do you think?"

Chapman could only nod. His face revealed a deepening confusion.

"We have access to certain powers, both natural and supernatural. You've come to the Wishing Tree no doubt to employ our powers to fulfill your wish. It's your wish to murder Helen or, should I say, to exact justice against Helen. Let me be clear, Mister Chapman, this is your wish, is it not?"

Chapman gulped. After a moment he muttered, "Yes, that's my wish."

"Do I sense some hesitancy?"

"Yes, because I'm not sure this is right. On the one hand, it is only just that Helen be punished for her greed. On the other hand, I don't want to be responsible for her punishment. That's how I got here, actually. I telephoned Saint Peter's Church in the city. The minister gave me your contact information."

"Mister Chapman, do you know of anyone at the Manhattan Opera who has had dealings with the Wishing Tree? Perhaps the talent? Staff? Business associates?

"No," replied Chapman with an expression that was both inquiring and bewildered. "None that I know of. I never heard of the Wishing Tree before the minister told me about you. And he said the matter was urgent. So, I came to Lake George as quickly as I could, without even saying good-bye to my staff."

Maletesto looked relieved to hear this.

CHAPTER 17

"WE CERTAINLY CAN MAKE this happen on your behalf, Mister Chapman. And we can do it within the bounds of the law. We curse. We curse during ritual. By cursing your wife, she will die as we determine."

"I thought cursing...well, never mind."

"Cursing is a form of free speech," continued Maletesto. "It's protected by the First Amendment. It's legal. And, because the Wishing Tree is registered as a religion, and because we rely upon the supernatural power of cursing...well, neither you nor any other person or organization can get prosecuted for criminal activity."

"No doubt you charge for this service."

"Well, yes, there is a price. But, in your case, the price is not measured in dollars."

"What do you mean?"

"We want your soul, Mister Chapman, your eternal soul."

"What do you mean?"

"Once you commit yourself to the Prince of Darkness, the Lord of Supreme Malevolence, your wish will come true. The curse will do its work. The Lord of Supreme Malevolence responds to human devotion with reward. If you demonstrate commitment, the Wishing Tree will bring forth the fruit of satisfaction."

"When I approached Saint Peter's Church for counsel, somehow this is not what I expected."

"We're grateful to Saint Peter's for the referral."

CHAPTER 18

"How old is she?" asked Graham Washington, who was kneeling on the floor near the United departure gate at O'Hare International Airport.

"Twenty months," answered the young mother in jeans and a tank top. Both the mother and daughter were Dravidian, perhaps visitors from India. The toddler had milky brown skin, shining black eyes, slightly curly black hair, and wore a fashion-forward single piece dress over black leggings with Velcro buckled booties.

"Would you like to visit with me?" Graham asked the tyke in a slightly high-pitched voice. He had caught her eye. She stared at Graham with interest. "You are just precious," declared Graham so the mother could overhear. The toddler registered no reaction to his voice, but she kept her eyes focused on his.

With both trepidation and curiosity, the tot moved slowly toward this most strange person who was asking for her attention. In her left hand she carried a string of licorice, already a third eaten and gummy with drool. As she approached, the giant man kneeling on the floor reached out his hand, palm up. She studied the hand. Then she placed her candy in Graham's palm. She stepped back, put her hands behind her back, and smiled the smile of victory.

"Oh, thank you!" exclaimed Graham, holding his hand steady. After a moment passed, the little girl reached back into Graham's hand and removed the licorice stick. She immediately put it into her mouth and then looked around the gate area for another adventure.

Graham seated himself next to his teenage protégé, Hillar Talin. Hillar's nose was buried as deep into his cell phone as a well point gets buried into the water table. He had not observed any of the previous interaction.

The public address speakers crackled briefly. "Attention, all those passengers scheduled on United Flight 288 to Albany. Our departure time has been delayed. We are waiting for the cockpit crew to arrive from Columbus. We apologize for the delay. A courtesy cart will provide you with water and a snack while you are waiting. Your patience is appreciated."

Hillar pocketed his cell phone and began to watch for the snack cart arrival. Once the cart had been wheeled into the gate area, passengers lined up to grab water bottles, apples, bananas, or small bags of chips or cookies. Most frequently all of the above. Hillar hurried over to the cart and returned to where Graham was sitting. He dropped down four bottles of water, two apples, and a fistful of chip bags and cookie bags. He stuffed numerous packets into his backpack. Graham looked up to see many of the other passengers stuffing snacks into their carry-ons.

"Are you going to eat all you've taken, Hillar?" Graham asked.

"Dunno. But, they're free. I'll take 'm just in case."

"That's hoarding, you know, don't you?"

"It's not hoarding, Graham. I'm just stocking up."

Graham laughed. "I think you've temporarily reverted to an earlier stage of evolution. Our Neanderthal ancestors hoarded—I mean stocked up—all summer so they'd have enough food for the winter. That's because food did not grow in the winter. But you, Hillar, will find food wherever you go on this trip. So, why stock up and then have to carry it?"

"Maybe I haven't graduated yet from the school of evolution," he said.

CHAPTER 19

Two of Sheriff Bolton's deputies, balancing in the boat bottom, carefully lifted the nude body up to the dock. Two forensic medics then lifted the woman onto a gurney.

"Where was she found?" asked Sheriff Bolton.

One deputy still in the boat answered. "Just floating near Diamond Island. Spotted by two jet skiers. They called it in. We borrowed this here outboard, rather than call for the lake police, just to save time. Gotta give the boat back now."

"Did you leave a buoy anchored to the spot where you recovered the body?" the sheriff asked.

One deputy looked at the other. Both shrugged. "Guess not, Sheriff. Sorry."

"Oh, never mind." The sheriff turned to study the body on the gurney. A petite middle-aged woman. Black hair slicked down by its wetness. No clothing. No obvious identification.

"Before you bag her, turn her over just in case there's something to see on the backside," grumbled the sheriff.

The two forensic medics followed the order. Once the body had been rolled with backside up, it became clear that this was no drowning accident.

"What's that between her shoulder blades?" demanded the sheriff.

One medic leaned over with an unneeded magnifying glass to study the wound. The length was nearly ten inches. The cross bar was six inches. "It looks like a cross has been carved into her back with a knife. It's a very deep cut. This could be what killed her, or at least rendered her unconscious before being thrown into the water."

"A cross, you say?" asked the sheriff.

"Yes. It's an upside-down cross."

CHAPTER 20

"GRAMMY, put your bags here in the front bedroom. I call it the blue room...blue bed spread, blue floor rug," directed Leona on the second floor of the Truesdale House.

Hillar and Graham had arrived a bit travel weary after their delayed flight to Albany from Chicago. They had rented an SUV with a back-up camera that Hillar immediately thought might have applications for Leona's CIA work. He hadn't quite figured out how, but the speculation kept his teenage nerd mind busy on the drive up the Northway to Diamond Point, New York. Graham was happy to keep his eyes on the road.

Turning to Hillar, Leona added, "Quasimodo, you're in here. Right across from my room and next to the bathroom. Choose the single bed next to the window. It's lumpy. But, you're tough."

When the two Chicago visitors had arrived just minutes prior, both pets came to greet them. Buck and Midnight followed every activity as they made their way through the parsonage, exhibiting an unusual sense of territorial ownership. Buck sniffed at the luggage as if he were looking for contraband, Midnight was simply curious as she hopped from tabletops to dressers, resting finally on Hillar's pillow. Both visitors easily passed the "pet test."

Graham and Leona had begun their friendship while she was shepherding the flock at Trinity Lutheran Church on Chicago's South Side. The dashing African American, a Creole, Graham Washington, doubled professionally: first as a full-time agent for the U.S. Central Intelligence Agency and, second, under cover as the assistant to the Churchwide Bishop, Justin Hurley.

Hillar Talin, about to enter his senior year in high school, was Leona's favorite teenager. She nicknamed him "Quaz," short for Quasimodo, the Hunchback of Notre Dame. This name was not because of his stature, but more metaphorically as someone unlikely who was there and cared for her and the church.

Hillar's hair was cut into a Psychobilly Wedge. A grotesque vulture tattoo was etched on his neck along with a twenty-gage stainless steel hoop in his nose. Secretly, Leona prided herself for her patience. Because no father was present in Hillar's home, she along with Graham gave the young man a good deal of parental attention and occasionally took him along on adventures. Hillar played it cool on the outside, but inside? Inside he was flattered that Leona chose him.

***

A COUPLE HOURS after the move-in, Graham fired up the Weber on the parsonage lawn. Leona organized the hot dogs and garnishes in the kitchen and brought them to the east veranda. Brenda Beale took a comfortable seat in a green wicker rocking chair to sip a Chardonnay. Hillar fetched a metallic medium-sized suitcase from his room, opened it, and extracted a mass of tangled wires and small boxes, along with miscellaneous electronic gismos.

Hillar assembled a drone in just minutes and sent it flying in circles around the yard. The drone performed acrobatics above the church roof, as if the circus had come to town. Graham, Brenda, and Leona watched in glowing amazement as Hillar's craft circumnavigated the cross-shaped weather vane atop the church's 120-foot steeple.

Once Hillar realized he'd drawn the grownups' attention, he sported a smug grin and stood just a little taller. "I've got a name for my drone," he bragged proudly.

"What's the name?" asked Leona.

"Genghis."

"As in Genghis Kahn?"

"The same!"

When Leona extended her attention, Hillar carefully described his homemade machine. "It has a front and a back," he said with confidence. "Here in the back I have a high compression tank. When I want speed, I release the pressurized gas. Genghis can jet up to a hundred miles an hour. For short distances, at least."

Leona feigned being impressed. Hillar continued. "It's got a computer chip. It's almost intelligent. And, I've installed my own bat radar. If Genghis is about to collide with an object, he takes evasive action. In only nanoseconds. Wanna see?"

"Of course," she responded.

"Get a baseball bat. I'll pitch Genghis to you. You see if you can hit him."

"I can't hit anything at 100 miles an hour."

"How about 70?"

Leona retrieved a baseball bat from the rear porch stash of recreational supplies. She took a position in front of the veranda stairs, standing in an imaginary batter's box. Hillar took a crouching position at the church's rear, some 60 feet away.

"Pitch it ta me, Quaz! Pitch it ta me!" she taunted.

With Genghis already whirling, Hillar jetted his drone toward the slugger at 70 miles per hour. Leona took a perfectly level swing. As her bat neared the middle of the swing, Genghis leaped up and over the bat, landing safely on the porch.

"Strike One!" hollered Graham.

CHAPTER 21

LATE THE NEXT morning Graham sat nursing his third cup of coffee at the kitchen table. Hillar stared at his cell phone, punching in letters and numbers at the speed of a chicken beak eating corn. The two heard the sound of high heels clicking as they descended the wooden stair case.

In moments Leona appeared in the kitchen wearing a black clergy shirt with a white tab clerical collar under a tailor-made black suit. The skirt hem hung tastefully just below her knees. Her nylon stockings disappeared into black mid-height heels.

Graham exclaimed, "Now, Pastor Lee, you should know that I have a Y chromosome. This morning you are a walking paradox. On the one hand, your feminine pulchritude stimulates in me an uncontrollable hormone flow, while your collar and suit prompt me to treat you as holy."

"I take that as a compliment, Grammy," she responded smiling. Hillar looked quizzically at both of them, not sure what that interchange was about, and then returned to his mobile phone.

After pouring herself a cup of coffee and sitting down at the table, she looked at Graham. "Here's my plan for the day. After a little office work, I will visit three shut-ins and make two hospital calls. I've got my home communion kit in the car. After I'm done with all this, Grammy, I want you to take me out to dinner."

"Sure," responded Graham. "Anywhere special?"

"Yes. I want to go to the Lobster Pot in Lake George Village. You'll just love it. I feel like sea food."

"You don't look like sea food," said Graham.

Leona stuck out her tongue and puffed her cheeks, making the kind of sound one would expect to hear in a commode.

At this Hillar looked up.

"Would you like to join us, Quaz?" asked Leona.

"No," he answered, "I don't like sea food."

"Good. I didn't want you to come, anyway," said Leona.

Hillar responded by blowing an obnoxious noise through his pursed lips.

Leona spoke. "Quaz, you can stay here with Buck and Midnight. The Pot Belly Deli just north of us on the Highway sells pizza by the slice. I'll leave a twenty-dollar bill here. But be sure you eat all the pizza you buy and bring home. Don't leave any."

"Why?" asked Hillar.

"Because any leftovers will be a temptation for Graham to eat. And we have to watch his cholesterol level."

"What's this 'watch Graham's cholesterol' stuff?!" interrupted Graham. "It's my cholesterol. Leave your hands off it. And, why are you disciplining my cholesterol but you tell Hillar to eat pizza?"

"Because Hillar still has time to develop good eating habits, Grammy," she said.

"Good eating habits?" said Graham, pounding the table top. "And you want to go to the Lobster Pot? First of all, such seafood is rich. Second, you dip it in drawn butter. What could be worse for your cholesterol, Miss Holy Pastor Lee?"

"You have a Y chromosome, Mister Graham. I have two X's. I have a right to be irrational at times."

"No, you don't. You're a pastor. You are obligated to be rational at all times," retorted Graham.

At this Leona puffed her cheeks and stuck out her tongue.

CHAPTER 22

Luciano Silvestri had just walked past the man in the Frankenstein costume when he raised his cell phone to check the time. *I'm a quarter hour early,* he murmured to himself. *Gotta kill some time.*

Luciano sat down on one of the many Canada Street benches backed against the ceaseless traffic. He placed his backpack next to him and reached for his water bottle. After a modest swig he relaxed and began to survey the sidewalk activities. He spotted a small tan dog wandering expectantly between the many legs partially adorned with shorts and flip flops. *Could this be a terrier of some sort? Norwich? Norfolk? Scottish? It can't be more than fifteen pounds. Skinny. Not well brushed.* Random golden hairs along with gray whiskers lined the dog's snout while other haphazard hairs covered portions of each bright brown eye.

"Here, boy!" he said just loud enough to perk the ears of the canine. The pup with only a minimum of caution approached the man seated on the sidewalk bench.

Luciano poured some water into his cupped hand and held it down. Having lost any sign of reticence, the tan terrier joyously lapped the liquid. "It's ninety degrees! I can see that you're thirsty, Puppy," he said in an affectionate voice. The dog looked up with her round brown eyes that clearly said *thank you*. Luciano tenderly patted the dog's head between the ears.

"I wonder if I might have something tasty for you to eat," mumbled Luciano as he rustled through his backpack. He found a partially eaten bag of roasted peanuts. "I wonder if you'd like these," he said invitingly while holding out a handful. His new four-legged friend gobbled the nuts and then licked the salt off his palm. Luciano repeated the hand-feeding until the bag was empty. The voracious pup vigorously licked the hairs lining her snout until every grain of salt had been swallowed.

Luciano looked again at his watch. With a hand on the pup's head he said, "Good-bye, dear friend. I now have to find a place called the Wishing Tree."

CHAPTER 23

Luciano's eyes struggled to adjust to the shock of passing from the 90-degree sunlit sidewalk into the air-conditioned and darkened interior of the Wishing Tree. He turned immediately toward the north wall and the glowing shark tank. He duly noted that a wild beast swam menacingly in the aquarium. As he scanned his whereabouts, he fixed next on the pine tree, lit from lights in the fountain pool beneath. Finally, to his extreme left, he first glimpsed and then stared at the reception desk. He walked slowly toward the woman with bleached blond hair and glasses hanging from a librarian chain.

"Welcome, Mister Silvestri," she said with no motion or emotion. "My name is Zuphlas."

Luciano looked at her quizzically. Because the darkness of the room suggested quiet, in a soft voice he asked, "How did you know my name?"

"We're expecting you," said Zuphlas. "Don't you have an eleven o'clock appointment with Mister Maletesto?"

"Yes, of course. Am I on time?"

"Unfortunately, Mister Maletesto has been momentarily detained. He'll return in a quarter hour. Perhaps while you're waiting you'll allow me to introduce you to the Wishing Tree."

"The Wishing Tree? I saw the name on the front door. But, Miss Zuphlas, I don't know what a wishing tree is."

"Then let me show you." Zuphlas walked around her reception desk and led Luciano toward the room's center.

Luciano heard the front door open and then close again. He turned to look and saw a man, perhaps thirty, wearing a blue maintenance uniform, enter. The entering workman was carrying a squirming dog. Upon looking closely, Luciano discerned that this was the same lost dog he had befriended only minutes earlier on the sidewalk. The dog fought unsuccessfully to free herself from her captor's vice grip.

Luciano turned briefly back to Zuphlas, but then reversed his gaze to watch what would happen to his new four-legged friend. The workman climbed a ladder adjacent to the aquarium. Without the slightest hesitation he threw the flailing pup into the shark tank. The surprised and petrified canine sank directly downward. Luciano raced into action. The Great White lost not a second before gripping the new arrival in its forceful jaws, crushing the hapless pup's bones. Blood spurted, turning the surrounding water red. The dog's eyes opened wide and locked onto Luciano. Those eyes were screaming, "Save me, Friend!"

The shark momentarily loosened its grip. Then it took a big gulp and the dog disappeared into the sea beast's digestive system. Only the pup's blood was left to swirl in the water.

"What the hell!?" shrieked Luciano.

The workman without expression descended the ladder and walked toward the front door.

"You can't do that!" shouted Luciano. "I've never seen such cruelty! Such, such..."

The workman paused. "Mister Silvestri," he began to say.

"How did you know my name?" screeched Luciano.

"Mister Silvestri," the workman continued without emotion, "the shark must eat just as you and I do."

"No! No! No! You don't feed a shark with an innocent pet like this. No! No! No!"

The workman approached Luciano and began to speak in a more hushed tone. "Do you eat hamburgers, Mister Silvestri? Barbequed steaks? Hot dogs? Some innocent steer died just like this in a meat packing plant so you could get your daily nourishment. So, what's the difference?"

Luciano stood frozen for a minute. He then turned to Zuphlas. "Please postpone my appointment with Mister Maletesto until tomorrow."

CHAPTER 24

"How DID the coroner's office fare during the illegal prescription drug scandal?" Leona asked Sheriff Bolton.

"Just a little mess. It got cleaned up quickly. Got a new coroner and chief nurse," he answered.

The two were talking as Leona walked into the Warren County Coroner's office. She had been called on her cell phone by the sheriff, who thought she might be interested in a new crime. The term *upside-down cross* had grabbed the pastor's attention. So she interrupted her day's schedule to visit the sheriff.

As soon as the body was uncovered, Leona immediately recognized the victim. "That's Sophia Korsky!" she exclaimed.

"Who's Sophia Korsky?" asked the sheriff.

"The wife of Stephen Korsky. The priest at St. Cyprian's, an Orthodox Church in Saratoga. I spoke with them only the day before yesterday, I think. She was very much alive and, well, you know, herself. At least I think she was herself. That's actually the first time I'd met her. This is just awful, Sheriff. This grieves me."

"One more very important thing, Pastor." The sheriff turned to the medic. "Please turn the corpse over."

"Oh, my God," Leona shrieked. "That's the upside-down cross

you told me about. Oh, no! This is...this is...impossible. Unbelievable. Oh, this poor woman. Who could have done such a dastardly thing?" Leona looked away. Then, she turned to examine the wound more closely.

"No doubt you think Sophia's death and what happened at my church are connected," said Leona.

"What do you think?" he asked.

"It appears that Sophia still has her heart, even if it's not working any more. So, she was not the victim of ritual sacrifice," murmured Leona, half out loud and half to herself. "But it looks Satanic, doesn't it?"

"I don't know what to make of it, Pastor Lee. But me and my deputies are going to consider that this murder and what happened in your church are somehow connected. Maybe the same people. I think our county is in grave danger. We've got to work fast."

Leona stood erect and looked directly at the sheriff, giving a slight nod of agreement.

"Do you have contact information for Sophia's husband?" asked the sheriff.

"Of course," answered Leona. "I'll provide it. Father Korsky must come up immediately to identify her. I can't imagine how he will feel."

Leona swept through her mobile and read aloud the Korsky contact info. Before clicking off, Leona could see that Angie was trying to call her. She clicked *Decline*.

CHAPTER 25

LEONA AND GRAHAM climbed the stairs to the second floor, the main floor, of the Lobster Pot Restaurant. Adjacent to the entrance stood a large sandwich board. The poster included a photo of Humphrey Crump, U.S. Congressman, standing with an outstretched hand on a ballistic missile. The large print slogan read: "Re-Nuke Now!" In the lower right corner was a picture of a peace symbol with President Andrew Dodge helplessly entangled in the lower filigree.

After pausing to study the poster, Leona and Graham followed the hostess to a table on the deck level close to the street. Over the railing they could watch pedestrians walking up and down Canada Street in Lake George Village. Leona had ordered a Sauvignon Blanc and Graham a Chardonnay to sip while reviewing the newspaper-sized menu. Leona told Graham hurriedly about the body of Sophia found floating near Diamond Point in Lake George.

"Do I know this person, Sophia?" asked Graham.

"No. I only met her shortly before you arrived. She's the wife of Stephen Korsky, an Orthodox Church of America priest in Saratoga. He seems to be well-informed about matters Satanic. I'm thinking about asking him more questions, asking him to help orient me in this strange world of the occult. I should think you'd find him interesting as well. After all, you are into new religious movements. Satanism counts as an NRM, doesn't it?"

"Yes, it counts as an NRM. But, as you can imagine, Satanism has been around for a long time and has some unique features that distinguish it from the others. Most new religions are not deadly."

CHAPTER 26

As THE DINERS perused the menu, the waitress set down water glasses. She stared at Leona's clerical collar. Her eyes fixed, almost trancelike, on the collar. "Father, I have sinned."

Graham and Leona locked eyes, both of them visibly surprised by the comment. The waitress did not notice their facial expressions. She continued to stare at Leona.

"I know this is terribly rude of me," said the waitress, "but my soul is in agony, an agony I never thought possible. I haven't been to church in a long time, but I see you here as a sign that I must confess my sin. I just must. Please, please, Father, could we go to the back of the deck? There's an empty table. Please come and hear my confession. This is so very, very urgent."

Chuckling quietly, Graham began a sentence. "Father?! Did you notice...?" Before he could finish, Leona stood up to follow the waitress toward the rear of the restaurant. Over her shoulder the waitress told another waitress to attend to the table at the front.

As they approached a distant table, the waitress made the Latin sign of the cross on her chest. Leona followed suit, crossing herself.

When the two were seated at some distance from other customers, Leona took the initiative. "What's your name? Leona asked this even though she could read her name on the restaurant identification badge.

"Shelly. My name's Shelly Wennes."

"How old are you, Shelly?"

"Twenty-three."

"Shelly, you sound like you're carrying a heavy burden. Want to tell me now?"

After a pause, Shelly launched in. "It's Mister Hagadorn. He's in hospice now. He could die any day. In fact, God forbid, he may already be dead."

"I'm sorry about Mister Hagadorn's situation," said Leona. "Is he a family member?"

"Oh, no!" responded Shelly. "Mister Hagadorn is the manager here at the Lobster Pot. Or, at least he was. Six months ago he was diagnosed with prostate cancer. But it was too late for any surgery or therapy to help. It'll be any time now."

"Why does Mister Hagadorn's cancer have anything to do with your feeling of sin?

Shelly looked at the floor. "I've worked here for two years. All year, not just summers. It's hard to get a year-round job here in the village, and I needed this one. But I did not like coming to work. Whenever I came near to Mister Hagadorn he would make comments. Sometimes he just said I was pretty. Other times he asked me to have sex with him. He said that if I would become his mistress that he would raise my hourly wage. It's not that he just asked. He badgered me. He kept it up and kept it up."

"This is a classical instance of harassment, Shelly. Did you report it?"

"No."

"Why not?"

"I needed the job. I thought I could just endure it. But over time I came to detest Mister Hagadorn. I think I even came to hate him. You see, when the time is ripe I want to find the right man, get married, and raise a family. I'm not the kind of person Mister Hagadorn wants me to be." She looked away. "I came to hate him, Father. I came to wish that the worst thing would happen to him."

Leona paused to allow Shelly to collect her thoughts. After a moment of silence, she asked, "Did you wish cancer on him? Is that why you feel guilty?"

"No, it was not the cancer."

"What then is the worst thing?"

"I said I wanted him damned to hell, to everlasting hell."

"And now with this cancer, it appears that your wish for Mister Hagadorn's everlasting punishment might be about to happen. Is that right?"

"Yes," sobbed Shelly. "I don't want my wish for his eternal damnation to come true. I don't. I don't."

"Well, Shelly, I suppose you said something like "goddammit" or "God damn Mr. Hagadorn." Let me ask you, do you think God is obligated to do your bidding? Many of us say these awful things when cursing, and certainly God hears us. But finally, it's God's decision whether Mr. Hagadorn is condemned or receives blessing. Not ours. This is a prayer that God probably does not honor when he hears it. The power does not lie with us."

A large tear fell from Shelly's left eye. She looked up. "It was not God that I went to for this wish, Father."

.

CHAPTER 27

"Not God? What do you mean?" Leona quizzed Shelly.

"I made my wish with Satan."

Leona was aghast. "*Satan*, did you say?"

"Yes, Satan. I paid money and I made my wish for Mister Hagadorn's eternal damnation. Then he got cancer. Now I'm sorry. I'm so very, very sorry. I can't live with myself. I feel like my soul has a big black spot on it and I can't wash it off. Can you help me, Father?"

Leona sat there saying nothing for a moment. "Shelly? Can you tell me just how you went about giving Satan your wish?"

"I went to the Wishing Tree."

"The Wishing Tree?"

"Yes. The Wishing Tree is a couple blocks north of here on Canada, just past the guy who stands on the sidewalk in a Frankenstein costume. You know."

"I don't recall having seen it. But let me ask: just what did you do at the Wishing Tree?"

"I paid twenty dollars and gave Satan my wish. And now, I fear, that wish is coming true. I'm so so sorry."

"Did you talk directly with Satan?"

"No. Some lady who runs the Wishing Tree told me that Satan himself would attend to my wish by cursing Mister Hagadorn. She invited me to come back, but that's the only time I've ever been there. Can there be any forgiveness for me, Father?"

"Yes, of course. The power of Christ's forgiveness breaks any and all chains the Devil might put you in. Do you want that forgiveness right now?"

"Yes. Now."

Leona raised her right hand. "By the authority vested in me as the representative of Christ on earth, I declare you absolved from this sin. Let your heart be at peace in the sure knowledge of God's love for you and God's promise of everlasting life. Amen." At that Leona once again made the sign of the cross.

"Thank you, Father," said Shelly.

"Well, Shelly, we're not quite done yet. I can see that your heart is changed. This is good. But, you've got one more thing to do. I suggest that you go to that hospice center and visit Mister Hagadorn. Test your heart. If you feel compassion for him, then convey to him that you forgive him. This could make a big difference in how he faces his own death. Do you understand what I'm saying, Shelly? You have an opportunity to help Mister Hagadorn."

"Yes," she said, with a small smile of victory. "Yes, I will do this. In fact, I will do it right now."

"You are forgiven by God," announced Leona. "Now, let's see how Mister Hagadorn takes it."

CHAPTER 28

GRAHAM ORDERED the two-pound lobster and Leona the Alaskan King Crab. Melted butter came in cups as if drawn from on tap. Their new waitress was named Veronica.

"What happened there, Father Lee?" asked Graham.

"Actually, my good friend, what happens in the confessional booth is a matter of confidence. I'm not supposed to tell you."

"I didn't see any confessional booth. It looked like you were sitting at a table. So come on. Out with it."

Leona considered the matter while both dipped their respective morsels of *fruit de mer* in butter. "After dinner, Grammy, I'd like to take a walk. I want to visit a place called the Wishing Tree."

"Anything you say, Father Lee."

CHAPTER 29

"COME ON, Buck! Let's go get some pizza," commanded Hillar. Boy and dog wandered across the rear lawn of the church toward the opening in the Diamond Point Road hedge. They turned right. At the corner of 9N they turned left and walked less than a football field's distance to the Pot Belly Deli.

Once inside the local equivalent of an all-purpose general store and pizza parlor, Hillar spotted some video consoles he'd not seen before. After ordering a large pizza with double cheese, mushrooms, pepperoni, and black olives, the teenager turned his attention to Monster Hunter: Interstellar.

Hillar did not give special notice to the shaved head in the jean jacket who entered the deli and wandered in front of the bins with charcoal of various brands and bag weights. The newly arrived customer took more than the usual time to make up his mind regarding what he might purchase.

When the pizza was ready, Hillar paid. With Buck at his side, the teen walked home with his evening's dinner. Once in the parsonage, the delighted teenager placed the take-out treasure on the kitchen table and opened a cola. He took a pizza slice along with a bottle of cola to the living room and sat in front of the television. He tuned into the first pitch of a night game between the Mets and the Cubs being played at Mets Citi Field. This meant Hillar would have to listen to New York announcers rather than the familiar Cubs play-by-play. He consented. He watched. He ate.

Hillar did not hear the almost silent footsteps on the east veranda. Nor did Hillar see the face looking at him through the dining room window.

Buck rose and walked through the dining room to the screen door to investigate a possible prowler. When the crowd roared and filled the living room with sound, the unlocked screen door opened slightly. The loud click of the tranquillizer gun could not be heard above the stadium din. In a minute, Buck's body lay motionless on the wooden floor.

CHAPTER 30

Leona and Graham wandered northward on Canada Street at dusk. Occasionally Leona, still dressed in her clerics, gripped Graham's arm just above the elbow to steady her high-heeled gait. Even though it might look odd to see a pastor on the arm of a tourist dressed in shorts and a T-shirt with an Adirondack moose on the front, the two walkers seemed oblivious when others looked up from their cell phones to stare at them momentarily.

As they passed the seven-foot Frankenstein on the sidewalk inviting the public to come into his wax museum, Graham announced that he was hearing a rock band play down by the lakeshore. "Should we go down and listen for a bit? I'd buy you an after-dinner drink, Pastor, er, ah, I mean, Father, Lee."

"Go ahead, Graham," said Leona. "I want to spend some time at the Wishing Tree. See the small sign? It's just up there on the left. We'll connect in a few minutes. I'll come and find you on the lakeshore."

The two parted. Leona opened the door of the Wishing Tree and entered the smallish shop. Air conditioning made her feel instantly cool. The interior was dimly lit. A spotlight drew her eyes to the middle of the room, to a Christmas-like pine tree with silver-tipped branch ends. She glanced at the giant aquarium and glimpsed the Great White swimming back and forth, but Leona did not feel compelled to stare at the fish.

"Welcome to the Wishing Tree!" Speaking was a sixtyish woman with bleached blond hair, thick lipstick, excessive make-up, and glasses hanging from a librarian chain.

"My name is Zuphlas," said the woman. "And you are, Pastor...?"

"I'm Pastor Lee. I serve in Diamond Point. If I'm not mistaken, your name, Zuphlas, means Angel of the Tree. Right?"

"That's right," answered Zuphlas with a broadened smile. "How do you know?"

Leona said nothing. She smiled slightly and sniffed while she surveyed the interior. She picked up an aroma of pine, coming perhaps from the scented candles or, more likely, the pine tree itself. The water surrounding the tree's trunk gurgled as in a fountain. Coins carpeted the pond's bottom. A hand-made sign painted in multiple colors asked, "What Do You Wish For?" Beneath this question was a list of suggestive words: FAME? POWER? ROMANCE? FAMILY SUCCESS? FINANCIAL SECURITY? GOOD HEALTH? REVENGE?

"Just how do I make my wishes come true?" Leona asked.

The shop's hostess smiled knowingly. "You fertilize the Wishing Tree."

Leona broke into a complementary smile. "And just what do I use for fertilizer?"

"Why, money of course. This tree grows on money. You've heard of money growing on trees? Well, the Wishing Tree does just the opposite. If you give me some paper money, I'll give you silver dollars. You could make one wish per dollar. Or, if you want to be more confident that your wish will come true, you could invest more per wish."

"So, fulfilled wishes are more expensive than idle wishes. Is that what you're telling me?"

"No. Our Lord of the Wish takes every wish seriously and grants fulfillment whenever he deems it deserving."

"This Lord of the Wish. He is the one who decides who gets their wish and who does not?"

"That's correct."

"Would you please give me twenty silver dollars, Zuphlas," said Leona. "Here's a twenty."

With her coins she walked over to the Wishing Tree. "Do I just make a wish and throw coins into the fountain?"

"Yes, that's exactly what you do. Are you ready."

Leona stood motionless at the fountain's edge. She closed her eyes. When she opened her eyes, she announced in a loud voice, "I wish for world peace, for the end of all war." Then, she ceremoniously threw five dollars into the water, one at a time.

Surrounding the tree was an aureole so bright that Leona did not notice a man entering the shop from the rear. The dim lighting beyond obscured the contours of his body as he stood motionless, observing and listening.

Zuphlas showed displeasure at Leona's wish ritual. "Most people who come to the Wishing Tree have a different kind of wish. They tend to wish for something, shall we say, personal?"

"Give me an example of a personal wish," requested Leona.

"Oh, you know, something for themselves. They wish for more money. Good health. Long life. Many wish for an exciting romance. Maybe a promotion. And, of course, we frequently get wishes for justice. You know, paying back someone who had done them wrong. That's the kind of thing we expect here."

"I see what you're saying," said Leona. She resumed her position at the fountain's edge. She trumpeted, "I wish that every human heart on earth be transformed to feel compassion and love for both God and neighbor." She then dropped the remaining fifteen dollars into the pond with a single throw.

Leona turned to look at the chagrin covering the face of Zuphlas. Feeling quite satisfied, Leona turned on her high heels and walked out of the shop.

CHAPTER 31

HAVING DEVOURED his plateful of pizza about the time a series of beer commercials filled the airwaves, Hillar rose from the living room couch and decided to walk through the hall toward the kitchen. There, he thought, he would pile more pizza on his plate and microwave it. Hillar was a teenager with a voracious appetite.

Hillar's eyes glimpsed Buck at the threshold of the door leading from the dining room to the veranda. The hungry teen stood perfectly still as the microwave hummed behind him. He fixed his vision on Buck at the screen door. *Did I see that screen door move slightly? Am I not alone?* Hillar immediately felt a strange and unfamiliar sense of danger pass through every part of his body. Perhaps someone or something might be lurking just beyond that door. *What should I do?*

Hillar ignored the beeping of the microwave. He turned and ran down the hall and past the living room for the front door. In seconds he was outside, leaping down the front porch steps, and running at top speed up the hill in the direction of the post office. *If there's only one prowler, then I'll get a big head start by running this way.*

Stopping and panting in front of the post office, Hillar rested his hands on his slightly bent knees. Adrenalin and fear mixed together to produce a slight nausea. He knew he needed to keep moving.

The fifth house up on the left belonged to Peter and Helen Simpson, good friends of Leona and members of St. John's. Hillar instinctively turned up the Simpson driveway. He knocked furiously on the side door. When Peter opened the door to welcome the frantic teenager, Hillar felt a wave of safety whirl through his psyche.

CHAPTER 32

CROSSING the street to get to the lakeshore where the live music wafted over the crowd, Leona pulled out her cell phone. *Graham can wait a few more minutes,* she said to herself while sitting down on a park bench in front of the library building.

After poking the phonescreen a number of times, Leona found the previous day's episode of the *Karen Foxx Spotlight Show.* Karen Foxx is Leona's mother, and her television talk show astringently confronts the challenges faced by the City of Detroit. Leona sat back to watch her mother in action.

Karen Foxx was interviewing three of the ten city council officers on Project Green Light Detroit. A number of restaurant and bar owners from Greek Town had just agreed to form a Safe Corridor, meaning they would install high-definition surveillance cameras and flash green lights to announce that theirs is a safe neighborhood. The introductory conversation alluded to how the Detroit Police Department was pressing for a public-private partnership to fight crime. Hostess Foxx easily elicited from her guests self-congratulations along with smiles and chuckles. This would turn out to be the calm before the storm.

"Each green business pays a $250 monthly fee. Is that right?" she asked.

The three guests nodded. One verbalized, "yes."

"Where does that money go?" she queried.

James Sheffield responded. "The fees go to the company that provides the camera installation and maintenance of the surveillance system."

Elizabeth Tate added, "This money subsidizes effective law enforcement. Our streets are much safer now." The third council member, Arthur "Chip" Onassis, said nothing.

"Now," Foxx began to speculate, "if we have, say, a thousand businesses paying $250 per month, that would net $250,000 per month. Over a year's period of time, well, that's a lot of money. Can any of you tell me how many businesses pay this fee?"

"I think it's about two thousand now," said Sheffield. Onassis did not stir.

"Remind me," said the show hostess, "which company handles all the details?"

"That's Troy Electronics," said Tate.

"Oh, that's right," acknowledged Foxx. "Troy Electronics." She put on her reading glasses and shuffled some papers in front of her. "I have the annual report here for Troy Electronics. I see that last year Troy's operating expenses were two million dollars plus change. Its income was six million. I wonder where that extra four million went. Does anybody know?"

Heads nodded negatively.

"Here in the report," Foxx went on, "it appears that Troy Electronics has a parent company. I wonder if that extra four million went to the parent company?

None of the three guests responded.

Karen Foxx paused. Then she pretended to look down at her papers. "It appears that the parent company is called Oakland Investments. It's located in Oakland, Michigan. Do any of you know anything about Oakland Investments?"

THE MOON TURNS TO BLOOD / 87

None of the guests responded. Foxx went on, again pretending to read something. "It says here that the chair of the board at Oakland Investments is..." Foxx took extra time to move the page up close to her eyes. "...one Arthur Onassis." She then removed her reading glasses and the camera turned to the face of Onassis. Foxx paused. An awkward silence intervened.

"Yes, I chair the board," Onassis finally admitted.

"Now, Mister Onassis, this seems to be a convenient arrangement. The DPD collects the money and pays Troy Electronics. After expenses, the profits go to Oakland Investments. And the profit margin seems to be quite high. I'd consider a profit of sixty-seven percent quite high, wouldn't you Mister Onassis?"

"Look. It takes big capital to start up a business large enough to handle the volume the police department wants to create. We at Oakland Investments raised the necessary capital to make things happen. We deserve appropriate compensation for our services to the wider community."

"Oh," said Foxx. "I had not realized that Oakland Investments is a charity! You serve the wider community of Detroit from, where is it? Oakland?"

"No, we're not a charity," said Onassis, stumbling. "We are an investment company and we expect a return. Just like any investment company."

"May I ask, Mister Onassis, just how much of Oakland Investments do you personally own?"

"I decline to answer that," said Onassis.

Karen Foxx put on her reading glasses and looked again at her papers. "I see here, Mister Onassis, that your personal earnings last year topped out at..."

Before she could finish her sentence, Onassis ripped off his microphone, stood up, and sprinted from the studio. Karen Foxx only chortled at his departure. Terror was written across the faces of Sheffield and Tate.

"Did you notice," said Foxx, "how Mister Onassis seems to

assume that he has a right to possess most of the money collected from Detroit businesses. Did you also notice that he sees himself as a public servant, contributing to the reduction of crime on Detroit streets? When he looks into the mirror, I bet he sees nothing wrong. I bet he feels justified, self-satisfied, perhaps even victorious."

After receiving a wrap-up signal from the engineer, Foxx turned to look straight into the camera. "Remember," she said, "in Detroit we have a motto: *Speramus meliori, resurgit cineribus.* Detroit will rise from the ashes. We hope for better things."

CHAPTER 33

WHEN LEONA LOOKED UP, she saw Graham just arriving, panting from running. "Gotta get back to the parsonage, Lee. Hillar's in trouble. I just got a text from Peter Simpson."

Leona jumped to her feet when she saw the grave look on Graham's face. "Let's go!"

Once Leona, Graham, Hillar, and Peter were together in the parsonage, they could tell that Buck had been temporarily sedated with a tranquillizer dart. Hillar's story was told, listened to, and evaluated. The parsonage was searched. No intruders hiding in closets, basement, or around the periphery. Buck showed signs of reviving after the sedation.

The house was pronounced safe. The dog was pronounced safe. Hillar was pronounced safe.

"I wonder if you might have a heart-to-heart talk with Hillar," Leona said to Graham after Hillar and Peter had drifted back into the kitchen to check on the now room-temperature pizza.

"What's this heart stuff? I've got a Y chromosome. I don't need a heart," was Graham's response, with a tone of humor in his voice.

Leona looked up at her partner with tear tinctured eyes. Saying nothing, she rested her head on his chest and wrapped her arms around him.

"OK," said Graham.

CHAPTER 34

As PARISHIONERS of the Saint John's Community Church wheeled their top-down convertibles and SUVs into the gravel parking drive the following Sunday morning, what they saw seemed strange. A yellow police ribbon crisscrossed the church's front door. On the south lawn folding chairs were arranged with rows and aisles. Once they had parked and entered the assembly area, congregants walked up the center aisle with Lena's Flower Garden on their right and the Jean C. Sliter Commemorative Garden on their left. The scent of mixed flowers was discernible. Ushers offered the weekly bulletin and the worshipers seated themselves, murmuring and whispering about the unusual situation.

In front of the assemblage with the white parsonage porch visible in the background stood a large table, covered with a white lace cloth. On it sat a large Bible, a chalice, and a paten with a loaf of bread. Also in the front but on the north side sat Ray Santucci at an electronic keyboard. Extension cords connected his keyboard with some outlet on the other side of an open stained-glass window. The Santucci trio normally played late Saturday nights at the Sagamore Hotel in Bolton Landing, making it a short night for the musician. But, with the exception of this day, Ray always seemed cheerful at the Sunday morning service.

Leona, the pastor, stood front and center in her white alb with a green stole. Her hair was neatly twisted into a tight Chignon bun, for this day in which she would be required to show maturity, leadership, and unflappability.

In her opening greeting, Brenda Beale welcomed everyone and stated briefly that this outside worship was due to most extraordinary circumstances. She promised that Pastor Foxx would tell what is known about the unusual events befalling the congregation. She asked for the hands of visitors. She asked for any announcements. Then Brenda walked to a front row folding chair and seated herself.

When Leona took over, she introduced her two guests, Graham Washington and Hillar Talin, visiting her for a week or two from Chicago. She added, "While my guests are in town, we'd love to do some boating. Now, none of us are sailors. No J-22s. But, if you might be able to loan us a boat that makes a noise—brooooooooom!—then, please mention it to me following worship." Leona then moved into the Call to Worship.

Immediately following the Responsive Reading, yet still early in the worship service, "Special Music" was listed in the bulletin. Ray introduced the morning's guest singer, Luciano Silvestri, visiting from the Adirondack Opera Company. In his late twenties, with dark curly head hair along with an open collar revealing chest hair, he stood to sing. Ray's accompanied Luciano's solo, "You'll Never Walk Alone." Even in the open air of the church lawn, his baritone voice seemed to reverberate off the clouds. Numerous eyes glistened with uninvited tears.

Biblical lessons followed. Then, Leona stood up to speak. "Our little church has stood here since 1876," she began in hushed but audible tones. "In the 1890s some parishioners had to be reprimanded for riding their horses into the church building. This might have been crude and rude, but not a sacrilege. To my knowledge never has a desecration occurred to render our sanctuary profane.

Until this past week. An unspeakable crime so heinous has taken place that we dare not sing praises to our eternal God in the church building until the altar has been re-consecrated to the one true and merciful Lord of heaven and earth."

During her momentary pause heads turned and mouths whispered. A muted uproar was heard rising. She regained control by beginning again to speak. "No doubt you have all heard something about the events of the past week. Let me provide you with facts and the status of the investigation as of this moment." The preacher dispassionately reiterated the details so that all would become informed. Then, she returned to her homily.

"Evil comes in two brands: ordinary evil and radical evil. Let's address ordinary evil first. Each of us here this morning is a sinner. We and everyone we know engage daily in sin, in what we might think of as ordinary evil. We might call it our dark side, our shadow side. Our dark side leads to a variety of pesky annoyances, embarrassments, and occasional distasteful repercussions. That's in part why we come to worship, to have such sins washed away."

The preacher continued. "Sometimes ordinary sinning leads to violence. When we treat each other violently, we do so in the name of the good. We justify our evil deeds by appealing to one or another good—to motherhood, or patriotism, justice, or ideology, or even our biased rendering of the will of God. We engage in gossip, backbiting, and character assassination, hanging someone in effigy, by measuring our victim according to some moral standard. We send our soldiers to war and drones to bomb and diplomats to intimidate, all to defend freedom or to extend our national interests, both good things.

We make others suffer, but we assure ourselves that we do it for the right reasons. The right reasons make us blind. As Jesus said, we try to take a speck out of another's eye while overlooking the log in our own eye. This is garden variety evil. It happens every day, perhaps every hour. On Sundays we sinners kneel before the cross, asking the God of grace to open our eyes and to forgive our trespasses.

What makes a person good is not good deeds, but rather the willing-ness to confess in the name of a still higher good."

Leona coughed briefly into her clenched fist. She turned her body slightly to the right while her head remained facing the worshippers. "But, there is also another kind of evil. It is very rare. We'll call it *radical evil*. In this case, evil is perpetrated in the name of evil. Whereas you and I may gossip, maim, or murder in the name of some higher good, there are some who wallow in evil like a pig washes itself in mud. What transpired in our sanctuary this past week was of the latter kind."

CHAPTER 35

AFTER A PAUSE, Leona continued her sermon. "I want you to remember the next thing I am going to say: You know it's Satan when you hear the call to shed innocent blood. Let me repeat: You know it's Satan when you hear the call to shed innocent blood."

After a gravid pause, the preacher continued. "Our ancestors heard this call and crucified Jesus. You today hear this call when a muffled voice from within tells you to commit suicide. You hear this call when the mob in righteous anger orders us to 'kill those gays' or 'shoot the police' or 'carpet bomb the Muslims'. You hear this call when our leaders rally our nation to take revenge, to nuke 'em." Leona hesitated for a few seconds. She attempted to re-center herself.

"The operative belief here is that the shedding of blood somehow leads to a resolution, to peace, to redemption. We kill for peace, either figuratively or literally. But this is a lie. And don't forget, Satan is the Father of Lies."

The congregants were listening but the expressions on their faces told Leona they were baffled by what she was saying. The hole she just dug was too deep.

Leona continued to speak in altered tone. "The altar cross in our church was turned upside down while the body and blood of an innocent victim was drained and, most likely...what we can imagine is perhaps the unspeakable. Innocent blood has been shed in our sanctuary. Our altar has witnessed a sacrilege. The sacred has been profaned. Evil and the symbols of evil have redefined our holy place of worship. The bloodstains are the stains of impurity, contamination, defilement. They symbolize death with no hope, not the promise of resurrection to everlasting life with God."

Leona was visibly grief stricken, yet somehow she found the courage somewhere deep inside her to remain composed. She proceeded to describe the altar and sanctuary as having been profaned.

"The altar was made profane by this unspeakable liturgy of death. Before we can worship again in this space, it needs to be reconsecrated to the God of grace and love. Two Sundays hence will be Reconsecration Sunday."

The pastor added that the altar and the chapel and the grounds would be rededicated to its original service, to praise and thanksgiving aimed toward the God of salvation. She entreated all to attend this most solemn and important ritual.

CHAPTER 36

As THE TIME drew closer for the Lord's Supper, the Sacrament of the Altar, Leona could not help but tear up. With glistening eyes, she held the bread and the wine of the Eucharist. On the outside she performed her sacramental duty with the depth of commitment for which she had been called. On the inside she could not expel the image of that victimized little Sarai, who died in the building next door. The pastor's tongue tasted like decay.

"In the night in which he was betrayed, our Lord Jesus took bread," she said, opening the words of institution. She held the freshly baked unleavened bread in her hands. She stared at it longer than usual. *This is bread,* she repeated to herself. *It is not the body of Sarai. O, is it?*

"This is my body given for you," she went on, quoting Jesus. *Yes, it's Jesus' body, but only in, with, and under the form of bread.*

"This cup is the new covenant in my blood," she continued while lifting the chalice to eye level. *Jesus' own blood in, with, and under ordinary wine. This is not a re-sacrifice we're doing here. It's Eucharist, a thank you to God for divine grace.* The presiding minister could not forcibly ban from her mind macabre thoughts.

CHAPTER 37

As was her custom, following the Benediction ending the worship service, Leona positioned herself at the exit of the assembly to greet parishioners as they depart. Now outside, this simply meant she stood with a foot in the gravel driveway. Nearly everyone lingered to discuss with her and with others the details of the shocking situation.

"Maybe you and your friends might like to borrow my boat," said Bill Orange.

Leona called Graham over to meet Bill and to talk arrangements. "Ya gotta have a boating license," said Bill. "Ya gotta know what a bouy is."

"I have a license, Mr. Orange," said Graham confidently. "I have piloted sail boats and cruisers on Lake Michigan. So we are good. Thanks for the loan. Where can we pick up the boat?"

"Just call me Bill. It's parked at my dock. I live halfway between here and the Lake George Club, north on Lake Shore Drive. Our little street only has three cottages. My name is Orange. I live next door to Mr. and Mrs. Brown on one side along with Mr. and Mrs. Green on the other. We live in the colored neighborhood."

Graham winced but said nothing. Bill and Graham walked over to meet Hillar. The line of hand-shakers continued.

"Have I met you before?" Leona asked a man with an outstretched hand, ready to shake. Leona's glance caught the golden tan on his square-jawed face. The glance was immediately transformed into a quick study. His Dockers complemented his Tommy Bahama Hawaiian shirt with the shadow of a palm tree. The Clark sandals revealed the tan was total in its coverage. Obviously, he'd spent considerable time in a boat on Lake George...and in the finer men's stores.

"No, Pastor. I'm Renard Maletesto. This is my first visit to your church. Despite the detestable events you have to deal with, I'm quite impressed with your spiritual leadership. I think I like it here."

"You are certainly welcome to return to worship with us, whenever. You may even wish to make Diamond Point your church home," she said.

"Yes, indeed. A church home? My, oh my!" He seemed to be momentarily pondering the significance of this prospect.

"Most of us gather on the parsonage veranda after worship, Mr. Maletesto, for a cup of coffee. Or, iced tea if you're too warm. Please join us."

"Maybe I'll just do that," he replied.

CHAPTER 38

"Pastor Lee, I want you to know Luciano," shouted Ray Santucci with an outstretched arm.

The guest singer and the pastor exchanged handshakes and "hellos."

"Your rendition of 'You'll Never Walk Alone' brought tears to many eyes this morning, Luciano. Thanks for bringing this exquisite offering. Are you permanent with the Adirondack Opera?'

"Nope!" Luciano replied. "I'm permanent with the Manhattan Opera at Lincoln Center. My boss's J. Holmes Chapman."

"Gotcha," said Lee. Small talk ensued.

The soloist mentioned that the Adirondack Opera Company was rehearsing for Alva Henderson's operatic adaptation of *The Last of the Mohicans*. "I will play the role of Uncas, the young Indian whose murder puts an end to the Mohican tribe. Do you know the story?"

"Oh, of course." Leona's eyes registered delight.

Luciano interjected, "Why don't you come to perform with us, Pastor Lee?"

"Oh no! I don't even chant the liturgy here at the church. I'm not in your league," she pleaded.

"You don't have to sing, of course," he added. "Leave the singing to the pros. What we need are supers. Supers are extras. We need bodies, not voices, to dress like British soldiers in the first act and French soldiers in the second. All you need to do is stand there and look mean."

"I don't think Pastor Lee knows how to look mean," said Ray.

"If you like the idea, Pastor Lee," said Luciano elatedly, "just show up at the Glens Falls Theater for rehearsal Thursday at 2:00pm. I'll introduce you to the director. You'll get a big kick out of this. In addition, you and I can get to know one another. I'd like to talk with a minister about something important. Something really important to me."

"Let me think about it," she responded. "I've really got my hands full these days. I'd better not add something like this, even though it sounds like fun. So, if I'm not there at 2:00 on Thursday, the show must go on without me."

The threesome shook hands, smiled, and began sauntering toward the veranda. *So, I might become an opera star,* Leona whispered to herself. *Who'd a thought?*

Then she reminded the group, "Coffee's on as usual. Iced tea too, but only for the faint of heart. Meet us on the porch."

CHAPTER 39

A HALF HOUR LATER, the churchyard was back to normal. Collapsible chairs had been returned to their storage place. Only a small group remained around the veranda coffee pot, talking with one another in various klatches.

"May I show Luciano your house, Pastor?" It was Ray Santucci asking. "I know my way around, you know."

"Sure. Give him the cook's tour, Ray, but stay out of my closets," shouted Leona over her shoulder while swatting a fly off her left arm. A wave of smiles and chuckles flowed over the conversation.

"I found the description of radical evil in your sermon most intriguing, Pastor Lee," said Maletesto, attempting to lasso her attention. The two were sitting adjacent on green wicker rocking chairs, sipping coffee. Others, including Brenda and Graham, sat in their vicinity with cups and cookies in their hands.

"How so, Mister, Maletesto?"

"Renard, please."

"OK. Renard."

"You described radical evil as evil pursued in the name of evil, if I heard you correctly. Otherwise, every day sinning is done in the name of one or another good. Did I get you right?"

"My, but you know how to listen carefully to a sermon, Renard. I'm flattered that you remember what I said with such precision. Most people who come to church listen for my jokes and then go home without recalling my message for the day."

"I didn't hear any jokes today, Pastor Lee," said Maletesto, leaning in and dividing the distance separating their faces by a third. "The matters discussed this morning were much too grave."

"Yes, much too grave for humor," responded Leona without shifting her posture.

"But," Maletesto continued, "I can think of one exception to your rule. I can think of an example where good is done in the name of evil."

"I don't expect my theology to be air tight, to be sure. I'd like to hear your counterexample. So shoot."

Graham inched his chair toward the debate. Hillar took up a position on the porch rail, with one leg dangling. He appeared disinterested, feigning playing a game on his device, but was close enough to hear every word. The topic of evil itself tempts curiosity.

"I don't know if you've ever heard of the medieval town of Regensburg. It's in Germany. Northern Bavaria, to be more precise. On the Danube. Early in the twelfth century, the citizens of Regensburg decided to upgrade their city by building two new structures, a cathedral and a bridge. A famous builder—today we'd call him a contractor—and his apprentice bid for both jobs and were awarded the contracts. The master builder got the cathedral, and the apprentice the bridge."

Leona rocked back in her chair with a knowing expression on her face. Graham and Hillar—even Buck—cocked their ears to listen for what would come next in the story.

Maletesto continued. "Now the master builder had both talent and experience. The apprentice lacked both. Yet, the competitive spirit of the apprentice made him want to win. He wanted to complete his bridge before the cathedral could be built. How could he accomplish this?"

Maletesto studied each listening face. No one spoke. Even Buck seemed to be curious. Luciano and Ray, having returned from the cook's tour, squeezed into chairs to listen in.

"Well," continued Maletesto, "the apprentice went to a special place, a wishing tree. There he met a most generous benefactor. We know this benefactor by many titles or names: the Devil, the Great Deceiver, Beelzebub, Lucifer, or Satan. We think of this benefactor as the Wicked One, the Evil One."

Maletesto seemed to enjoy the rapt attention of his listeners. "What happened is this. The apprentice explained his situation to Satan. Now, Satan liked the idea of delaying the building of a cathedral. So, Satan listened quite sympathetically and announced that he could provide the apprentice with just what he needed to build that bridge over the Danube River. So, they struck a deal."

"What did the apprentice have to give Satan?" asked Graham. "The Devil usually demands payment, doesn't he?"

"Yes, of course," answered Maletesto. "Satan asked for three souls. Satan asked for the souls of the first three to cross the bridge. For the price of only three souls, the apprentice would not only build a fine bridge but complete it ahead of schedule."

"What happened?" asked Hillar expectantly, allowing his cell phone to drift downward.

"The construction went surprisingly well. Satan caused a drought that temporarily dried up most of the river, so the apprentice could easily lay the foundations for fifteen support columns. Between an island and the shore, the apprentice ordered the construction of a dam. Then, when the rains came and the water level went back to normal, he could build the bridge on a dry surface. In only eleven years the great Stone Bridge, longer than a football field, was built. This bridge has continued to carry all sorts of traffic right down to the present day. In fact, if you ever go to Regensburg, you can walk across this very bridge."

Maletesto turned to Leona. "Now, isn't this an example of evil— in this case the Evil One himself—doing something good?"

Leona sat in her green rocking chair with a pensive look on her face. Brenda and the other listeners stared at her, anticipating her response to this challenge.

CHAPTER 40

"HAVE you actually been on site in Regensburg, Renard?" Leona asked. "Have you stood on the bank of the Danube near the *Steierne Brücke,* I mean, the Stone Bridge?"

"Why, yes of course," responded Maletesto. "I'm very familiar with Bavaria. I know firsthand everything there is to know about Bavaria. Everyone in Bavaria knows how the Evil One helped them."

"Renard, do you recall seeing on the surface of the river the swirls and eddies? Do you recall seeing the whirlpool patterns of the water's flow?"

Maletesto nodded ambiguously. Leona went on. "There is more to this story, Renard. You left something out. Yes, indeed, the apprentice agreed to pay the Devil with the first three souls to cross the bridge. But, here's what you left out."

Now the porch audience was fixed on Leona. What would she say next?

"On the day the bridge was to be inaugurated, the city officials showed up for the celebration. The first three scheduled by the event committee to lead the parade across the bridge were: the Bishop, the Mayor, and the Duke. The very thought that these three community leaders would spend eternity in hell frightened the poor apprentice.

He could not let this happen. He had to think of a plan to fulfill his bargain with Satan yet preserve these noble people."

"What did he do?" asked Hillar, now fully and obviously engaged in the story.

"Here's what that clever apprentice did. Ahead of the parade, he shooed a dog, a cat, and a chicken. These three animals ran ahead and were the first to cross the bridge. So, the Devil would have to take these three animal souls and be denied any human souls."

Maletesto's face showed disgust. Hillar's showed delight. Graham's showed incredulity. The faces of Luciano and Ray revealed they were still trying to keep up.

"There is even more to this story that you have not told us, Renard," Leona said. "The Lord of the Abyss became enraged. He had been tricked, after all. So, Satan tried to knock the bridge over. He wanted to smash what the apprentice had built. But, no matter how hard he tried, he could not destroy the bridge. It was built of stone. And its pillars were solidly grounded in bedrock. So it would not yield."

"Then what happened?" asked Hillar, leaning in with intense interest.

"Satan..." said Leona as she turned to lock eyes with Hillar. She paused. Then continued. "Satan was now frustrated along with being angry, so he took the souls of the three animals and threw himself into the river. He swam all the way down to the abyss, to hell. On his way down he uttered curses. His angry curses are what causes the river water to swirl and whirl. If you go to Regensburg today, you can still see Satan's anger in the Danube. But the Stone Bridge stands strong. So, I ask you, Renard," she said turning toward the visitor, "is this really an example of doing good in the name of evil?"

"Neither of you have said anything about that cathedral?" interjected Graham.

Maletesto nodded in Leona's direction. She responded by speaking. "After more than a century, the cornerstone for that cathedral had still not been laid. Then, in 1273, construction began on what would become a giant gothic behemoth, the St. Peter's Dome. Well, they're still working on it as we speak. I have no idea when it will be completed."

Maletesto then turned toward the pastor. "You seem to know a great deal about Bavaria, Pastor Lee."

"I'm a bit of a Germanophile. That's how I realized that you told only part of the story, Renard."

"I've got a question, Pastor Lee," interjected Hillar. "Does this mean that Buck and Midnight have souls? Will I see them in heaven?"

CHAPTER 41

Soon Ray and Luciano were picking up dirty napkins and used coffee cups to take to the kitchen. The coffee klatchers were drifting down the porch steps, onto the grass, strolling toward their cars. Leona offered a "good-bye" to each in turn.

When Maletesto found an opportunity to arrest Leona's attention, he spoke in a loud whisper. "Do you have a favorite wine, Pastor?"

"Now, that's a personal question, Renard. Yes, I happen to have a favorite wine."

"Well?"

"Are you into wines, Renard? Why do you ask?"

"Just tell me what it is."

"I hate to, because it's so expensive. It's Silver Oak cabernet sauvignon. Ever heard of it?"

"Of course. Everyone knows that exquisite taste. Speaking of taste, I wonder if you'd like to come over to my cottage early this evening for a barbecue."

Hillar's ears pricked up, so he moved closer to monitor the conversation. Leona looked up at Renard and smiled.

"Because you are a Germanophile, Pastor Lee, I will plan a special barbeque. We'll do what Bavarians do. We'll grill some *Weisswurst*, you know, the white dinner sausage they eat in Regensburg. What do you think?"

"How about sauerkraut? Sweet mustard? Beer?" Leona interrogated Maletesto. "You know, what Bavarians do in the evening."

"Yes, of course. Will you come? Bring your friends here. I will send a boat for you and pick you up about 6:00. Okay?"

"No. I don't think we can make it tonight. But Renard, thanks for asking," she said with a note of sternness.

"Perhaps another occasion, then," Maletesto said while departing for his car.

Hillar seemed excited. "Why did you say 'no' to that invitation, Pastor Lee? I'd like to go to that barbeque."

"Yes," added Graham. "That was a tad abrupt on your part."

"Sorry to spoil our evening. But the man's a liar. Anyone who genuinely knows northern Bavaria knows that Regensburgers eat their *Weisswurst* in the morning, about 9:30. The sausage is eaten with sauerkraut, sweet mustard, and a pretzel. Yes, they sometimes accompany this coffee break with beer. Better than coffee. Here is the key point: this is not their evening meal. Maletesto tells half-truths, incomplete stories, and pretends to know more than he does. And I ask: why?"

Ray gulped. Graham pondered what he was hearing from Leona. This was a detail he could not have predicted she would know.

"So?" asked Hillar.

"So, I don't want to jump into a social relationship too quickly here. If Renard Maletesto lies so unashamedly, it makes me suspicious, Quaz. Doesn't it make you suspicious?"

Graham merely grinned. Hillar looked confused. Luciano and Ray were now in the huddle.

"And you all remember who is the Father of Lies, right? Jesus told us."

Every face turned blank. Leona looked up at a passing cloud and exclaimed with her hands stretched out sideways, "Why do I do this?"

CHAPTER 42

"I've really missed you, Grammy," said Leona, her eyes looking down at the glass in front her.

"If you've really missed me, Lee, then why do you live at Lake George and I live in Chicago?" he replied sternly, looking directly at her, but seeing only the part in her lustrous auburn hair rather than the depth of her blue-green eyes.

"This is not the time to talk about that," she said, attempting to avoid tension before the topic took control over the evening. "Another time."

"Another time. Another time. Another time! That's all you ever say," responded Graham with unambiguous irritation in his voice. "What are you so damn afraid of, anyway?"

Leona shifted in her chair and reached for his hand resting on the table. She gently squeezed it. Graham's face softened a bit, but Leona knew that she couldn't keep avoiding this discussion simply by showing appreciation. She avoided any talk about their relationship regardless of the niggle in her stomach.

"But I can't even begin to express how truly grateful I am to have you here."

The two sat at a table on the east veranda of the Lake George

Club. They had left Hillar at Pete and Helen Simpsons' instead of keeping him at home. Now alone, the two watched the early evening sun begin its end of day ritual. Bobbing sailboats at anchor shimmered in the light. Nubile young beauties in skimpy bathing suits wandered the dock and occasionally dipped their feet in the ice-cold lake. A muscular male lifeguard surveyed everything behind dark sunglasses. The setting sun's rays struck the eye like a horizontal arrow even though the day was readying itself to transition to night.

"I don't know what any of this means, Graham. I have suffered through Iranian prisons, the murders of people I love, PTSD and moral injury, and through the crisis and victory of faith. But this? This makes no sense to me. I don't know where to put this gratuitous act of evil in my psychological file cabinet."

"I understand, Lee. It is nothing I have ever had to confront either. The symbolism is obviously ritual blasphemy. Instead of the blood of Christ transubstantiated from wine on the altar, it's human blood. Ugh. Could it be Satanism or pseudo-Satanism? If so, this is not typically on the to-do list for a CIA agent, or even for a bishop's assistant, for that matter. "

"Not bread and wine, but a little girl's body and blood. Graham, this is too atrocious to even think about! And then there's Sophia."

"Have the police given you any more information?"

"The police? They are as helpful as mice in a cheese factory. It seems they nibble away at what they think are clues, without a shred of awareness that they don't have the requisite understanding of cults needed to actually *solve* something like this."

"What about Sheriff Bolton? Does he seem to know what's going on?"

"Not a clue. His theory is that Sarai is the rope in a marital tug-o-war. The losing parent supposedly murdered the daughter out of spite."

"But that wouldn't explain the religious symbolism."

"Of course not. And it seems like quite a reach to me, like they can't think of anything else," Leona said, shaking her head slightly as she looked at Graham.

Graham waited. Leona spoke again. "The sheriff brought into the investigation a guy from the NYPD nicknamed Mohawk. I think he's a descendent of the Mohawk tribe. Fancies himself an expert on the Six Nations. He's got his own theory."

"Pardon me, Lee. The Six Nations?"

"Oh. When the Europeans arrived in this part of North America, many of the natives they mistakenly called *Indians* were organized into a confederation of tribes. Since I've been living here, I've gotten kind of interested."

Graham sipped his water.

Leona continued. "This group of Indians was sometimes called the *Iroquois Confederacy* or the *Five Nations* or the *Six Nations* or the Haudenosaunee. It included the Mohawk, Onondaga, Oneida, Cayuga, and Seneca, if I recall correctly. And, to make a sixth, I think, the Tuscarora moving north from the deep south joined the confederacy. But they had no vote at the council. I think the Tuscarora were somehow attached to the Onondaga and spoke through them. Anyway, decisions about war and peace were made at a council representing all six tribes. They met around a council fire among the Onondaga. In fact, that very fire burned for three centuries before it was extinguished, at least that's what we are told. They extinguished the fire only when the tribes could no longer agree on which white men to fight with a united army."

It was Leona's turn to sip from her glass. "Look at the lake, Grammy. If we were sitting here in the summer of 1757, we would see the French army along with the Huron Indians canoeing southward. Right there, Grammy, right there," she said pointing to the water.

Without warning, the blue sky turned dark gray before their eyes. After a few minutes a down rush of heavy rain pelted the tree leaves, dock surfaces, and deck chairs. Thunder could be heard in the distance. The two watched the changing colors of the waterscape.

They listened to the roar of the wind and the rhythm of raindrops on the awning that sheltered them. They felt the dampness of the ambient air, even though they remained dry.

"Just this fast the sun will return, Graham. It'll be as though God turns the heavenly light switch on and off as a sort of game."

After a pause, Leona continued. "In the French and Indian War, the Mohawk sided with the British. Even though Marquis de Montcalm was a brilliant French General, the British eventually won. That's why today we speak English, not French. Only a hundred and sixty miles north of here they still speak French."

"I've got French genes in me, you know," interposed Graham. "I'm Creole, after all."

"How much French do you speak, Mister Creole?"

"Get back to your story."

"OK. The Mohawk fought with the British in the French and Indian War and later in the Revolutionary War. Siding with the British a second time was a big mistake. Because the Americans won, that left the Mohawks without any European friends. So many of the Mohawks moved up north and now have a single reservation that straddles the St. Lawrence, half in Canada and half in the U.S."

Leona switched from water to Sauvignon Blanc, sniffed the bouquet, and took a sip. "Back to the period just prior to the revolution. The Huron fought for the French, as I said. They treated both the Mohawk and the British with utmost cruelty. Torturing, murdering, scalping. The Mohawk today have not forgotten this history, although they mostly joke about it. After intermarrying with so many Huron and even German settlers, today's Mohawk only read about their ancestors in school."

Suddenly, dazzling sunshine enveloped the dock area and spotted the lake vista with pools of yellow glow. The trees of Long Island burned in bright light, while the green-gray mountains of Queen Anne, New York, two miles beyond the island, provided a dark backdrop. A double rainbow appeared linking New York State to Vermont, which lay beyond those mountains.

"Frankly, Lee," said Graham, picking up the conversation, "I don't see any connection between this near three-century-old history and our crime scene."

"Frankly, Graham, I don't either. But I think this New York detective does. His name is Mohawk, Mohawk Evans. Did I say that already? He's got a corncob up his ass, to put it mildly. He thinks falsely that ancient Huron sacrificial practices were of the type that killed little Sarai. But, had it been Huron *redivivus,* her scalp would be missing, not her heart. The guy's confused. I fear he's going to lead both the NYPD and our sheriff down a blind alley."

"Do we have to follow down that blind alley?"

"Of course not. We follow our own alleys."

CHAPTER 43

THE FOLLOWING DAY, after parking Graham's rental in Bill's neighborhood, a party of four descended the log stairs to the Orange boathouse. They were gratified to see docked there a hefty seventeen-foot Starcraft with two Mercury 35-horsepower outboard engines bolted to the transom. Once Graham, Hillar, Leona, and Buck were in the boat, Graham piloted the craft slowly and carefully into open water. Then he gunned it.

The brisk morning air, combined with the bright sunshine and occasional water spray, elicited a feeling of near euphoria. To bounce across wave tops is to experience the elixir of the universe running through one's veins. Even Buck felt it, as he leaned over the Starcraft's edge staring forward with wind in his eyes.

Graham led the crew on an aimless drive on the watery road with no lane striping. "Grammy," asked Leona. "Do you know the artwork of Georgia O'Keefe?"

"Yes, of course. I regularly go to the Chicago Art Institute, you know."

"Who's what's-her-name?" Hillar interrupted. He wanted to be let into the conversation. Buck did not seem to mind not being addressed on this topic.

"Georgia O'Keefe is an artist famous for painting scenes of Lake George and New Mexico, Quaz. During the 1920s she lived in that house over there with her boyfriend, Stieglitz, one of the most famous photographers of all time. It's the gray mansion with the reddish-brown roof. See it?"

The other humans in the boat glanced incuriously at the Stieglitz mansion. Buck kept looking forward, apparently enjoying the wind in his face.

"Let's go around the southern end of Long Island," First Mate Lee said to Captain Graham. "This island's a mile long. All wilderness," she announced, as if she were a tour guide. After rounding the southern tip, they navigated northward with Harris Bay and Ripley Point on their right. Just beyond they could see the tree-covered Pilot Knob Mountain in Vermont.

"I think I see birds' nests," exclaimed Hillar, pointing to tall pines in the island's center. "They're giant nests."

"Eagles," added Leona. "Bald Eagles. When they're young, they have just one color. But, after six months or so, the fledgling feathers drop out, leaving the magnificent white headdress."

"I wanna see," stated Hillar forcefully. He opened his metallic suitcase and drew out electronic paraphernalia. Soon, Genghis was assembled and switched on. Captain Graham parked the boat with engines in idle so that the group could quietly watch the drama about to unfold. Eventually, Graham cut the engine entirely so the boat would drift. The crew felt an unobtrusive rocking motion that did not interfere with their concentration.

Genghis soared upward toward Long Island. Pilot Hillar carefully guided the aircraft with his cell phone into a hovering position above the tree holding the giant nest. He then switched on the camera as Genghis began his descent.

The audience of three watched the show on the cellphone screen. One full sized eagle, complete with white mane, was feeding three fledglings that were jostling, poking, and yapping. Each of the little ones demanded food, showing no interest in sharing. "Kinda reminds me of the human race," remarked Leona.

Buck said nothing.

CHAPTER 44

ONCE GENGHIS HAD RETURNED to the drifting boat, Graham returned to his driver's seat and gripped the steering wheel. Before he could restart the engine, Leona whispered loudly, "Listen! What's that noise?"

The three humans froze momentarily while Buck cocked his head to listen. "I think it's a drone," offered Hillar. "Another drone!"

Despite the strong sun, they all visually searched the sky. After a few seconds, Graham pointed upward toward a small four-propeller craft hovering only two hundred feet above. "I get the feeling it's watching us," he said. "Too far away to see if it has a camera, but I bet it does."

"Why would anybody want to spy on us?" queried Hillar.

"No reason I can think of, Quaz," commented Leona with an open hand shielding her sunglasses while watching the object above. "Unless, of course, it's got something to do with the church desecration. I wonder if we have enemies we don't yet know about."

"Want Genghis to go get it?" Hillar asked with a tone of challenge in his voice.

"What do you mean?" asked Leona.

"Let me show you," said Hillar proudly as he prepared Genghis for his next flight. This time he would guide the drone with his now open laptop computer. "I'm going to affix my net pack. I designed it myself. It's a drone defense against drones. This'll be its first actual test. It takes two of these compressed gas tanks, not just one."

"Go get that Red Baron," growled Graham.

After a few short minutes Genghis was ready for the dogfight that was to come. Genghis began a slow and deliberate ascent under Hillar's remote piloting. "If the Red Baron holds still, I'll be able to capture it," said Hillar while concentrating on Genghis.

The alien drone appeared to remain in place as Genghis approached. Suddenly, the Red Baron accelerated and headed directly toward Genghis. Because of its computerized avoidance mechanism, Genghis dodged upward at the last second and the Red Baron flew past its target and missed.

"Strike two!" hollered Leona.

The anticipated dogfight was on. The two drones zoomed past each other, one diving below the other, then reversing the attack. The confrontation repeated itself for a full two minutes, each drone missing the other by a hair. Eventually the Red Baron circled around as did Genghis. The two flying machines now hung in midair, facing each other at a distance of only a hundred fifty feet. "I think it's time for my jet blast," said Hillar. With this, Genghis shot toward its target at lightning speed. But the Red Baron popped sideways, and Genghis was left with a harmless pass to the side. "I think the Red Baron's got something like I've got," announced Hillar.

This time the foreign drone followed Genghis. Hillar guided his craft toward Long Island and into the forest at a high rate of speed. A competitive joy took over Hillar's face as he zigged and zagged between trees. Yet, the Red Baron seemed equal to the combat task and followed Genghis at almost the same speed and with matching agility.

"I can't see them anymore. They've disappeared into the woods," commented Leona.

"I can see everything with my cameras," said Hillar with glee and a sense of youthful pride. His computer screen looked like a video game without a points tally.

A moment later Genghis emerged from the woods at an altitude of only a hundred feet. The Red Baron zoomed into view only seconds behind. Once Genghis had passed the boat, Hillar guided him into a large elliptical pattern. When Genghis had turned back in the pattern, the alien drone followed. Then Genghis could approach the Red Baron from the front. Hillar exclaimed, "Watch this!"

The Red Baron suddenly ceased its forward motion. It simply hung in a hover, engines running but going nowhere. With a gleeful expression, Hillar exclaimed, this is my version of the X-MADIS drone slayer. I've got it paralyzed."

"What's X-MADIS?" asked Graham, partially shouting over the boat engine noise.

"It stands for eXpeditionary Mobile Aerial Defense Integrated System. The drone slayer works up to three kilometers away. What I did is jam the Red Baron's signal and took it over. Do you wanna take it home as a souvenir? If so, watch this!"

Something shot out from Genghis. The projectile slowed just above the Red Baron and then spread out a large net. The net completely enshrouded the alien drone. Its four propellers abruptly stopped turning. Before the Red Baron could begin its descent, a small parachute opened and the entire assembly floated downward toward the lake's surface. "Awesome!" shouted Leona.

Graham and Leona applauded, while Buck looked on with expectant eyes. Hillar brought Genghis back in just as a fowler would land a falcon. Graham started the engine and headed the boat toward the debris field. Just before they arrived at the site where the drone landed, something exploded. "Pop!" It was the alien drone. The Red Baron had exploded, with pieces spreading about and then sinking.

"Some sort of self-destruct mechanism, I bet," murmured Hillar as he reached over to scoop up what was left of the drama in the sky.

"Somebody does not want us to identify them," commented

Graham. "Otherwise, it would be ridiculous to equip a drone with a self-destruct mechanism. So what was this all about?"

CHAPTER 45

"Thanks, Quaz," Leona said to Hillar as he placed a cup of hot coffee on the table next to her. Leona was sitting in a wicker rocker on the east porch of the parsonage talking with Angie in Michigan on her cell.

"Why don't you take my calls?" growled Angie.

"I'm in a whirlwind here, Angie. Sorry."

"Frankly, Lee, it's a lot of work to be your BFF. I'm worried. I don't know what's going on from day to day. I don't know whether you're dead or alive." After a pause, Angie continued. "Are you being careful?"

"Yes, yes, of course. I *am* careful," Leona assured Angie, in a tone that tried not to reveal how irritated she could get when her best friend acted more like her mother than her surrogate sister.

Hillar could hear only Leona's voice. "Yes, yes, Buck is fine. Graham and I were worried about him, but he seems to have recovered. We think he must have eaten something when he was out on his exploratory treks by the creek. Actually we were more worried about Hillar. He was visibly shaken....yeah, Graham plans a man-to-man talk with him and he seems better....Yeah. Gotta go. Somebody just drove up. Love you too. Bye"

Both Hillar and Leona turned to watch while a Warren County sheriff's car rolled slowly through the hedge opening and onto the back lawn of the church, parking in front of the parsonage veranda. Out stepped Sheriff Bolton and Detective Evans. The two cops ambled up to the porch, assuming they would be welcome. They were definitely welcome, in Leona's mind.

"Hillar, would you kindly bring our new guests some coffee," Leona ordered through the window screen after hanging up with Angie.

With a sense of duty, Hillar served the coffee on a tray with spoons, sugar, milk and small napkins, all neatly arranged. He appreciated that he was able to contribute in small ways to what he was beginning to accept as his family. Buck settled on the porch steps; Hillar pulled up a chair to listen. The two law enforcement officers, with somber expressions on both their faces, hesitatingly engaged Leona in conversation.

"There's been a new development," tendered Sheriff Bolton. "Don't know if it's relevant or not. This morning a man was found dead in Saratoga. A death blow to the head."

The sheriff pulled his small notebook from a shirt pocket and studied it. "He's known as Bishop Tikhon. Some kinda church big shot. Might you have any knowledge or thoughts about this, Pastor Lee?"

After a few moments of dead silence, Leona responded pensively. "If I'm not mistaken, I believe Bishop Tikhon is Stephen Korsky's superior in the OCA."

"OCA?"

"Yes. Orthodox Church in America."

Silence again as Leona dropped her head into her hands. "Now, Sheriff, let's backtrack for a moment. What happened when you brought Father Korsky to the coroner's office?"

"Well, he was quiet. Moved kinda slowly. He identified his wife's body. And, of course, he showed shock, sadness, and even cried. Strange though, now that I think about it. He seemed to recover quickly for a guy who just lost his wife and lost her in such a horrible way." The sheriff paused to think about what he'd just said. Then, he continued. "He made arrangements right away with the coroner for a funeral home to receive the body. Like he was in a hurry. Like it was a business deal of some sort."

"Hmmm...that does seem unusual, especially for a clergyman," Leona responded and then shifted her focus. "Okay, what about the autopsy? The autopsy show anything important?"

"Yes," answered Mohawk. "Along with the sheriff here I read the report. Bruises suggest that Mrs. Korsky and her murderer were fighting. She lost the fight, obviously. No doubt the assailant was larger and more powerful."

Mohawk continued. "A blunt instrument damaged her brain. Perhaps the killer hit her in the head, and this knocked her unconscious. The upside-down cross carved into her back might have been added later, after she was dead. Because of the lack of blood on the wound, the upside down cross was undoubtedly a postmortem incision. It was the brain damage that most likely caused her death."

"This fight. It could've happened with her clothes on, right?" asked Leona.

"Yes, most likely," said Mohawk. "Only after she was unconscious or even dead were her clothes removed and the symbolic cut added to her back."

"Did the fight occur out on the water? In a boat?" she asked.

"Not necessarily," interjected the sheriff. "Mrs. Korsky could have been murdered anywhere, then later, her body dumped out of a boat into the lake. The coroner reported that there was very little water in her lungs. If she had no water in her lungs, she probably was murdered somewhere else, and her body dumped after she stopped breathing."

"This sounds premeditated to me," said Leona.

"Certainly looks that way," said the sheriff.

"Now, back to Bishop Tikhon. Was there any symbolism at the death site?" Leona asked, looking at both of her visitors.

"Actually," said the sheriff, "There was. This is what I want to ask you about. The body of the bishop was found in his bungalow living room. He was dressed in his pajamas. We think the time of death was morning, perhaps right after breakfast. But, here's what's curious."

The sheriff pulled out his cell phone and swept his fingers across the screen a few times. Finally, when he had found what he was looking for, he showed the screen to Leona. Hillar moved quickly to look over Leona's shoulder. Buck lifted up his head but remained disinterested.

On the screen was the body of the dead bishop, lying face up, in his pajamas. Around his neck and draped across the front of his torso was a stole, a liturgical stole. This stole was not clean. It was smeared in red and ragged, as if someone had punctured it in many places with an ice pick.

"Do you know what we're looking at, Pastor Lee?" asked the sheriff.

"I'm not totally sure. It doesn't immediately make sense. Why Bishop Tikhon would be wearing vestments in his pajamas is beyond me. I don't get it. This stole is called an Epitrachelion. Both priests and bishops wear it for the sacrament. Not with pajamas. And, what's this red stuff? Blood?"

"Yes, blood," interjected Mohawk.

"Well," pondered Leona, "it appears that the Epitrachelion has been deliberately defiled. And it was punctured while it was worn—before or after he was dead—to insure that the Bishop's innocent blood would stain it. Why?"

"That's what we're asking you," said Mohawk.

"What is the cause of death?" asked Leona.

"We're waiting to find out," answered the Sheriff. "It does not appear that he was wearing the stole when he died. It appears the stole was added after the death. We won't know until we have examined everything."

Leona sat back in her green wicker chair. Everyone sipped coffee in silence. Then Leona spoke. "I don't know if this is relevant. When

Father Korsky and Sophia visited me, something was said. Evidently, Father Korsky could become a bishop only if he wasn't married. And, of course, only if a bishop's slot opened up." Then, Leona paused to let the matter sink in.

"On the one hand," Leona surmised, "it's likely that these two deaths were perpetrated by the same group that murdered Sarai. On the other hand, it's very possible that the death of Sophia and that of Bishop Tikhon are not connected to the ritual sacrifice here at Saint John's. But, of course, the evidence is too scanty to tell. Yet."

CHAPTER 46

WITHOUT BEING ASKED, Hillar emerged through the screen door onto the veranda with a fresh pot of hot coffee. He offered refills. Everyone accepted.

"Mister Mohawk," Leona said, addressing her guest. "I am still not clear. Just why did you come from New York City up here to Diamond Point? Please tell me again."

"Well, Pastor, as I mentioned, we've had a number of unsolved crimes in the Red Apple. Murders, actually. Let me tell you about one in particular. This Bishop Tikhon case looks almost like a copy cat."

"What was the first case?" asked Graham with interest.

"The victim was a singer. Opera. Internationally known star."

"Who?" asked Leona.

"Vivian Champagne," answered Mohawk.

Leona's eyebrows went up. Graham nodded to acknowledge having heard the name.

"She had been singing the lead in Bizet's *Carmen*."

"So, what's the connection with Diamond Point?" quizzed Graham.

"When we found her body in her apartment, her heart had been surgically removed. It was gone. In addition, her larynx had been removed. It was a bloody mess."

"This does not sound at all like Bishop Tikhon's case. No missing heart. No missing anything. Only a gash in the head," said Leona.

"Well, Pastor," continued Mohawk, "what did you notice about that stole? What did you call it, a, a...?

"Epitrachelion," she interjected.

"Yes," acknowledged Mohawk, "one of those. Well, Vivian Champagne did not have one of those. But, she was wearing a nun's habit. It was not a real habit. It was a costume taken from the opera house. And it was put over her following her murder. We know this because it covered up the missing body parts, the heart and larynx."

"So," paused Leona, "I bet you see symbolic meaning in this nun's habit, right?"

"Well, asked Mohawk, "what do you think?"

Leona turned to look toward Graham. After a couple seconds, Graham began to speak. "Obviously the removal of the heart and the larynx are symbolic. The nun's clothing is definitely intended to convey desecration. Now, just what could all of this mean?"

"Certainly, Mister Mohawk, you are testing one theory or another," added Leona. "Just what's your best guess?"

"Well," began the detective. "I think there's a single group behind what's happening both in the City and here at Lake George. I think that the heart removal means that someone is eating those hearts. It's some sort of ritual. Some sort of empowerment ritual."

"Do you suspect it's the Hurons?" asked Leona.

Mohawk said nothing. He sat looking straight ahead.

"Well, with all due respect," Leona continued, "I think that theory is ludicrous. There is no evidence of any Huron organization —let alone conspiracy—either in New York City or here at Lake George. A ritual heart removal? Yes, of course. But definitely not Hurons."

Mohawk only shrugged his shoulders. So did the sheriff. Silence followed.

"Who, may I ask, replaced Vivian Champagne in *Carmen*?" It was Graham speaking.

The sheriff looked at Mohawk. So did Leona. The NYPD detective said only, "Lilian Serano."

Sheriff Bolton and Mohawk departed, thanking the pastor for her cooperation. Leona walked into the house and into the telephone booth to find the Korsky phone number. She dialed it.

CHAPTER 47

A LITTLE WHILE LATER, from the north porch, Graham watched while a UPS truck parked along the front hedge. The driver asked Graham to sign for a package, a large and heavy box with Silver Oak listed as the return address. Graham picked up the box and walked it around the house to where Leona was sitting.

"Silver Oak, Lee," he announced, paying no attention to Leona on the phone. "Now, I know on your salary that this is unaffordable. And I know that Doctor Neshat is dead. So it must come from a new admirer, a rich admirer at that. And how the hell would he know that this is your favorite wine?"

"Gotta go, Stephen. Again, my condolences on your two losses." Leona hung up.

Once the mystery box was set on the wooden veranda floor, Hillar opened it and pawed through the contents. He victoriously raised a bottle of the most cherished cabernet sauvignon, cherished at least by Leona Foxx. "How would anyone know what you like, Pastor Lee?" Hillar asked with amazement.

"I can't imagine," she answered.

After reaching into the box, Graham pulled out a card and proceeded to read it aloud.

Out of admiration and affection I send you this card,
With a fruit of the vine tasteful in your churchyard.
Gaining knowledge of good and evil
is not only primeval or medieval;
it is avant-garde. Yours truly, Renard.

Graham feigned looking aside as if to grant Leona privacy. Then he turned his eyes back to the card. "It appears that your new admirer, Renard, would like to host you for lunch. He'll have a boat waiting for you at the Lake George Club day after tomorrow at 11:30. Wanna go?"

"I know I'm not invited this time," said Hillar. "But, if I were, I would not go. Where I want to go is over to the Pot Belly Deli to get a slice of pizza. And right now. Come on, Buck."

CHAPTER 48

GRAHAM BROUGHT out two wine glasses partially filled with Silver Oak Cabernet Sauvignon and sat on a wicker chair on the pillared east porch of the parsonage. A moment later Leona let the screen door slam behind her as she took her chair and began to sip the cab.

Midnight the miniature black panther sat on the white railing and, along with Graham and Leona, watched the activities in the yard between the church and the white house. Hillar and Buck, back from the Pot Belly Deli, were sprawled out in the lawn wrestling. The dog droned a continual growl, a playful growl. Hillar growled back. The two tumbled, first with Buck on top and then the reverse.

Buck would occasionally grip Hillar's head in his enormous mouth, but never did he clamp down or inflict any injuries. Simulated violence was play for the giant canine. The worst Hillar suffered was an excess of dog saliva, unappetizing to Leona but a delight for Hillar.

Midnight leaped off the porch and ran toward the wrestling match. She grabbed Buck's left rear paw and nipped it with her teeth deep enough to make the husky yelp. Buck reared up to attend to the annoyance and then realized he'd been attacked. He turned immediately toward Midnight, who then streaked toward the ravine's edge. Buck followed, picking up speed with each stride. The black cat found a tree and clawed her way to a height of ten feet or so. Buck circled the tree trunk, growling with both joy and mock aggression.

Abandoned by the canine and feline, Hillar made his way to the veranda after opening a canned soda. Soon the three *Homo sapiens* were in conversation.

"Dogs come from wolves, y'know," announced the teenager to the grown-ups. "I've been reading the New Skete brothers on dogs. The New Skete monastery is not far from here, over in Vermont. The brothers say that dogs evolved from wolves gradually. First, some wolves hung around human camps to snitch scraps of discarded food. Next, the wolves lost their fear of people. Eventually, people took wolf puppies and raised them. As time passed, nature selected those wolves that could get along with people and their genomes changed. Now, dog puppies open their eyes later and take longer to grow up, meaning they develop more sensitive relationships with their human owners. But," Hillar spoke with philosophical emphasis, "the tie with wolves was never fully broken. They can still interbreed, yaknow."

"Buck looks like a wolf to me," commented Leona. "I am really impressed, Hillar! Where did you learn all this?"

"Oh, I just was lookin' around the Internet one day after Buck and I were wrestlin' and I found out about huskies and then wolves and then the New Skete brothers. Interesting, huh?

"You see, in one sense, Buck is a wolf. But, in another sense, he's only a dog. He gets along with people because he's always been with people. Jack London would say that if we put Buck back into the wild, pretty soon he'd turn into a wolf again."

"I thought Jack London was discredited," said Graham with his eyebrows raised.

"Not in my book," retorted Hillar. "He's my favorite author. New studies in ethology confirm what he said about dogs and wolves."

"*Ethology?* How did a kid your age learn such a big word?"

snipped Graham. "Did you graduate or flunk out of the school of evolution?"

"Graham!" snarled Leona.

"That's all right, Pastor Lee," interjected Hillar. "We just need to educate this Princeton grad and get him up to speed." Hillar turned to Graham with a slight smirk on his face. "Wanna know about eye contact?"

"Yeh, sure. What about eye contact?"

"This is fascinating." Hillar went on exhibiting his glee at getting an attentive audience. "Wolves in a pack make eye contact with one another. The dominant wolf, the Alpha Male, stares down the others and establishes his authority. But, wolves in the wild never make eye contact with a human being. They want to avoid human dominance."

"This is why I never look Pastor Lee in the eye, Hillar," remarked Graham with a chuckle. "I want to avoid her dominance."

"Stop that, Mister Washington!" commanded Lee, laughing.

"Now, Hillar, if I stop talking to you, then I concede that Pastor Lee's my Alpha Female. So, I'd better..."

"Cut it out, Grammy. Let Quaz get on with it."

"Dogs are different," Hillar proceeded. "They look us in the eye. They accept that we humans are their Alphas. They read our eyes for information about how we feel and whether we're happy or angry or whatever. You know that when you're angry at Buck you look him straight in the eye and scold him. Or, when you're feeling cuddly, you look Buck in the eye and coo. That's what makes Buck a dog and not a wolf."

"I thought it was genes that distinguished a dog from a wolf," said Leona.

"Oh yes, dog genomes have changed through evolution. Most dog genes are still wolf genes, but a few separate the two. But, it's more than genes. It's the way they are social that makes the difference. I read all this on the New Skete website, yaknow."

"So, Hillar," said Graham, "if I call Buck right now and he comes up on the veranda with us, then I can look him in the eye. Is that right?"

"Right."

"Well, if I look Pastor Lee in the eye, will she look me in the eye too?"

"I think I'd better go to the ravine and see how the animals are doing," said Hillar.

CHAPTER 49

HILLAR HAD TAKEN ONLY a few steps when Midnight came scurrying across the lawn with Buck racing on her heels. The black cat leaped up to the first branch of the birch tree in front of the veranda. Buck stopped at the steps. He rocked back and forth lightly on all fours and seemed restless, apparently wanting to bark, but not doing so.

Buck's attention turned toward the hedge separating the church property from Diamond Point Road. A male black Labrador retriever had wandered through the driveway opening into the churchyard. Buck and the Lab spotted each other simultaneously. Both cautiously but hurriedly moved toward each other, meeting in the middle of the large lawn. At first, they simply stared at each other, heads erect, tails moving to indicate both joy and curiosity.

Neither dog made a noise. After a moment, the two repositioned themselves so that their noses could smell what was under each tail. Taking small steps, they began marching comically in a circle.

Graham, already prone to laughter, snorted and chuckled out loud.

Hillar, watching the show intently, spoke so that all could hear.

"I've often wondered why dogs do this. Why in the world do dogs sniff each other's butts?"

"I think you'd better ask the pastor, Hillar," said Graham.

Hillar looked at Leona. Leona began to speak. "We have to go back to the beginning, Hillar. When God was first creating the world, he made dogs to be friendly. Dogs did not fight. They got along quite well. On one occasion, an international dog convention was held in a very large auditorium. All the dogs in the world attended."

Hillar looked at the pastor quizzically. "Pastor Lee, this does not sound like a scientific account of dog evolution. Are you sure of your facts?"

"This is a mythical account, Quaz. It's an origin story. So, listen carefully." Leona paused and then continued. "Because dogs' fannies are stinky, the ushers told the attending dogs to hang their fannies on hooks in the vestibule. Once all the dogs had assembled in the auditorium, there was no uncomfortable odor. The program went on."

Now Hillar was looking at the pastor incredulously. Leona continued. "Unfortunately, during the program a fire broke out. One dog yelled, 'fire!' All the dogs scrambled and raced to the exits. They simply grabbed whatever fanny they could and put it on. Then, they ran to all four corners of the Earth."

"What?"

"Ever since then," concluded Leona, "every dog has been on an incessant hunt to find his or her own fanny. So, whenever two dogs meet, they check to see if the other one is wearing his or her own fanny."

Graham was now doubled up in laughter. However, Hillar looked dumbfounded. Hiller spoke. "I'm not sure people should trust what you say, Pastor Lee."

CHAPTER 50

"COULD THAT BE THUNDER?" asked Graham.

"Nope," responded Leona. "I think it's a stampede of Harleys in the distance. Bikers coming our way, I bet."

Leona was right. The roar grew in intensity. Soon a roaring mass of black-leather-vested drivers, along with some riders, paused near the Diamond Point Church driveway. Then the cycle parade poured into the churchyard on the gravel driveway. One biker turned from the circling posse and drove across the lawn to the parsonage porch. After shutting down his machine, he dismounted the bike as he would a horse and approached Graham and Leona, who were now standing.

"May I speak with the pastor," said the lead biker in a most courteous tone of voice.

"You're looking at her," answered Graham, pointing toward Leona.

"I'm Pastor Lee Foxx," Leona said, holding out her right hand to shake. They shook briefly.

"I'm Artie."

"I can see that you're Artie. It says so right here on this sign." She pointed to his brown leather name badge just under his left shoulder. Both smiled.

"Me and my gang need a lawn or some flat place to just park for a while. Would you give us permission to park and rest for an hour or so?"

"Please make yourself at home," said Leona. "I'll unlock the external rest room, complete with wash basin. Just up the path here. I don't have enough beer in the refrigerator for everyone. But, you're still welcome."

"Much obliged Pastor Lee. Toilet access is what we need most." Artie motioned to his riding posse, who then shut off their engines and parked their bikes.

"I can see by your shirt that you're called *Rolling Thunder*," observed Graham. "Are you the guys that Rocky Lynne sings about? You know the song—*Thank You*."

"Yeh, that's us," answered Artie. We're rolling with Harley thunder on behalf of vets, especially vets who are MIA or still in prisons over in Iraq and Afghanistan. Even some Nam vets are still MIA. Our government doesn't give a tinker's damn about 'm. They just write 'm off. But, we remember. We organize for legislation, and we press the VA to take care of our comrades with PTSD or other injuries. Rocky Lynne is one of those who says *thank you*."

"Did you fight in Viet Nam?" asked Graham.

"Yep. See, I was Army." Artie pointed to a badge on his black leather vest. "We'll roll on until we've done right by every name on that black wall in Washington."

"Let me look at you," asked Leona. She stretched out her feminine fingers and touched Artie's vest in various places, spinning him slowly around. "Here's the *Ride for Freedom* patch. Here's a patch with a coiled cobra. It says, *don't tread on me*. And, Graham, look at this one: *In His Service: Jesus Christ the Son of God*."

Leona turned to look Artie in the eyes. "Welcome, Brother. Blessings on you and your important work. Make yourself at home."

CHAPTER 51

AFTER ROLLING THUNDER HAD DEPARTED, nature's own thunder growled in the distance. Shortly, a roaring rain pounded the parsonage roof, sounding more like air hammers than Harley David-sons. When she thought she was hearing the phone ring, Leona leapt from her porch chair. She raced in to catch it on the third ring.

"Saint John's Community Church. Pastor Lee Foxx speaking." Leona sat in the telephone booth. Unlike telephone booths of recent antiquity, this telephone booth, curiously, was a transformed closet. It stood adjacent to the fireplace in the parsonage and only five feet from the dining room table.

"Hello, Pastor Foxx. My name is Leonard Hicks. I'm senior pastor at St. Peter's Church in New York City. We're the parish in the City Corp Building. Perhaps you've heard of us."

"Yes, indeed. I've worshiped with you. Not recently, however. Great liturgy. To what do I owe the pleasure of receiving this call?"

"This will be a pastor-to-pastor call. May I presume professional confidence, Reverend Foxx?"

"Yes, you certainly may. Tell me what's on your mind. And just call me Lee."

"Okay, Lee. I'm Len. I need a pastor in the Lake George Village area. I found your name in a directory on line. I hope you'll understand what I am about to say. If you can help me, this will be fine. If not, perhaps you could direct me to someone who could."

"I'll see what I can do."

"Recently something peculiar happened. It may mean nothing. But, I have a niggle that it could be quite important, perhaps even deathly important."

"Go on."

"On the off-hours answering machine here at St. Peter's I listened to a somewhat puzzling and disconcerting message. The voice was that of a man named J. Holmes Chapman. Mr. Chapman asked to speak to the pastor. Evidently, he did not know me or any of my assistants. Perhaps he got our church number online or something. But that's not the important thing. He wanted to know if, during the Sacrament of the Altar, we would drink actual human blood and eat human body parts. In addition, he asked if such ritual sacrifice could guarantee the answer to prayer."

"That *is* puzzling. And disconcerting. What could he have meant? That is so archaic."

"I just don't know what had prompted this question, Lee. But, as you can imagine, I felt I needed to take this seriously as a possible pastoral matter."

"I think I'd take it seriously too," said Leona. "Go on."

"Well, let me continue the story. I telephoned Mr. Chapman's office immediately and set up an appointment. I did not want to let this matter wait. I showed up the next day at the appointed time. But...now it gets even more weird...the receptionist said that I had already been there, and that I had already left with Mr. Chapman. Now, she did not mean me personally, of course. It was an imposter, someone pretending to be the pastor from St. Peter's Church. Can you imagine?"

"No. This sounds very weird."

"The bottom line is this: Mr. Chapman is missing. Gone. The receptionist said Mr. Chapman had left a message with her saying he would be traveling to Lake George Village. That was a week or so ago. I check twice per day with the receptionist, who has agreed to contact me when she gets word. She's polled the Chapman family and associates and others. But, nothing. So, the trail ends at his departure for Lake George Village."

"How might I be able to help?"

"Honestly, Lee, I don't know. I don't even know for certain that anything's going on worth investigating. And, you're a pastor, not a detective. So I'm stuck. Yet, I felt I should contact somebody."

"Did you tell the police?"

"Oh, yes. And this is curious too. After I'd explained the situation over the phone, the policewoman I was speaking with asked me for the name of the man who left the message. I told her it was J. Holmes Chapman, who just happens to be the owner and manager of the Manhattan Opera. Then she told me that Mr. Chapman's case is being handled by a certain detective. Case! What's this about a case?"

"What's that detective's name?"

"Let me see, I have it written here. Oh. I've got it. Detective Sherman Evans."

"What did Detective Evans say when you related your story?"

"Mr. Evans never called me back. He never heard my story. I've left messages on his individual answering machine, but there has been no reply as of yet. So I fear he may not be following up at all."

"Len, let me report a couple items. First, I've heard of Mr. Chapman. He's a public figure. But I've never met him personally. Second, I have met Mr. Evans. He showed up here at Lake George a week ago. He keeps matters close to the chest. I have no idea what melody he hums. Let's exchange mobile numbers in case we need to follow up with one another."

After details were settled, Leona continued. "Before we hang up, do you know why Chapman apparently went to Lake George

Village? It's only four miles south of Diamond Point. Do you have even the slightest lead?"

"Maybe one thing. Is Lake George Village kinda honky tonk?"

"Yes, the village is to tourists what a Macy's Black Friday sale is to shoppers."

"Does the Wishing Tree ring a bell?"

.

CHAPTER 52

THE FIRST OF Leona's rehearsals for *Last of the Mohicans* went satis-factorily. She was filling in an open super spot. The core singers had been rehearsing for weeks. The show would open on the weekend after next and run through the following Saturday. Leona thought it would be fun to join a theatre troop and an opera to boot. Maybe, she also thought, she should explore the opera path to see whither it might take her.

In the first act, Leona stood erect as if she were a British soldier at attention. She duplicated her non-speaking and non-singing role as a French soldier in the second act. She would not appear in the third and final act. Jokes had been made about her, a woman, dressing like a man. But, then she thought, *what else's new?*

"Can we talk privately, Pastor Lee?" asked Uncas. Uncas, of course, is the role sung by Luciano Silvestri. They took their coffees to a quiet location in the theater's rear, by some display tables.

"How can I help, Luciano?" Leona asked.

"Well, this is difficult," he stammered. His eyes looked away for a moment. Leona waited without stirring. "I am not sure I can talk about this." Luciano's lips quivered. After a few seconds, he reestablished eye contact. "They say that if I sell my soul to the Devil that I'll become a famous opera star."

"For the sake of Calgary, who's 'they'?"

"The Coven."

"For the sake of Cambridge, what do you mean, 'coven'?"

"There's a secret coven within the Manhattan Opera company. The stars, the real big stars, belong to it. Lillian Serano and Juliet Johns are world famous. They got that way by selling their souls to Satan. Satan made things happen. Satan has that power."

"I can't believe what I'm hearing from you, Luciano," said Leona, unable to contain her astonishment. "This sounds just like *Faust*. This sounds just like *The Devil and Daniel Webster* all over again. Are you serious?" Leona was well aware that her skepticism had led her to break her pastoral composure of unconditional positive regard for someone in a counseling situation.

"I *am* serious. I worried about talking to you, fearing you might not believe me."

"Luciano, it doesn't matter whether I believe you or not. What does matter is that I'm concerned about you. About *you*. Please continue."

Luciano suddenly looked away. They were being approached by a third person. The unbeckoned visitor walked up to within fifteen feet and stopped to glare at Luciano. Dressed in an Indian costume, bare-chested, a single feather in his folded hair, this was Magua. In both Cooper's novel and the opera, Magua is the treacherous Huron responsible for kidnapping, insurrection, mayhem, and scalping. In this actor, Leona thought she perceived the same fire in the eyes she would expect of the real Magua, should there ever have existed a person such as Magua.

"He doesn't like me talking to you," Luciano murmured from the side of his mouth to Leona. "He's my recruiter for the coven. He's already sold his soul, and now he wants mine. He's afraid you'll convince me not to go through with it."

Magua's eyes seemed to say, "Pastor Whoever-you-are, I want

you dead. This prey is mine." Without saying a word, the actor turned and departed. After a few strides he connected with a teenage boy. Magua put his hand on the teen's shoulder. Then the two exited together.

Leona turned her eyes back to Luciano, who eventually turned his attention back at his pastor. She said nothing. He paused, evidently unaware that silent time was passing.

"In real life he's actually a Huron," said Luciano. Leona waited. "I think he likes singing the part of a Huron in the opera, even if he has to be so evil. He kills me in the final act, you know."

"It sounds to me like he's evil both in fiction and reality, Luciano. Is this what you're telling me?"

"Yes." Luciano paused to think some more. Leona said nothing. "But it wasn't like that at first. He was really welcoming and helped me to learn the ropes, so to speak, for the company. Showed me the way the wardrobe mistress liked to have the costumes returned, showed me where the coffee and snacks were, offered to help me with any of the blocking if I was unsure about where to stand. You know, little things. But things that put me at ease."

"I understand that," said Leona. "Go on."

"Well, he invited me to join him for lunch one day and we talked about where we grew up, where we studied music, family, things like that. I told him that I only had one living aunt and she was quite old now, living in a retirement home in New Hampshire. I was an only child and I never found the right woman to marry, so I am alone. Music is my life."

Leona gazed intensely at Luciano, feeling empathy for him as she heard the brief history of his life. *How alone he must feel.*

"Well, we spent quite a bit of time together, listening to music at the lakeside, things like that," Luciano's eyes began to tear.

"I thought he was my friend, Pastor Lee. I thought he was my friend."

Leona placed her hand on his shoulder and whispered assurance that she was there for him.

"This one night after dinner, he asked me if I wanted real success in the Opera. Would I want to be a star, in New York City, not just a lead in a second-rate opera company in a resort town. Of course, I answered, 'Yes!' And then he said, 'It's possible. You just need to have faith'."

Leona looked at Luciano intently.

He continued. "I thought he was going to talk to me about having faith in God and living a positive life."

Luciano was visibly nervous. His eyes flitted back and forth, watching for Magua to reappear.

"You wouldn't believe it, Pastor. He said that God created Satan, and it is with Satan that there is power. If I would give my soul to Satan, he would make all my dreams of success come true."

"This must have been a shock for you, Luciano," said Leona in a comforting, steady tone. She could feel the anxiety build inside of her, but she knew she needed to keep calm, especially in her pastoral role. "Tell me the rest."

"I was so stunned I didn't know what to say. I found myself unable to say, 'No.' But I couldn't say, 'Yes' either. I was scared, Pastor. Really scared. It felt like my voice and mind were frozen. I finally just said, 'Let me think about it.'"

"Are you still thinking about it?"

"Well, I think I made up my mind. They took me out last night."

CHAPTER 53

LEONA CONCENTRATED on suppressing the depth of astonishment she felt when she heard this story. So her face remained neutral. "What do you mean you went out last night?"

"Coven people blindfolded me and drove me to the shore, I think. We rode for a while in a motorboat. I was led onto land and through a forest to a meadow. There, my blindfold was removed. I could see some of the singers from the Manhattan as well as others I did not know. The high priest was Baphomet. You know, the goat-headed Devil? He slaughtered a chicken on an altar. He poured the blood into a cup, a cup kinda like our communion chalice. We all drank some of this blood to confirm our solidarity and loyalty. Next time, he proclaimed, it will be a human, and we'll both eat the body and drink the blood. Then, the deal will be finalized."

"Luciano!" exclaimed the pastor. "You can't be serious about this! You're a baptized Christian."

"Catholic, actually."

"But..."

"We have to renounce our baptism at the ceremony.... We renounce the Apostles' Creed."

"Luciano! You can't do this. It's not who you are. You're baptized.

You're a kind person. You have a compassionate heart. You're honest, as far as I know. You have no truck with any sort of evil, especially radical evil in the name of the Devil. For the sake of Columbus, can't you just say 'no'?"

"But, Pastor, you gotta know how much I yearn to see my name up in lights. I want to see my name on the opera program. I want people to line up at the box office to hear me sing. All this can be mine. The coven has promised this to me. Is it worth my eternal soul? Well, I think it might be."

Leona frowned and looked at the floor.

"Obviously, I have many doubts, Pastor. Second thoughts. This whole thing scares me. That's why I thought I should talk to you before I make this final."

"Well, Luciano, I seldom tell a person what to do. But I will in this case. Say 'No!' You don't need to have your name in lights or on opera programs. Your relationship to God and your warm and loving heart are far more valuable than fame. And God's love lasts forever. I command you as your pastor—say 'no'."

Luciano stared at the floor.

Leona spoke again. "Besides, Luciano, you are a child of God, and how do you know you won't achieve stardom because of your own talent, guided by your own moral compass? You might be selling your soul for a hollow promise."

Luciano continued to stare at the floor. Leona rested her hand on his shoulder. The two sat quietly, while Leona prayed. She prayed quietly at first, but then uttered aloud, "Amen."

CHAPTER 54

"There's someone I'd like you to meet," said Chapman to Lilian Serano and Juliet Johns. Then he waved at Karl Sogaard to come and join them. "Right in here," said Chapman, leading the trio from backstage into the empty theater manager's office.

They settled into armchairs and the divan. "I'd like to introduce you to Mister Renard Maletesto."

At that Maletesto walked into the small office. "Oh Renny!" exclaimed Serano, who stood up and shared a two-cheek kiss with the arriving Maletesto. Similarly, Johns stood with a gleeful, "Renard the Subtle One." They exchanged a hug. "Of course, Renard and I go back some," murmured Sogaard.

Chapman appeared surprised. When all had taken seats, Maletesto looked at Chapman. "As you can see, Holmes, we all know one another. Perhaps we should let you in on a little secret. I've been a good friend to the Manhattan Opera for some time now. You might say, I'm a benefactor of considerable proportions."

"Do you mean I'm the new kid on the block?" Chapman asked.

"That's right, Holmes," said Johns, with a crooked smile. "Renny the Subtle One has, shall we say, found the secret to success. And he's shared it with some of us in your standing cast. We owe him a great deal. A great deal!"

"Perhaps, Holmes, you'll join us," added Serano. Sogaard said nothing.

"Why do they call you the subtle one?" Chapman said, turning toward Maletesto.

Maletesto smiled. "Perhaps it's because I so frequently understate things. Or, perhaps it's in remembrance of the serpent in the Garden of Eden, the most subtle of God's creatures. Or, perhaps it's because Cooper's anti-hero was Le Renard Subtile. Or, well, take your pick." Maletesto paused to observe the confusion on Chapman's face.

"Actually, I have a purpose for our meeting," declared Maletesto, addressing the larger group. "Our friends overseas are in need of some money. Quite a bit of money, in fact. With your permission, I would like to ask Mister Chapman here to deduct a portion of your pay checks for the next six months. This money will contribute to a very good cause, I assure you. In due time, you will be repaid. For the moment, however, this is a rather urgent matter."

"How much?" asked Johns.

"Eighty percent," responded Maletesto. "With the big bucks you make, your Big Apple life style will not suffer. And, as I said, your rewards will come in time. They're in the mail, so to speak."

None of the three—Serano, Johns, or Sogaard—expressed any hesitancy or objection. They placidly accepted their foreordained fate.

"Might you tell us just who needs this money? And why?" asked Sogaard.

"For the moment, no," answered Maletesto. "Just trust me."

CHAPTER 55

BUILT in 1909 in the then-popular Tudor revival style, the Lake George Club stands today as a testimony to the reverence the Lake George community holds for its tradition. The Club was built by the newly-rich elite from New York and environs, those tycoons who had made fortunes in the booming new industries, businesses and finance centers of the era. They first built their own lavish homes along the shores of the Lake where couples and families whiled away the warm summers in elegant comfort, engulfing themselves with the beauty of nature far from the clamor of the city. They played tennis and dined on exquisite seafood dinners at the Club, which served as the center of their transplanted society.

Those were the days when women stuffed themselves into tightly-cinched corsets, regardless of the heat, and dressed in long white cotton dresses, each embroidered with distinctive patterns. Whenever Leona visited the Club, she took a moment to review the photographic archive that lined the walls, preserving memories of chapters of the Lake George saga, written long after the Iroquois Nation was dissolved.

In current times, the Club has become a family hub where children chase each other as they scamper in and out of changing rooms, lunch on hot dogs from the Lakeside Grotto Food Bar, and build sand castles on the small beachfront. Elegant dinners, special events, yacht races and weddings are still the Club's calling card.

Leona and Graham were enjoying their "talking breaks," as Graham called them, on the veranda of the Club. It was a quiet time for the two to have uninterrupted conversations, peppered with bits of shared wit and accompanied by a buttery Chardonnay and a tart Sauvignon Blanc.

After all that had happened in the past few days, the veranda might have been their sanctuary, but not today. After parking the car in the small lot, Leona and Graham walked through the front doors into the circular atrium where rich, dark wood planks, meticulously sanded and polished in that bygone era, braced the walls and floors. Narrow sturdy timbers encircled the room, arching upward 20 feet to the original wrought iron chandelier. The chandelier was once gas-lit, but now it is kept in its original state though converted to electricity. The small, authentic, leaded-glass panes of the windows added to the elegance of the room.

"I'll find something to do here at the club," said Graham, wishing Leona good luck. "I'll see you when you return."

Leona walked straight through the atrium and down the exterior cement stairway toward the dock that extended a hundred feet out into Lake George. A twelve-year-old bounced on the diving board, while three women too old for their bikinis sipped their martinis in plastic cups while reclining in Adirondack chairs. A dozen J-22s, scheduled to race every Saturday, bobbed at anchor to her left. To the right of the dock Leona spotted the Chris Craft Cruiser, or at least a facsimile of this wood-paneled classic. On the bow she could read, NY 4489 MK. On the stern she found what she was looking for —*Fuzzy Logic.*

"Are you Reverend Foxx?" hollered the youthful captain, a college-aged Amerindian man, head shaven, wearing a billed cap. After she'd nodded affirmatively, he invited her into the boat and sat her in the open stern. "Please wear this lifejacket, Reverend Foxx.

Just for safety reasons. The trip will take the better part of half an hour."

The driver took his place behind the windshield. He backed the boat gently away from the dock, shifted, and began driving forward toward open waters. Soon the inboard engine was whirring at top speed and the bow of the Chris Craft Cruiser lifted well above the water. Leona's view of the Lake George Club receded toward near oblivion.

Maybe I'll take an Instagram photo of the scene, she thought. But, when she reached into the leg pocket of her sweat pants, she discovered her cell phone was missing. *Musta left it at the club. Hope Graham picks it up.*

The engine and water noise were so loud that no conversation could take place. Her black-capped captain remained nameless. Evidently, anonymity was prescribed.

CHAPTER 56

"I'D LIKE one of those beers. There, the one with the picture of the I-87 sign on the label," Graham told the bartender in the Lake George cocktail lounge. "I've driven more than a few miles on the Northway."

"One Glens Falls IPA Comin' up!" It was the voice of the triple X sized man tending bar. He sported a freshly shaved head and a big smile revealing a single golden crown among his upper front teeth.

Due to the time of day, no one else was seated in the bar. Too early for all except career bar flies. Bar buzzing was not Graham's usual portfolio, but he made himself comfortable on a bar stool as a way to pass the time.

"I don't think I've seen you in here before, Mister? Mister...?"

"My name's Graham," said the guest, stretching his right hand out for a shake. "Graham Washington."

"I'm Al," replied the bartender with a welcoming smile. "Nice to meet you."

"I'm a partner, so to speak, of someone who's a club member. Reverend Leona Foxx. Do you know her?"

"Oh, yes, Pastor Foxx. I think I just saw her get into that imitation Chris Craft a moment ago."

"Yes, that was her. I gather you are acquainted."

"Of course. Mighty nice person, that Reverend. Tips well. She remembers the little guy. That's important when so many of our club members are successful business people from the City and Jersey. Those big shots sometimes forget us little shots, ya know. They look right past us without seeing, it seems."

"Yeh, I getcha," said Graham, sipping his beer straight from the bottle. "Did you grow up here in the Adirondacks, Al?"

"Yep. This is my home. Except for college, I've never left this place. I kinda feel like I belong to the land. Where my family lives is where my family has lived for, well, I don't know how far back it goes. A long time. Even before the colonists arrived."

"Before Lake George became a vacation spot? Was that 1832? Did I read that somewhere?"

"Long before 1832," emphasized Al. "My ancestors go way back."

"So, what nationality are you, then? Native American?"

"Well, Graham, whatever you do, don't call me *Native American*. My people never met Amerigo Vespucci. As I said, my ancestors and this land predated the French, the English, and you black people too."

Graham smiled, acknowledging a minority kinship. "Be more specific, Al. Did you come from the Algonquins, the Hurons, the Iroquois, or what? Are you the last of the last Mohicans?" Graham sipped his beer and reached for some bar snacks.

"Maybe the last of something, anyway," Al responded with a chuckle, appreciating the quip. "I got both Huron and Mohawk blood in me. You might say I'm a mixture. You might say that I'm a garden variety Indian, or something like that. When it comes right down to it, I'm just a human being like you are. Isn't that good enough?"

"Good enough for me!" Graham raised his beer bottle in a toast. "Now, Al, you called me a black man. Look closely. Are you sure."

"Well, you certainly are colored. But, you're not real dark. Anybody who's colored is black, even if they're not black, right?"

"Are you black then?"

"No. I'm a so-called red man."

"But, Al, you don't look red to me. You just look human. So, where does this red and black bullshit come from?'"

"Dunno." Al paused as he lowered his head to stare as he was drying newly-washed wine glasses. "Just the way those early colonizers labeled us so they could feel superior, so they didn't have to think of us as equals. Maybe that was it."

"Let me tell you something," said Graham, beginning a dissertation. "I'm what you call a Creole. I've got French in me. I've got African American in me. And, I've got Native American, I mean Indian, in me. I'm a card-carrying member of the Choctaw tribe. This means, Al, that I'm a red man just like you. Do you believe me?"

Al looked puzzled. "Well, Graham, if you say so. Does that make us reds-in-law?"

Both laughed.

"How much do I owe for the beer?" asked Graham.

"You can't pay me. We don't sell anything here. I'll just put what you owe on Reverend Foxx's account."

"Well, then, I'll order another one. I've gotta wait for a while."

CHAPTER 57

THE CHRIS CRAFT veered toward the north end of the mile-long Long Island, which stretched north and south on the east side of Lake George. Once around the horn, they headed south and east toward Ripley's Point. Off to her right Leona strained to see any possible activity in the eagles' nest. *I hope you're all getting enough to eat.*

Once they had arrived in Ripley Point cove and were putt-putting toward the boathouse dock, Leona spotted some exceptionally comfortable swimmers in the water. Rather than swimming, they were sitting in floating Styrofoam chairs, sipping gin'n'tonics, while soaking in the sun. The fully tanned Mr. Maletesto seemed to be holding forth, while two other men, without tan, but with a bit of sunburn, listened intently.

Immediately upon docking, the Chris Craft captain disappeared, saying nothing. Upon disembarking, Leona was met by another Amerindian man; but this one was wearing black tuxedo pants with a tux shirt and black bow tie.

"Would you like a changing room, Ma'am?" he asked.

"Oh, no," she replied. "I'm wearing my suit under my sweats." Leona quickly disrobed and handed her belongings to the patient young man in the tux. All male eyes within sight turned to review the statuesque new arrival in the aqua bikini.

From the house, forty feet inland, a second Amerindian man dressed also in a partial tux came running with a drink in hand. "Here you are, Ma'am. A gin'n'tonic for the guest." In a matter of moments, Leona found herself floating and conversing and sipping just like her hosts.

"Is this standard clergy issue attire," asked Renard while holding his glass up for a toast? "Prosit!"

"I'm frugal with my material," she responded. "I'm the kinda girl who makes her own clothes. Prosit!"

"When I was in my college fraternity," one of the as yet unintroduced men began, "we brothers would describe a girl nobody would want to date: 'she makes her own clothes'."

"I bet I never dated anybody in *your* fraternity," Leona said with a wry smile.

"No one would ever guess you make your own clothes, Pastor," said Renard with a trumpet tone. "Lee Foxx, meet J. Holmes Chapman." Leona and Holmes clinked their plastic cocktail glasses. Her facial expression signaled no hint that she'd heard this name before.

The other floater and gin-and-tonic drinker was slight in build with distinguished white hair, perhaps in his sixties. Maletesto panned a hand and said to Leona, "meet Karl Sogaard. Karl is a *basso profundo* with the Manhattan Opera. He will be singing Tamenund in the Adirondack Company's production of *Last of the Mohicans*." The regal white-haired man tipped his glass toward Leona and winked.

Was that really a wink? Leona quizzed herself silently.

From the beach the two Amerindians walked right into the water. Instead of tux pants, they were now wearing black boxer bathing suits with their white shirts and black bow ties. Both were holding trays, strutting without even a splash to the floaters. To each floating chair they connected a tray, on which was displayed Maine lobster salad, fresh French bread, and a glass of iced tea. They departed without a word.

"Time for lunch," announced Renard. "We'll skip grace," he added while glaring with a superficial grin aimed at the pastor.

CHAPTER 58

WHILE DINING ON LUNCH, Leona turned her attention toward the mysterious visitor from the Big Apple. "Mr. Chapman, what brings you to Lake George? Vacation? Profession? Investigation?"

"It's curious that you should list investigation, Pastor Foxx. I am in fact looking for something," he said.

"I understand you own the Manhattan Opera Company. Are you here for rehearsals?"

Chapman's facial expression registered a touch of anxiety. "No. I mean, yes. I expect to be on site when the Adirondack Opera opens *The Last of the Mohicans* later next week. Some Manhattan singers are on loan to the Adirondack, as you may know, Pastor. This includes Karl here. My local staff have matters quite in hand, as you can imagine. So, I don't plan on supervising anything."

"I've met Luciano Silvestri. I gather he'll sing the part of Uncas. Quite a tenor."

"Luciano Silvestri, did you say? No, I don't recognize the name. Probably somebody new to the cast." Karl nodded that he knew Luciano. Chapman continued. "Perhaps you know our stars. Lilian Serano will play Cora. Juliet Johns will sing the part of Alice. And, as

I just mentioned, our *basso profundo* will be Karl Sogaard singing Tamenund."

At that Leona puffed up her chest and began to pump her fist while singing in a parody of a bass, "My day has been too long!"

"Oh, you know this opera well," responded Sogaard with delight. Maletesto's face registered that he'd missed something. Chapman turned to Maletesto to say, "Pastor Foxx just sang part of the opening and closing aria."

"For anyone who lives in this part of the country, we dare not forget the discouraging closing speech by Tamenund in Cooper's book," added Leona. "The aging elder, Tamenund—the wise Sagamore—is grieving over the death of Uncas, who is the last of the Mohican tribe. Uncas was killed by the treacherous Magua, a Huron disguised as a Mohawk. It is bad enough for the French and English to go to war on Indian land, but the Hurons and Mohawks and other tribes do themselves no service by fighting among and within themselves." Leona then recited Tamenund's oration from Cooper. "The pale-faces are masters of the earth, and the time of the red men has not yet come again. My day has been too long."

Maletesto expressed impatience at hearing more than he wanted to know. He took over. "We call Serano and Johns the 'Soprano Superstars.' They have shot up to the stratosphere like rockets. Serano just sang *Aida* in Vienna and Johns sang Mimi in *La Boheme*. Where was that, Holmes?"

"Berlin," added Chapman.

"The Adirondack summer stock program is unusually fortunate to get them for this season," said Maletesto with the pride one would expect of the chamber of commerce. "Thanks to Mr. Chapman, it's happening."

Leona turned her face toward Chapman. "You described this visit to the north country as an investigation. Surely you're not investigating your own opera company."

"Actually, I am, Pastor Foxx. Sorta. More importantly I am searching for something intangible, yet very real."

"What is intangible yet real to you?" she asked.

"Justice."

CHAPTER 59

EVENTUALLY LEONA FOUND herself thinking about Graham waiting
for her back at the club, so she conspicuously looked at her watch.
"Oh, for the sake of Chattanooga, look at the time. I think I've got to
get going," she announced.

Maletesto arranged for the previous boat driver to pilot her back
across the lake. After climbing over the gunwale and into the cruiser's
helm area, Leona could not help but notice a change. The pilot did
not offer her a lifejacket. He wore one, but that was the only one in
the boat. Curious.

"Are you and your friends Indians?" she asked inquisitively.

"Yes," he mumbled and pretended to be preoccupied with
readying the craft.

"Could you be descendents of the Hurons?" she pressed.

At this he turned the ignition key, starting the inboard engine.
The engine noise drowned out what could have been an answer.
Leona settled herself into the stern, sparing herself any rocking as the
bow lifted itself high above the water's surface with wash waves on
both sides.

The cruiser was aimed southward, not north. This meant the trip
to the Lake George Club would take a bit more time because they'd

have to pass Harris Bay and Assembly Point before turning west, adding almost a mile total to the trip's distance. Leona said nothing.

When they had rounded the southern end of Long Island, Leona fixed on the *Lac du San Sacrament,* the largest of the three ships owned by the Lake George Steamboat Company. The steamboat was making its way south, probably on return from a thirty-mile ride up to the portage route linking Lake George with Lake Champlain. The bright white *Lac du San Sacrament* looked majestic in the late after-noon sunlight.

As the minutes rolled by, it appeared to Leona that the Chris Craft Cruiser was heading dead north. Any slight directional change toward the port side would place it on a collision course with the steaming *Lac du San Sacrament.* The two boats—one a Goliath giant and the other a miniature David—approached one another. Leona watched with growing anxiety.

She opened the stern's lazaret, but to her chagrin she found no stored lifejackets. She took stock of her environment. She sensed that a crisis moment was about to commence. She was right.

Without warning the Huron pilot spun the wheel to the left, causing the boat to swerve aport. He shut off the engine and threw the ignition key into the water. Then, he leaped out of the boat on the port side. Once in the water he began swimming southeast.

The now powerless cruiser began to yaw in the very path of the rapidly approaching steamship. With no hope of starting the cruiser's engine, Leona leaped into the icy cold water and began a vigorous swim eastward. The captain of the *Lac du San Sacrament* could not actually see the drama unfolding down on the water's surface, so high up was he situated on the steamship's bridge. A collision was imminent.

Without enough time to swim out of the way, Leona took a full breath and plunged down underwater. Down and down she stroked, trying to get as deep as possible. When she could no longer stand the increased pressure, she leveled off and continued in her eastward direction. Just as she was about to gasp involuntarily, she risked a return to the surface. After her first inhalation of fresh air, she witnessed the passing of the giant steamship. Even though tossed about by the ship's wave wash, Leona was relieved that she'd avoided a hit and run by the *Lac du San Sacrament*.

What she had not witnessed was the direct hit. The steamship split the cruiser and plunged it beneath its own massive hull. Eventually planks and splinters would resurface while the heavier engine would sink a hundred feet to a lake bottom grave.

Leona allowed herself some recovery time while treading water. Then she laid her sights on Long Island's west coast and set that as her destination. Only a thousand feet to her right she watched while another small cruiser picked up her previous driver and ferried him presumably back to Maletesto's cottage. As far as she could tell, her would-be killers had no idea that she had survived.

Once she had pulled herself on to the shore of Long Island, Leona rewarded herself with a quarter hour of convalescence. Then, she set out to find some campers with a working mobile phone.

CHAPTER 60

AFTER RECEIVING Leona's SOS message, Graham drove Bill
Orange's boat to Long Island to rescue the tired and weary and frightened pastor. Leona thought she was never so glad to see Graham. As
he stepped out of the boat and moved towards her, the anguish of
what she had just experienced surfaced and burst forth in a flood of
tears.

"Oh, Graham, you can't believe what just happened to me,"
sobbed Leona as she wrapped her shivering arms around his neck.
Graham held her and felt a small exhilaration: Leona exhibited a
vulnerability that was usually buried deeply below her confident
exterior.

Leona slowly released her arm hold, then tightly held Graham's
hand as they started the boat trek home.

Back at the parsonage, Leona's compatriots shuttered at hearing
her account of the near-death experience. No doubt at some point an
official investigation would commence and a search for the body of
anybody drowned would be undertaken. At Graham's suggestion, the
parsonage trio considered reporting versus not reporting the
attempted murder to the authorities. "I vote that we keep this to

ourselves for a time," advised Graham. "Let's let them think they were successful, at least for a few hours."

"Should I call Sheriff Bolton and Mohawk Evans?" asked Leona.

"Yes," said Graham, "tomorrow. Let's try to enjoy a normal evening, if we can."

"What in the name of Carson City counts as normal around here!?" stammered Hillar. All laughed.

At that moment Leona's cell phone, now in Graham's pocket, vibrated. After answering and speaking. Leona announced that Sheriff Bolton was attempting to make contact. Graham shrugged his shoulders in defeat and gave her an awkward wave of the hand before walking out of the room.

"Sheriff? Thanks for calling. I've got some rather confidential yet very important news."

After providing Bolton with the details of the incident, the sheriff offered his sympathies. "Why might Maletesto want to see you dead, Pastor Lee?"

"Let me ask this question: could Maletesto be the one behind everything? The child sacrificed on St. John's altar? The skyrocketing success of the Manhattan Opera Company? Lillian Serano becoming an opera star because someone got murdered? The Wishing Tree? The recruitment of J. Holmes Chapman? The courting of Luciano Silvestri to join a cult? The murder of Sophia? The murder of Bishop Tikhon? The attempted murder of me? Just as all roads lead to Rome, all evidence seems to lead to Mister Maletesto."

"Again, Pastor Lee, why would Maletesto put you in his cross hairs?"

"My guess is that he fears I might know too much. Maybe he's afraid I could expose him. Satanism gets its power from symbols, you know. Evil is pursued in the name of evil, which is very rare. We mortals almost always cover our asses with sugar. That is, when we pursue evil we pretend it's good. But once you've signed up for Satan's army, then you march under the flag of evil. Figuratively speaking, of course. Maybe Maletesto fears that I'm learning too much from Luciano and the Wishing Tree. And, most importantly, that I'm capable of grasping what went on with the infant sacrifice on the St. John's altar. Well, Sheriff, that's my best guess."

They discussed whether or not to keep the attempted murder confidential. "I'm afraid I can't do that, Lee," he said. "Time is important here. If there's really something going on at Maletesto's cottage, then we should move in before he moves out or attempts an additional murder. I don't think we can wait until tomorrow."

"I can understand, Sheriff. It's your call."

"I will let Mohawk in on this, but we will muster help and begin surveillance tonight. We'll wait to determine when to move in for an arrest. You'll just have to be prepared to make a statement in court."

Leona phoned Leonard Hicks at St. Peter's to let him know that Chapman had surfaced and was now interacting with his singers. "I've reached out to Chapman's wife, Helen," reported Hicks. "I'll pass this news on to her."

Then, Leona walked out to the east porch where Graham, Hillar, Buck, and Midnight had assembled. "Okay, now we can begin our normal evening. Let's get the barbecue going."

CHAPTER 61

"CANDIDLY, I'm skeptical about anything and everything having to do with Satanism." This was Graham speaking. It was the next day. Graham along with Leona sat at the ends of the antique oak dining table in the parsonage. On the window side sat two guests, both clergy: Father Stephen Korsky along with Daren Richardson, an Episcopalian serving in Bolton Landing. Across the table, with his back to the fireplace, sat Father Ernan McMullan from Queensbury, fifteen miles south of Diamond Point. Next to him was Brenda Beale, congregational president. Leona had called this meeting to seek planning advice for her proposed reconsecration service. All had expressed sympathy and condolences to Father Korsky.

Graham continued to hold forth with an expertish tone to his voice. "Satanism is almost always an imaginative creation of the anti-Satanists. Think historically for a moment. Remember the *Witches' Hammer*? It was the Dominican inquisitors who published *Malleus Maleficarum* in the fifteenth century, a book describing sorcery that actually defined what sorcery would be. This made things easy for the Inquisition. Whenever inquisitors found something that looked like what was described in their manual, they would have evidence of witchcraft. Think of the travesty perpetrated against the women of the day and against old-fashioned nature worshippers!"

Each listener around the table was quiet and intent, taking in what Graham was telling them. They anticipated more. "Remember also the scare over Satanic ritual abuse in the 1980s. Again, it was the anti-Satanists who described to the media what the purported Satanists were like. The whole fiasco turned out to be an urban legend disseminated by religious psychotherapists who wanted to increase their business by specializing in childhood ritual and sexual abuse. They used hypnotic regression to drum up all sorts of weird stories about children being abused. This led to the prosecution of family fathers and preschool teachers. It was madness, mass hysteria. Finally, a group of anti-anti-Satanists rose up to combat the hysteria propagated by the anti-Satanists."

"Now, for the sake of Calistoga, I simply disagree with Graham," said Leona sternly to the group. "If you dismiss the 1980s scare as merely an urban legend, you'll also dismiss the claims of the women who were abused as children. In that era of fighting against social repression, women with nightmarish childhoods needed to be listened to. Listened to by somebody. Those anti-Satanist therapists listened. Without that listening, the atrocities perpetrated against young daughters would have remained invisible."

"I think that what Graham is saying is that the very idea of Satanic Ritual Abuse was a fabrication," interjected Richardson. "Forgotten memories of childhood sexual abuse was one thing. Satanic ritual abuse was another."

"I hesitate to agree, Daren," said Korsky. "Even if claims of abuse were sometimes overblown, there must have been a core phenomenon of ritual abuse that was real. Ritual abuse is one form of sexual abuse. It's more than that—it occasionally includes murder. Just because some therapists were found leading their clients does not mean we should dismiss everything that was reported."

McMullin took his turn. "As I remember the hysteria of the 1980s, the anti-anti-Satanists contended that the anti-Satanists were the real danger to society, not the Satanists themselves. They concluded that the anti-Satanists were just witch hunters."

"Precisely my point," announced Graham triumphantly.

"That's not good enough, Graham," responded Korsky. "The Church of Satan and Temple of Set in San Francisco and the Charles Manson murders were a lot more than merely the concoction of overly imaginative therapists. This applies to the Marquis de Sade a century earlier too. These past Satanists were as real as Al Qaeda or ISIS in our century."

"Arguing about the Inquisition or the 1980s will not help me today," broke in Leona. "Here is an empirical fact: the mutilated body of a baby girl was left on the Saint John's altar. Here is a theological fact: you know it's the voice of Satan when you hear the call to shed innocent blood. I call this *Leona's Law of Evil*. Leona's Law was true when the Pharisees and Romans called for the crucifixion of Jesus, and it is just as true for this sacrificed little girl, whom I call Sarai. What God did was to raise Jesus from the dead on Easter, disarming Satan and his minions. That's all we need to know to move forward today."

Korsky shuffled some papers he had previously placed on the table. "Because you're planning a reconsecration, Lee, I brought some prayers we use in the Orthodox tradition. This one by Tarsius, Patriarch of Constantinople, fits well when an altar has been desecrated by heretics. Are Satanists heretics? Well, regardless, it may help you as you do your planning." Korsky passed photocopies of the prayer around for all to read. Each skimmed the page.

"Pardon my asking," opened Ernan, "but don't you Orthodox presume that God *permitted* the defilement of the altar? Do you attribute defilement to the punishment of Christian sinning rather than to the profane perpetrators of the violation?"

"Yes, Ernan, that's true. Here's how one of our prayers reads. I think I've got it here," said Korsky, thumbing through his papers. Then he quoted: "On account of the multitude of our sins, Thou hast permitted it to be defiled."

"I find that disgusting, frankly," responded McMullin. "Why should we pray for *our own* forgiveness when someone else is responsible for the defilement? This sounds like you're blaming the victim, not the perpetrator."

Korsky looked flummoxed, not taken aback or defensive. "Well, I think asking in prayer for our own forgiveness is something we *can* do. It's difficult to ask God to forgive profane culprits who do not ask for forgiveness. I believe we're praying for our own reconsecration without rendering judgment about the heretic or outsider. That's the best I can come up with, Father." McMullin nodded in gratitude.

"Well, Lee," said Daren, addressing Leona, "are we helping you yet? Just what do you envision at this liturgy?"

"First of all, thanks again for coming here today," she said. "I want each of you to attend and to lay hands on the altar when I pray. Brenda and I are scheduling the service for two o'clock in the afternoon Sunday after next. You can take care of your own duties at your home parish in the morning, and then you can come here to join us. This ecumenical solidarity will mean a great deal to me and to the congregation at Saint John's."

CHAPTER 62

As the dining room assembly dispersed, Father Stephen Korsky requested a visit to the restroom. After saying goodbye to her guests and after Graham disappeared upstairs, Leona escorted the empty coffee cups to the kitchen. The Orthodox priest was passing the refrigerator when Leona stopped him. "One more cup of coffee, Father?"

While sitting at the kitchen table each with a coffee mug in hand, Leona pressed her visitor. "In your ministry, Father Stephen, have you performed exorcisms?"

"Yes, I have. Not frequently, to be sure. But, the matter has come up from time to time. By the way, we call it *deliverance ministry*."

"May I ask some questions about deliverance ministry?" posed Leona.

"Yes, of course," said the priest. "Good coffee."

"How does demonic possession come to your attention?"

"Usually, a family will bring the troubled soul to me. They phone me at the church, describe the symptoms. If in my judgment it sounds like a possession, we make an appointment."

"Then, what?"

"I ask all of them to meet as a family in the sanctuary in front of the iconostasis. All the icons are visible, especially Jesus with his hand raised in benediction. I watch carefully the facial expressions of the person who allegedly is possessed."

"Are you looking for contortions?"

"Yes. The Christian symbols prompt a demon to recoil like a cat's paw from water. But that's not what's important. The most important thing is to get the demon's name. You have to get the name! So, I address the demon directly. I ask, 'Demon! Tell me your name!'"

"Do you get an answer."

"Oh, no. At least not at first. The demon wants to avoid exposure. So, I ask questions and listen carefully to the answers. If the person is possessed, I start to hear lies. Satan is the Father of Lies, recall. But I keep pressing— 'Demon! Give me your name'."

"Can't the demon simply sandbag you?"

"No. Because lies are irrational. Evil is irrational. After some time spent on interaction, I catch the demon in a contradiction, and then the demon feels like giving up the name. So, I get it."

"Once you've got the name, then what?"

"At that point I pronounce the name loudly and command in the name of Jesus Christ that the demon depart. Jesus Christ is the demon's lord too. This is true everywhere in the world, regardless of culture. Once I've issued the exorcism command, I have to send the demon somewhere, into a tree or animal or something. Usually, I send the demon to outer darkness. Oh, they hate that."

"Will demons obey you?"

"Oh, yes. They don't like it. The parting shot the demon leaves is a convulsion. Looks kinda like an epileptic fit. The possessed person is thrown to the floor. He or she writhes and screams. After a moment or so, we pick up the person. Soon a calm consciousness takes over. Then, it's done. I admonish the family to take the person home and show care."

"The people who come to you, who are they? Any Christians? Anybody who is already baptized? Because the Holy Spirit is present in a baptized person, I should think this would make him or her immune to possession. Inoculated, so to speak."

"Well, almost. Most possessed persons I see have never been baptized. But some are. I guess if you really want to become possessed, you renounce your baptism. I'm just not sure."

"What do you mean, 'want to become possessed'?"

"Nobody makes a home for a demon against their will."

"Huh?"

"A Satanic force will not enter you unless you're open."

"What makes us open?"

"Greed or grudge. If greed gets out of control, we might be willing to sacrifice our integrity to our passion. But, the almost sure way to put out a *Welcome, Demons!* sign is to demand revenge for some injustice. If we become obsessed with a grudge, if our desire for revenge grips our consciousness and our mind obsesses about it, the demon will have an opening. Maybe a Christian can override baptism with vengeful desire, I'm not too sure. But clearly, when we confess our sins and forgive the person who wronged us, no self-respecting demon is going to want to hang around us."

Leona leaned down to the floor and picked up Midnight. "Black cats are the favorite of witches. Does Midnight come from hell?" she asked.

CHAPTER 63

"LET ME CHANGE THE SUBJECT," said Leona. "This must be a difficult time for you, losing your wife and then your bishop. And both so violently. I cannot imagine what you are feeling. I know this is a delicate question, but does all this mean that you might become bishop?"

"Prospects for that are quite good, I think, after a while, and after the church Fathers consider it."

"Have you had a desire to become bishop for a long time?"

"My desire doesn't count, you know. It's a question of God's will alone, apart from my desire. I'm persuaded that it's God's will that I become bishop."

Leona paused, aghast. "It's God's will that you become bishop. Is that what I heard you say?"

"Yes, that's what I said. I am very confident that God wants this for me."

"Do you desire what God wants for you?" interrogated Leona.

"Yes, of course. I want my desire to conform to God's desire."

"But, a moment ago, I thought you said that your desire could be set aside so that you could follow God's will alone, apart from your desire. Did you say that?"

Korsky said nothing.

"Does this sound like a contradiction?" she asked.

"Well, I guess I desire what God desires."

"How do you know it is God's will and not Satan's will?" she pressed.

"I think I know the difference between God and Satan, Lee. For heaven's sake."

"Let's speculate, Stephen. Suppose Satan wants to place you in a high-ranking office in the church. Suppose Satan wants to plant you in the City of God like the Hellenes planted the wooden horse inside the city of Troy. Once within the citadel, then the soldiers could wreak havoc. Could you possibly be a Trojan horse, Stephen?"

"No, of course not. As bishop I would dedicate my ministry to Christ and Christ alone."

"Do you recall Leona's Law of Evil? *You know it's the voice of Satan when you hear the call to shed innocent blood.*"

"Well, Lee, let me assure you: I have never shed innocent blood."

Leona said nothing.

"LEONA," interjected Graham, walking hurriedly into the kitchen. "You've got a Skype call coming in upstairs. I think you'll want to take it."

"Oh, Stephen, I hope you'll excuse me," apologized Leona as she left the room. Graham saw the guest to his car and bade him goodbye. In moments Leona had settled herself before her computer screen and greeted her friend in Lahore, Pakistan: "In the name of God, the Most Compassionate, the Most Merciful."

"In the name of God, the Most Compassionate, the Most Merciful," she heard in response. "Lee, you're looking beautiful, as always."

"You're not supposed to notice a woman's beauty, Muzaffar," she said, jesting. "You should keep your mind on Allah alone. No shirk."

"But you are the creation of our good God, Lee, and when I admire you I am thanking God," said Muzaffar Haq.

"Boy, you got out of that one like a fish leaping out of the net!" exclaimed Leona.

"As much as I would like to engage you in electronic flirting, Pastor Lee, my matter is urgent. May I proceed?"

"Yes, of course."

"Here at the university, we frequently receive colleagues from other parts of the world. This past evening, I spent some time with a physicist from Malek-Ashtar University of Technology in Tehran. I dare not give you his name over Skype. He is fleeing Iran. He's seeking asylum. I don't know exactly where."

"And?"

"What he reports to be secretly happening has shaken me," Muzzafar stated with an emphasis in his voice that gave Leona a chill. Then he paused.

"Some of his colleagues have begun construction on a portable nuclear weapon. This will not be attached to a missile or dropped as a bomb. No. It will be placed in a truck or other vehicle and driven to the spot of detonation."

Leona was stunned. Seeing her own face on the Skype screen shocked her, and even Muzzafar could see the reaction.

"So," she asked with a quivering voice, "they can park it anywhere? A market? A school? A government building?"

"Yes, anywhere. And there would be no hints about what lies within."

"Oh my God! In a way, they make nuclear warfare invisible! Unpredictable?"

"That is the sad truth, Lee."

The two friends, Leona and Muzzafar, bound together as colleagues by their mutual fight against terrorism, quietly stared at each other from opposite sides of the one globe. Each felt the overwhelming sense of dread these facts portended.

"So, walk me through the way they might execute this plan," requested Leona.

"First, they will demand a ransom. A big ransom. So big, only a wealthy government will be able to pay. Unless the ransom is paid, the bomb will be detonated from a satellite signal. This insures the nuclear blackmailers can be safely protected on another continent. This will radically change geopolitics, Lee."

"We have been expecting nuclear blackmail for some time, Muzaffar," said Leona. "So—the darkness is nigh."

"What's so devilish, Lee, is that the conspirators have found a way to disassemble and reassemble the components, making it undetectable when transporting it across borders. By the time any security agency wakes up, it will be already planted and ready for detonation. I had not dreamed the technology was this advanced. But it is."

Both paused the conversation. Then Leona spoke. "Motive? What the hell is the motive?"

"Well, Lee, this might be a theological question. If Satan himself is truly behind it, then the sheer shedding of innocent blood would be the motive. If we all shake our heads in horror, that would make Satan's day. But, if it's not Satan himself, then some person or clique or syndicate is pursuing what your New Testament calls the root of all evil, namely, money."

"The Bible should've said 'power.' Because that's what people actually think they're getting when they get money." Leona fell silent for a moment.

"Some kind of world dominance. That's what Ghengis Kahn wanted. That's what Julius Caesar wanted. That's what today's oligarchs and presidents and prime ministers and dictators want. You've told me about your friend Maletesto. Maybe he wants mere bloodshed or the threat of bloodshed for profit, and he thinks you stand in his way. Pastor Lee, you're an inconvenience. He needs to get rid of you."

"I'm not afraid."

"That's what worries me, Lee. You should be afraid. It might make you safer."

Leona paused before responding with a change of subject. "Did your physicist friend provide names and places and such?"

"He's keeping it to himself until he can trust the representative of an international power, he says. And, as you know, we don't have anyone we can trust in my home country. That's why I'm calling you."

"Spell that out for me, please," she requested.

"I hesitate to say it on an open network such as this. But, shall we say, you have contacts who would know what to do with this information, don't you?"

"Muzaffar, I will take it from here. It's probably the case that those very contacts are monitoring my Skype. So, it should not take me long."

CHAPTER 65

THE FRONT DOORBELL RANG. Leona descended the steep wooden stairway to the landing, where she opened the door to the expansive front porch. It was Susan.

"Hello, Susan," said the pastor welcomingly. "Would you like to come in?"

Without speaking, Susan crossed the threshold with a slight lumbering gait. She followed Leona into the living room. She spotted the chair she had sat in previously and made a bee-line for it, as if there were a sense of order, as if that chair was there especially for her. Leona smiled knowingly.

"How are you, Susan?" asked Leona.

"I am fine, Pastor Lee," she responded.

"How did the ashtray turn out?"

"It's not an ashtray," said Susan, digging into her bag. "It's a gift for you, Pastor. And I know you don't smoke."

"Oh, how lovely to have you think about me."

After some effort Susan withdrew a handful of newspapers wrapped around a solid object. Then, she handed the fistful of newspaper to the pastor, who proceeded to unwrap the mystery gift.

"Is this a cross?" asked the Pastor. It was a ceramic cross about six inches long and an inch thick. It was glazed in browns and greens with a smooth glasslike finish.

"Yes, it's a cross. Jesus died on a cross, you know. I made this for you because I thought it might help you when you pray."

"Help me when I pray?"

"Yes. You could look at this cross and hold it when you pray. This will help you to remember that God loves you even when you are having a bad day."

"Why, thank you, Susan. I will look at your cross the next time I pray alone."

Susan abruptly stood up and turned her body toward the door. "I need to go now, Pastor."

CHAPTER 66

THE BEDROOM LIT UP. The light came through the east window of Leona's second story bedroom. She sat up in bed. Curious. Alert. Her ears picked up a distant growl, which quickly became a deafening roar. The parsonage was engulfed in light and sound.

Leaping from bed she slipped on a pair of jean shorts and a sweatshirt before she hastened down the hall toward the stairway. Leona descended two steps at a time. At the bottom she turned and ran through the living and dining rooms to the east porch door. Once through the door and on the porch steps, she looked upward. The bright light and roaring noise came from a landing helicopter. The bird was settling in on the large lawn on the south side of the church.

The spotlight shut off, but the rotors continued to turn. This would not be a long visit. Leona recognized this particular helicopter. Few could mistake Marine One.

Hillar and Graham scrambled down the stairs and joined Buck, already on site, asking, "What's happening?"

One lone figure exited Marine One and walked briskly to the veranda steps to greet the three humans and one husky. Buck, who normally does not bark, was agitated and prancing with a mixture of confused anxiety and protective anger. As the helicopter passenger approached, it became clear that it was a man. He was dressed in a neatly pressed black suit, white shirt, and silver tie. The ear wire made it clear: he represented the Secret Service.

"Reverend Foxx?" he asked in a raised voice to carry above the din. When Leona nodded, he continued. "I'm Elliott Groome, Secret Service Attaché to the President. Would you please come with me?"

"Now?!" she exclaimed.

"Immediately, please."

"But, I just got out of bed. I need to dress."

"No. This is a come-as-you-are party." He reached for her arm and began to escort her toward the waiting craft.

"Wait!" screamed Hillar, holding Buck still by the collar. "You can't do that! Bring her back."

Leona stopped and turned. "Hillar and Graham, everything is okay. You need not worry. I'll be back soon. Take care of Buck." Then she turned her back on them and entered the craft. In a moment the helicopter had ascended and the motor could no longer be heard at ground level.

Hillar stood aghast. His eyes pleaded with Graham for an explanation. Graham looked at the teen with a weak expression of assurance. "It's going to be okay, Hillar. It's happened before. Pastor Lee will return and things will go back to normal."

"Nothing here is normal, Graham!" Turning to the canine, Hillar muttered, "Come on, Buck." Then he walked back into the house, head down in bewilderment, watching his own steps as he made his way into the kitchen. Graham followed at a comfortable distance, knowing that Hillar needed some space as he was trying to process what had just happened.

"How about a cup of my world-famous hot chocolate?" Graham asked once they reached the kitchen table.

"Sure," said Hillar without making eye contact.

After half an hour of relative silence, they returned to their respective bedrooms for the remainder of the night.

CHAPTER 67

THE FLIGHT WAS long and Leona dozed off in her seat, wearing ear phones turned to Mute. She awoke when the whine of the rotors changed and the craft made its landing within the White House perimeter in the nation's capital. She and Elliot Groome were greeted by uniformed aides and ushered toward the building.

"Where?" breathed out Elliott.

"Red Room," said an aide. "No tourists this time of night."

Leona followed Elliott in her bare feet up the stairway and through the State Dining Room into the Red Room. "This is where I leave you, Reverend Foxx. I'll see you again shortly." Then, Elliott closed the door, leaving the guest alone.

The Red Room in the first White House was where John Adams routinely ate his breakfast. The room's appointments belong to the *American Empire* period between 1810 and 1830. The Italian white marble mantel was installed in 1818. The red carpet and red uphol-stered chairs gave the room its name.

Anxious while she waited, Leona studied the Red Room, admiring the exquisite appointments and how the color energized the room. At the same time, she felt the entire experience to be surreal.

Leona stroked the edges of the marble mantel, admiring the

beauty of its symmetry and wondering if John Adams himself might have done the same.

Her thoughts were interrupted when she heard the door behind her open. A presidential aide leaned in to allow the door to open without himself entering. There stood President Andrew Dodge. The head of state stepped in as the aide closed the door.

"Oh, Andy!" she exclaimed in a loud whisper. She ran to his open arms that embraced her with both tenderness and passion. Leona nestled her forehead between his neck and ear. He held her without speaking for what seemed like an endless time.

CHAPTER 68

WITHOUT HURRYING they settled into two adjacent chairs, facing one another at the corners. "I'm really worried about you, Lee."

"What do you mean?"

"Satanic ritual abuse is worse than just violence," Lee. "It can have eternal consequences."

"How do you know about that?"

"You'd be surprised about what I can know if I want to."

"I'm so confused, Andy."

"Yes, I know that too. That's why I sent for you."

"But, how?"

"That's for me to know."

"Don't treat me like a child, dammit."

"I won't. Before we go any further, I'd like to bring someone else into our conversation." The president pressed an electronic button located just behind him on the wall. The president spoke softly yet distinctly: "We're ready for Gary."

Momentarily, Gerhart Holthusen walked through the door. Leona leaped to her feet and embraced the Director of the CIA.

"My, My, Gary, what a nice surprise! Are you in the habit of hiding behind the president's door to be summoned at any time?" Leona quipped.

"I do whatever I can in the service of our country...but I must admit, this meeting tonight was not on my calendar. The White House does make a respectable late-night snack, however."

"Eggnog, anyone?" asked the president.

"One thing I like about you, Mr. POTUS, is that you like to entertain with a certain sense of singularity. So, eggnog this time of year? Sure. Why not?" responded Leona, smiling while reaching for her taste of Yule Tide.

Once they had settled down with eggnog in hand, it was time for a nose-to-nose discussion. "Please tell us what has been happening at Lake George," queried the president.

"But I don't see how this could be a national security matter," protested Leona mildly.

"We'll be the judge of that," said Holthusen. "We want to know what things look like from your perspective."

Leona began with the gruesome discovery at Saint John's, her interactions with Sheriff Bolton and Detective Evans, the Faustian contract offered to Luciano Silvestri, the suspicious behavior of J. Holmes Chapman and Renard Maletesto, the murders of Sophia and the OCA bishop, and the attempt to drown her in the waters of Lake George. "Even though this seems to involve radical evil in its ugliest possible form, it appears to me to be local and not international."

"Gary?" said the president, looking at Holthusen.

CHAPTER 69

THE CIA DIRECTOR BEGAN. "We have good reason to believe that the organization is international in its structure. The semi-secret corporate name is *Cultus Satanas*. On the one hand, it's a federation of local cults, including both theistic and atheistic Satanic groups. On the other hand, it's tightly organized. Even authoritarian. It leases franchises. The coven within the Manhattan Opera is actually a relatively recent franchise. Maybe only a couple years or so."

Leona asked, "How could *Cultus Satanas* possibly include both theistic Satanists, who believe in supernatural sorcery, and also atheistic Satanists, who simply sell debaucheries?"

"Control," answered Holthusen. "*Cultus Satanas* maintains tight control over the local groups. The threat of releasing evil in either its supernatural form or common thuggery is surprisingly effective at maintaining internal group authority. And, of course, in shuttling money and talent from the local to the international levels."

"Human sacrifice," began Leona, "should I presume it belongs to the classic *Missa Solemnis Satanis*?"

"Yes," responded Holthusen. "The worshippers literally consume body and blood. They believe they ingest the life-power of the sacrificed person. They further believe that if they offer this sacrifice to

Satan, that Satan will respond by bestowing blessings. The Faustian pact with the devil is sealed by sacrifice."

Leona dropped her head into her hands. "This is just so wrong! The whole point of the death of Jesus on the cross is that there is no mechanism of sacrifice. Sacrifice does not compel any divine power to reward us. The cross is intended to put an end to all sacrifice and announce God's grace as unconditional. What you're describing is so perverted! And then, the horror faced by little Sarai as she was being slain!"

"The Satanists are twisting precious symbols so as to reverse their meaning," Holthusen continued. "It gets worse, Leona."

The director paused to catch his breath. "*Cultus Satanas* is creatively connecting the core doctrine of sacrifice to other traditions. It applies reverse Christian theology to the Aztec practice of cutting out human hearts and eating them. In your situation in the Adirondack Mountains, the Manhattan Opera coven is trying to connect heart-eating with the ancient Indian practice of scalping enemies. The coven is trying to revive tribal identity through stealing life-power from sacrificial victims. It is a multicultural form of Satan worship." Holthusen laughed.

"This is all going somewhere," Leona speculated. "Where?"

"Well," interjected the president, "what do you think might count as the most horrendous and unthinkable form shedding innocent blood might take?"

Leona registered surprise and bafflement.

"Try a nuclear explosion," added the president.

"That's unspeakable," declared Leona.

"Well, Lee, that's what we're up against. It's not clear that each and every Satanist upholds an ideology, but the net effect of the momentum we've been tracking leads in this direction. The international core of *Cultus Satanas* has been negotiating with a number of terrorist groups, offering to supply the financial where-withal to acquire a nuclear weapon. They say it's for nuclear black-mail. Allegedly, the group with the dirty bomb could blackmail any government by simply threatening detonation. But *Cultus Satanas* does not want to stop at the threat. They want to go all the way. They'll go all the way even if it means self-destruction. More than political ideology is at work here."

"Who is the target?"

"No particular target. Mass murder on any continent will do. Washington? Moscow? Beijing? This is death for death's sake on a scale of millions," answered Holthusen. "On one level, it looks like we have nuclear blackmail to deal with. On another level, some Satanists want to bypass the blackmail and go straight to war. Maybe blackmail will be the opening salvo, but the Satanists want to be sure that some bombs go off somewhere."

"Not just the Satanists," interjected Dodge. "What about that asshole congressman, Humphrey Crump?"

"Let's get back to the Satanists," said Leona. "Can *Cultus Satanas* deliver the weapons technology? Do you two know what I know after talking with my biologist friend in Lahore?"

"Yes, we know," said Holthusen. "I could apologize for monitoring your private communications, Lee, but I won't. I think you understand. And, as you can imagine, we will follow up with Professor Haq."

Leona nodded without verbalizing anything.

Holthusen went on. "Back to *Cultus Satanas*. By continuing the recruiting program, the cult hopes to raise enough funds to bribe or buy or steal what they need to entice a terrorist group to do the dirty work under one or another political ideology. The high priest may select a current Middle-Eastern terrorist group or create a new one. More than likely, he'll try to contact the Tehran group. We will need to beat him to the punch."

Leona gave a thumbs-up signal. "I trust that *Cultus Satanas* will want to remain in the background and give somebody else the notoriety, right?"

Holthusen answered. "Exactly right. *Cultus Satanas* will groom its own terrorists with their own identity. Cult emissaries will kindle

196 / TED PETERS

the flames of anger at the injustices perpetrated toward a selected group until wrath boils over into chaotic violence. Once a group becomes convinced that it is the victim, then it easily becomes motivated to engage in revenge. The target will be blamed for whatever injustice is responsible for the victimization. Propaganda will be spread via the Internet to make the entire plot look like the pursuit of justice, just to slow down the debate process for approving the ransom. Some group or another will do Satan's dirty work, I predict."

The three sat quietly, sipping their drinks with only a passing glance at one another.

"Have you been watching Mohawks in upstate New York?" asked Leona, breaking the silence.

"You bet," said Holthusen. "Hurons too. After this recent incident I had one of my team, a native American herself, investigate."

"Well, I can't believe that Mohawks have any inclination to organize, let alone radicalize," offered Leona. "Nor the Hurons."

"Exactly." Holthusen nodded in agreement. "Actually, my investigator found it offensive that anyone might even think that. Native Americans, to her knowledge, have never overlaid these ancient war practices onto the religious practices of Europeans."

"From what I know, I agree," said Leona. She continued. "What is the endgame for *Cultus Satanis*—ransom or death? Ransom for Satan's followers. Death for Satan himself."

"Death, and on an apocalyptic scale," said Holthusen. "But they may take the ransom initially in order to pay their bills....and just for the love of money. As the Bible says, the love of money is the root of all evil. And this is evil in spades. Finally, though, it's the incineration of a portion of the human race they're after. The detonation of one or more bombs will so terrify the survivors that the cult's power will become absolute overnight. Finally, even in hell, it's about power."

"Who and where is the head of *Cultus Satanas*?"

"It has a moving head in the person of Renard Maletesto, the high priest," said Holthusen.

Leona shook her head slightly to acknowledge what she'd just heard. "No doubt you've thought of, shall we say, decapitation? How did you get all this intelligence?"

"A well-placed informant," answered Holthusen.

"Do I know the informant?" asked Leona.

"You've met him," Holthusen said. "His name is Karl Sogaard."

"My day has been too long," sang Leona.

"What does that mean?" queried the president.

"Oh, it's just the aria Sogaard sings. Gary, does Sogaard know who I am?"

"Yes, indeed. But he will not drag you into this unless it's unavoidable. In fact, Lee, I recommend you avoid *Cultua Satanas* whenever you can."

"It's too late for that, Gary. I'm in this one for both time and eternity."

CHAPTER 70

Leona was returned to the parsonage lawn via helicopter, landing well after sunrise yet before breakfast time. Buck watched her arrival from the dining room window and gave her a wiggly greeting as she walked through the door. *I think I'll skip my morning jog,* she mumbled to herself. In just moments she was snuggled under her bed covers and asleep before Hillar or Graham arose.

When the groggy pastor finally descended the stairs and headed out to the veranda to sip her first cup of French Roast coffee, the day was already in full swing. Graham sat at a green wicker table hunched over, concentrating on his computer screen. Midnight had perched herself on the porch railing where she could get a panoramic view.

Hillar sat on the porch steps with his cell phone, directing Genghis as it flew between the church and the parsonage. From the bottom of the drone on a foot-long string hung what looked like—*yes, it was!*—a bone. One of Buck's doggie bones. Buck furiously chased after the bone. When the dog would get close, the drone would move upward or sideways, eluding Buck's snapping mouth. Each miss only excited the husky all the more, and he would then chase the drone more vigorously. At one point, Hillar had drawn Buck into running in a wide circle. Hillar's delight expressed in his guffaws was sufficiently contagious that soon Leona was laughing at an equivalent volume.

"Life is great, Grammy! Aren't you glad to be alive?"

Graham did not look up from his screen. He waved his left hand, signaling he did not want to be interrupted.

"Think of it, Grammy. You exist. You are here. You are in this moment. In just the flash of one little ol' nuclear bomb, you and I, along with Hillar, Buck, and Midnight, and everything you love and hold dear could be incinerated. Good morning, Grammy!"

Graham showed no reaction.

"What's going on?" asked Hillar. Leona looked up to see that two pick-up trucks had parked in the gravel drive circle near the front of Saint John's. Workmen were busy unloading folding chairs and setting them up on the lawn between the church and the memorial garden.

"This afternoon the League of Women Voters is hosting a town meeting," said Leona loud enough for both Hillar and Graham to hear. "They want an open discussion of platform planks before the national party conventions begin. I told them they could use Saint John's as a venue, but that was before what happened. So, if it doesn't rain, we'll hold it on the lawn."

Leona turned back to her coffee and stared for ten seconds each at Midnight, then Buck, then Graham, and finally Hillar. *Thank you, God, for what we have when we have it,* she prayed to herself. *Oops! Here I am praying and I'm not looking at Susan's cross.*

CHAPTER 71

"WE ARE GOING to need more fissionable uranium 235 and plutonium 239," said Maletesto to his co-conspirators in the teleconference. Even though the teleconference link was thought to be secure,
the face of each interlocutor was still pixilated and voice disguised.
No names were used.

"Transporting fissionable material across borders is nearly impos-
sible these days," responded one voice with an Eastern European
accent that could not be entirely disguised by the voice changer.
"Security is so tight and inspections so thorough."

"That's right," said Maletesto. "But our situation is by no means
hopeless. On the one hand, by disassembling and reassembling the
parts of each unit, we can transport many components which are by
themselves unidentifiable. This will work just fine in the Middle East
and Far East, so our planning for Europe, Russia and China will go
unimpeded. And, on the other hand, we will not need to rely on
international transport in the case of the United States."

"Why is that?" a voice asked.

Maletesto continued. "The Americans will provide us with all
the ingredients to make bombs inside the country, including the
fissionable material. Everything we want sits idly in pools of water at

nuclear power sites. The plans prepared by President Jimmy Carter back in the 1970s to bury high-level nuclear waste in deep mines by 1997 were scrapped by President Ronald Regan in 1980 and never revived by subsequent administrations. So, seventy metric tons of high-level radwaste are stored at seventy power generation sites in thirty-nine states. For us, this'll be like picking oranges off trees in Florida."

"Just how will we pick this radioactive fruit?" asked a third voice.

"We have followers—soul-signed, committed followers—at four key nuclear power plants already in place," bragged Maletesto. "Here's what already happens. Spent fuel rods and radioactive effluent are stored onsite for a number of years, to allow a certain amount of cooling. Then the spent fuel rods are transported to another, more permanent site for packaging. The rods will be encased in a set of copper sleeves, perhaps a half dozen or so in a single copper cylinder. Then, the cylinder is sealed and stored. Here's what we plan. We want to catch those fuel rods during the transport phase. Or, to say it another way, we will provide the trans-portation. And we will reassign the destination."

Maletesto got affirming nods from those listening. "When our trucks roll up to the power plant, highly enriched plutonium will be loaded into lead-lined compartments and shipped to our assembly plant. No one will even miss the radwaste before it's too late."

"Then what?"

"The driver will then take the payload to our facility near Colum-bus, Ohio. Each bomb will be assembled and stored in a warehouse already prepared with lead-lined walls, floor, and ceiling. We plan on manufacturing forty very dirty bombs in the U.S., along with an equal number in Europe and Asia. When the time comes for detona-tion in the continental U.S., we will hire a truck driver and provide delivery to the destination, an address in the targeted city. Once the driver nears the address, the bomb will be detonated remotely by satellite signal."

"How will you get truck drivers to volunteer for this suicide run?" asked a fourth voice.

"Each driver will not be part of the conspiracy. We'll hire Teamsters. In 1980 each Teamster earned about $24 per hour. Then the White House broke the unions and the hourly wage plummeted to $14 per hour. The original level has never returned. So, if we offer $50 per hour, we'll get all the suicide drivers we want. And they might even be dead before they can cash their paychecks."

An additional voice with a skeptical tone entered the conversation. "You don't plan to blow up forty U.S. cites all on one day, do you? I thought we were planning nuclear blackmail. I thought we would only threaten in order to collect ransom. This means we get rich without blowing up anything. Right?"

"Nuclear blackmail is only phase one," responded Maletesto. "Yes, we will threaten to destroy one American city and demand that Uncle Sam pay us a very large ransom on the promise that we will refrain. Yes, those of us on the planning committee will become instantly wealthy, to be sure. But this is only phase one."

"What comes next?" someone asked.

"In phase two," Maletesto continued, "we actually detonate the first bomb in a selected city, such as Houston."

"Really? Why? If we already have collected the ransom, then why do we need to blow up anything?"

Maletesto paused and then spoke. "Remember whom we work for. We work in the service of the Prince of Darkness, the Father of Lies, the author of broken promises, and the principle of evil for the sake of evil. Our long-range goal is to convert the ordered human spirit to chaos so it will self-destruct. After the first bomb is detonated we go on to phase three."

"Phase three?"

"Yes, phase three. In phase three we stimulate the human propensity for scapegoating. We spread the rumor that China is responsible for the destruction of Houston and that all Chinese-looking persons within America's borders are in collusion with the mainland. Can you just imagine the riots and burning of Chinese restaurants all over the country?!"

"This is getting ugly," voice three offered.

"Yes, delightfully ugly," interjected Maletesto. "As I said, the spirit of America will devolve quickly into uncontrollable mob violence. Our Lord of the Underworld will find this gleeful, and we will be properly rewarded in his kingdom."

Maletesto allowed a moment of silence before continuing. "But then, there's phase four. In this phase we will blow up one city per day for the next thirty-nine days. After only a couple detonations, the U.S. government will be convinced that a foreign power is responsible and launch an all-out missile barrage against China. In addition, we will selectively detonate nuclear devices in Russian and European cities. Russia, not knowing whom to blame, will retaliate against both China and the West. The apocalypse will have begun. The moon will turn to blood. It will be war of all against all. There will be no children of light to fight against the children of darkness."

A pause followed. Maletesto continued. "What is important for us is not the destruction of civilization per se, but the anxiety people everywhere on the globe will experience from anticipating death. What we want to see is the disordering of the souls of those fearing their imminent demise. Each person will die in terror, flailing away at evil in the fruitless pursuit of self-preservation."

"This is much more drastic than I had anticipated," someone remarked, aghast.

"Just remember whom we serve," said Maletesto.

CHAPTER 72

"I THINK MIDNIGHT MIGHT BE MISSING," said Hillar, walking from the kitchen into the dining room.

"What?" asked Leona.

"Neither the litter box nor the food dishes have been touched in a day," he reported.

"Graham!" Leona hollered loudly over her shoulder. Soon the three humans and Buck were embarked on a search of the parsonage, the yard, and the ravine. Buck took charge of searching the ravine all the way down to the creek.

"Hillar, would you please examine the roads? Just in case the worst has happened," requested Graham. Hillar began with Diamond Point Road and then searched Lake Shore Drive. He found nothing. Nor did anyone else find a sign of the missing black cat.

When the empty-handed and discouraged search party convened on the east veranda, three faces looked worried. Buck, sensing something wrong, laid himself quietly at Leona's feet.

Hillar spoke first. "Back in Chicago, ya know, sometimes at Halloween, black cats go missing. Teenage Satanists sacrifice them. It's pretty ugly."

"Thanks for that cheery note, Hillar," said Graham. "It's not Halloween."

While Graham was speaking, the parsonage phone rang. "Saint John's Church," said Hillar in a courteous tone. A moment later he passed the cordless phone to Leona. "It's for you."

"Pastor Lee Foxx here," she said.

"Pastor Foxx, this is Doctor Daniel Beard. I'm calling from the Adirondack Urgent Care Center. We have a patient here asking for you. Miss Shelly Wennes. Do you know her, by any chance?"

"Let me...yes, Shelly Wennes. She works at the Lobster Pot. What's wrong?"

"That's right. The Lobster Pot. Well, Pastor, it seems that Shelly attempted to take her own life. Overdose of opioids. She has gone through quite an ordeal, but she's going to make it. She's resting now. I'm calling you personally because I made her a promise. I promised her that if she'd pull through I'd find you and call you. She's very insistent."

"Well, Doctor, I'm very glad you did!"

"She calls you 'Father.' You know that, don't you?"

"Yes," said Leona, smiling into the phone.

"To find you I telephoned Ernan McMullin. He's my priest. When I described you he said, 'Well, that can only be Leona Foxx at the Saint John's Church in Diamond Point'. He was right."

"I'm on my way. What room number?"

CHAPTER 73

AT SHELLY'S BEDSIDE, Leona heard from a still groggy Shelly Wennes an account of her suicide attempt.

"When you and I parted at the Lobster Pot, your soul seemed content, at peace," observed Leona. You left with a sense of joy. You were going to see, what was his name? Mister Hagadorn? You were going to offer him your forgiveness. How did that go?"

A tear dropped from Shelly's eye onto her cheek. "When I got to the hospice, I was told to wait in the entrance. Evidently some sort of medical emergency was taking place. After a half hour, a nurse or someone came out to tell me that Mister Hagadorn had died. He died right then. He died while I was waiting to see him. He died before I could forgive him. Oh, I'm so miserable."

Leona placed her hand on Shelly's. Shelly sobbed.

"Now, if Mister Hagadorn goes to hell, it'll be my fault. I feel so...so covered with dirt. Scum," said Shelly.

"What happened then?" asked Leona.

Shelly explained that she had gone home, that she'd become depressed. "Then, I heard this voice."

"What voice, Shelly?"

"I don't know where it came from. I was alone. I was in the bathroom. That's where I heard it."

"What did this voice say?" asked Leona.

"'Kill yourself, Shelly. Die, Shelly.' That's what it said."

"What did you think when you heard this?" asked Leona.

"I was feeling so awful. So dirty. So evil. I felt that I should leave this world before I could make any more mistakes like condemning Mister Hagadorn to damnation."

"So, you obeyed what this voice told you? Is that what happened?"

"Yes." Shelly continued to sob. "I took those pills. Lots of them."

Leona allowed for a moment of silence. Then she spoke forcefully. "Shelly, I want you to listen to me. You are not responsible for Mister Hagadorn's damnation. Believe me, you are not responsible. Here is why. That curse you uttered came from Satan. God is not bound by any curses from Satan. In addition, it is God and God alone who determines what happens to us after death. And we know something for sure: God is gracious. God is loving and forgiving. On the other side of death's veil, Mister Hagadorn will meet only a God who will take care of all such matters of conscience. You have got to trust that what I say here is true. Do you understand me?"

Shelly looked Leona in the eye. She nodded affirmatively.

"That voice, Shelly. That voice enticing you to put an end to your life. That is the voice of Satan himself. Your blood, Shelly, is innocent. Do you hear me? It's innocent. No need to shed it."

Shelly nodded. Shelly's facial expression registered a hint of confusion right along with gratitude for this pastoral presence.

"You are such a fine young woman, Shelly. I so very much want to see you grow up and enjoy that family you are planning. Don't, don't, don't listen to that voice."

Shelly simply stared at Leona.

Leona spoke next. "You were baptized in a Catholic church, right?"

"Yes. When I was a baby, of course."

Leona stood up and walked around, evidently looking for some-thing. In a moment she was holding a plastic bottle of baby oil. She picked up a small pill cup and poured a thimble's worth of oil into the pill cup. Then she resumed her seat on Shelly's bed.

"Hold still, Shelly. I'm going to anoint you, just like the prophet Samuel anointed Saul and David." Leona painted the sign of the cross in oil on Shelly's forehead. "I anoint you in the name of the Father, the Son, and the Holy Spirit."

Then, Leona put the cup on a nearby shelf. She turned to look Shelly squarely in the eyes. "With this anointing, Shelly, you have the power at any moment to draw up the Holy Spirit given you in baptism. With the Spirit's power, the Devil will be annihilated. If you ever again hear that voice telling you to kill yourself, here's what you do."

Leona paused.

"What?" asked Shelly.

"Here's what you do," continued Leona. "Say this: 'Satan! Get the fuck oughta my life!"

Both laughed.

CHAPTER 74

HILLAR RETREATED to a corner of the living room sofa, took out his mobile phone, and stared intently at the small electronic screen. Playing *Gunblood* transported him from the present moment into the isolated world of cyberspace.

Graham casually leaned against the doorframe that led from the living room to the hallway, and quietly observed Hillar. This vantage point allowed him to watch Hillar without seeming intrusive. If Hillar noticed Graham standing there, he did not let on. After a few minutes, Graham broke the silence.

"This was quite an experience for you, wasn't it, Hillar."

"Yeah," Hillar responded without looking up from his game.

"Sort of scary?" Graham said reflectively, while maintaining his distance.

"Yeah, I guess," replied Hillar, still fixating on his game.

"I sure was scared when I heard about it," said Graham.

"Yeah," said Hillar flatly, without a hint of emotion in his voice.

Graham walked over to the sofa and sat down at the opposite end, leaving enough space between him and Hillar to assure him that the man was not intending to intrude on the boy's private space.

"Hillar," said Graham. "Can we talk? Just you and me?"

"Yeah, I guess," said Hillar, continuing to play his video game.

"I would like to have a *real* conversation with you, Hillar. Not just phrases volleyed through the air with no sense of connection," Graham stated, with a new sense of firmness.

"I really like you a lot, Hillar. I think you know that. Pastor Lee and I include you in what we are investigating because we like you, not just because you are so good at the tech stuff. Understand that?"

Hillar looked up to acknowledge that he was listening.

"At the same time, I realize there is so much that I don't know about you. And so much you don't talk about."

"I know. Yeah," said Hillar. "I don't much like talking, especially about myself."

"*That* I do know about you, Hillar," said Graham, now tempering his firm voice with a slight chuckle and a smile. "I know that. But I think it's time for you to open up and let me in. It doesn't matter what you tell me. I will always be your friend."

Hillar stared at his phone again, then looked up at Graham with watery eyes.

"It's really hard, Graham," said Hillar with a quiver in his voice. "You and Pastor Lee are the only people in the whole world I feel I can really trust. I feel like when we are all together, we are sorta like a family. I never had a real family. My family was like pieces of a family. When I go away by myself, sit by myself, it is because I don't feel that I really belong anywhere."

"I can understand that. We all have a little of that feeling inside. But for you, I think, it is a lot deeper. Am I right? Tell me what it is you carry with you all the time. What thoughts go on in your head."

"Sure you want to hear all this?"

"Of course. We are family, sorta..."

"Well, I think it goes back to before my dad left. I was only twelve and my brother Jerry was sixteen. I never knew why he left. Mom never said. She would only start crying and go into her bedroom and slam the door. She started drinking a little, then a lot. I thought maybe my dad didn't love me or my brother, or maybe we were too much trouble. Sometimes I didn't want to do my homework. One time I stole some candy from the 7-11. Dad found out and he was so mad he beat me so bad I couldn't go to school the next day."

"Did he beat you a lot?"

"Yeah. And he beat Jerry too. And my mom, too. We never saw him hit her 'cause he did it when we were in school. But she sometimes had bruises that weren't there when we left in the morning."

Graham continued to listen without interrupting. Hillar went on. "When he beat us, he would swear in Estonian, sometimes in Russian. So I couldn't understand him. He never wanted us to learn his languages. Then he would shout in English, 'America is no good for opportunity!' I think he was just angry that he couldn't get a really good job and had so much trouble with English."

"After he left, I cried every night for maybe a year or so. I think my brother did too. But he thought I didn't notice. We shared a small bedroom. It was the only place we both felt safe. Jerry was my best buddy."

Hillar shifted his body back and forth on his corner of the sofa, appearing to make himself more comfortable but actually giving himself time to compose himself. He put down his game and used both hands to wipe his eyes.

Graham placed a gentle hand on Hillar's shoulder. "I know when Jerry committed suicide, you were devastated, Hillar. PTSD is a terrible affliction. It is especially so when those who suffer from it are the best guys, the ones who want to protect our country."

"Yeah," stuttered Hillar. "I thought life was over. Maybe I should do the same. You know, end my life too. You and Pastor Lee were there for me. I couldn't have made it through without you."

"Of course. We know what a good guy you are."

"Thanks, but I don't always feel like I am good."

"Those doubts are part of being human."

"Yeah, I guess. So, I think when scary things happen, like all this murder stuff, I go back to being little and my dad beating me. Sometimes I can't even breathe. I think about Jerry and how they found him. I think of my mom: how when she is there she isn't really there. Then, I am afraid of being left all alone again. So I go off and be alone."

Hillar began to sob. "Crazy, isn't it?"

"Not at all, Hillar. It was good you could say it."

Graham paused for a moment and allowed the boy to take a few deep breaths.

"Your mom has been really good about having you stay with Pastor Lee and letting us take you places."

"Yeah, she has. Mostly because she finds it easy to not take care of me. She drinks a lot, especially during the day, so by the time I used to get home from school she was asleep. She would buy vodka and groceries in the morning and then...."

"I hope you are calling her while you are here in New York. I bet she loves you more than you think. She just isn't able to get over all her losses. I know Pastor Lee has tried to get her to go to AA or get into counseling, without much success."

"That would be admitting that something is wrong. She took me to church when I was little, in Chicago, the church that Pastor Lee came to. She was much happier in those days. That changed my life. Not just the Jesus part, but having someone like Pastor Lee to really care about me. Now, mom just lives in la-la land"

Graham reached over and hugged Hillar with a big strong bear hug. "Don't forget about me. I care about you too," asserted Graham as he pulled back and patted Hillar on the back and looked him straight in the eye.

"Never," said Hillar with a smile.

"Thanks for sharing all that with me," said Graham. "I knew some, but I appreciate you connecting the dots."

"That's okay. It wasn't as hard as I thought it would be."

CHAPTER 75

By four o'clock the church lawn was full of milling visitors looking for a seat in the assembly. Brenda Beale took her position in the front of the gathering, inviting everyone to find a seat so that the forum could begin. Once conversation had subsided, she welcomed all in attendance on behalf of the Saint John's congregation. Brenda introduced Pastor Lee, who then introduced Mary Anne Kelly, Chair of the Education Committee for the League of Women Voters.

Mary Anne Kelly took over the meeting, carrying herself with appropriate confidence and authority. Her opening included a brief description of the League's work in the state of New York, inviting volunteers to join either the Environmental Action Committee or the Campaign Finance Reform Committee. She then turned to the matter of the day, a town hall meeting on two Capitol Hill bills, one in the House and one in the Senate, both aimed at enlarging America's nuclear arsenal.

"We are the *hoi polloi*, the average Joe and Jill," announced Kelly. "We are what politicians allude to as *the American people*. Politicians ask us what we think, but they close their ears. They are deaf to us. So we need to yell so loudly they cannot not hear us!"

That brought applause. Kelly proceeded. "But before we yell, we need to think. We need to think out loud. That's what we're here for today. The Lake George chapter of the League is glad you all are here for this forum on national security and national defense. Thanks for coming."

By this time Leona had taken a seat in the rear row next to Sheriff Bolton and Mohawk Evans. Graham slid in. All four listened intently. Leona noticed something not acknowledged by her seat mates. Hovering silently above the meeting was Genghis. *I bet Hillar's filming the forum,* she said to herself. *That boy's just too much.*

Kelly continued. "Our question for today is this: shall the United States modify its present policy toward international military threats and domestic terrorist threats? Specifically, should the Pentagon enlarge the national debt and invest that money in enlarging our nation's nuclear arsenal? Speaking on behalf of expansion is Congressman Humphrey Crump. Let's give a warm welcome to the Honorable Humphrey Crump."

With this round of applause, the congressman, dressed in a pinstripe light gray suit, with no necktie, and wearing a red baseball cap one size too small for his head, stepped to the podium.

"The greatest danger from both abroad and within," announced Crump after a welcome and an opening joke, "is our own nation's president, Andrew Dodge. This president has weakened our military by cutting its budget. Meanwhile, through his bilateral peace negotiations, he has strengthened enemies such as Iran, Russia, China, and North Korea. Our enemies are now stronger than ever. America is now in grave danger."

Applause, though sparse, responded positively to the congressman.

Crump continued with a verbal paragraph on each of America's archenemies. Iran is evil. North Korea is led by crazies. China and Russia are out to dominate the world. "The only way to eliminate any threats is through strength. The only way to defend against our enemies is to eliminate them first, before they can attack us. As President Reagan said many years ago, we need to be ready to win a limited thermonuclear war. We have the weapons advantage now. That margin of superiority may not remain as other countries develop their own nuclear arsenals. Now is the time for a preemptive strike. We could win an exchange with any enemy on the globe and lose a maximum of forty million American people. We could survive a forty million loss. But once the battle is over, world peace would reign and America would become, once again, world dominant."

Now the clapping was vigorous. Leona kept her hands in her lap.

CHAPTER 76

Mary Anne Kelly introduced two women, who appeared to be around thirty, to represent the opposing position—Nancy Shields and Rosemary Jenkins. The two women rose from their front row seats and placed themselves at the speaker's microphone. Each of the two brunettes wore jeans, horse-riding boots, short-sleeved checkered blouses, and leather vests. Wild west clothing stores could be found only ten miles south of Diamond Point, but it was not clear that these leather vests were merely tourist trophies.

With unusually soft and halting voices betraying that public speaking was not something they did regularly, Nancy Shields defined the position they would be defending. "We would like America to become less of a threat to other nations and remove from terrorists the reason for hating the American way of life. Although it is not our intention to take sides in national politics, we would like to express our gratitude to President Andrew Dodge for his vigorous pursuit of non-proliferation and for making international agreements that help insure peace," she read from a small piece of paper.

Despite their humble demeanor, the two women demonstrated that they'd done their political homework. Rosemary Jenkins took her turn at the microphone. "My friend Nancy is a Huron Indian. I am a

Mohawk. We are both mothers. Nancy has three children. I have two. We want to raise our families in peace, not war. We want to raise our children to become good citizens, not warriors. We want to raise our girls and boys to have children and live in this beautiful land next to this beautiful water in perpetuity."

The audience registered a level of dismay. Rosemary continued. "Now, you might say, 'I never see any Indians around here.' Well, we are here. We never went away. Even if you don't recognize us daily, we work as your restaurant waitresses, boat mechanics, and school teachers. Our young people serve in the U.S. military. Yes, our ancestors are the ones you read about in the history books. But today we all paddle in the same canoe. We are all citizens of this one nation, in war or peace."

She paused. Then she continued. "The French and Indian War, which once divided us, is over. There are no more savages, whether Indian or European. Or are there? We have just heard that America could lose forty million of its precious mothers and fathers and children in a thermonuclear battle that would put our nation on top of the world. Well, Nancy and I do not believe it is worth the life of a single American or a single citizen of any country to achieve such a goal."

Leona looked at Mohawk, who returned eye contact. The Indian smiled—almost a victory smile.

CHAPTER 77

As THE TWO Amerindian women were seating themselves and Mary Ann Kelly was striding to the podium, thunder roared close by. It was Harley Davidson thunder, and it was increasing in volume.

In moments the roar of motorcycles enveloped the assembly on the lawn. Harleys buzzed and circled around those seated, like prancing painted wooden horses circle the center of a calliope. Those attending remained seated, waiting for what would happen next.

All Harley engines turned off at precisely the same second. Leather and lace alighted from motorcycle seats, and each biker or pair of bikers stood almost at attention facing the assembly. Artie took long strides from his bike to the podium. With a gentleman's bow he greeted Mary Ann Kelly and respectfully beckoned for the microphone. His body language conveyed its own message: *it's my turn to speak.*

Artie paused before speaking to look around the gathering, making eye contact with virtually every individual in attendance. He gained their undivided attention.

"If you don't know us," he began slowly yet deliberately, "we are Rolling Thunder. Our mission is to remember the soldiers and the families of those who sacrificed for our nation's freedom. This is a freedom which everyone here today enjoys. Our heroes of previous wars won this freedom the ol' fashioned way, with courage and conviction in the face of danger. Each man and woman you saw straddling a bike here today is one of those veteran soldiers."

One member of the audience clapped. Then another. Artie waited long enough for the entire gathering to applaud.

"We thank you for that applause. We know your gratitude is sincere. We also know that the sacrifice of the soldier brings Americans together—people of all ages, ethnic backgrounds, and races. The soldier, especially the dead soldier, makes us all one as Americans."

Artie paused. Leona and Mohawk looked at one another quizzically.

"Unfortunately, this national unity comes at a cost. That cost is not just the lives of our soldiers either killed or taken into an enemy's prison. That cost is neglect here at home. The ranks of the homeless in our cities are swelled with wandering soldier souls, home from battle but now losing a war with their own psyches. Those who find their way to a VA hospital are told to wait. They wait sometimes until they are dead before they get admitted. They die from either unattended bodily injuries or moral injury, a hurt that leads to suicide. We lose more veterans to suicide than we did on the battlefield. Here is my point: it is the *symbol of the dead or captured soldier*, not the flesh-and-blood soldier him- or herself, who unifies our nation."

After another pregnant pause, Artie continued. "But this is not why I have asked to speak to you at this event. Rolling Thunder is present today at the involuntary invitation of the Honorable Humphrey Crump. No doubt you have heard what Washington has heard: Representative Crump wants to launch a pre-emptive nuclear strike against..."

Artie turned to look at the congressman. "Who is it today, Mr. Crump? Russia? China? North Korea? Iran? All at once?"

Artie turned back to the audience. "Before you take Representative Crump's recommendations at face value, please look at the face behind the face. Notice three features of the second face. First, among Congressman Crump's most generous donors are the nuclear power industry and defense contractors."

Having established the pause as integral to his message, Artie took a moment to let this point settle in before continuing. "Second, a nuclear attack we launch against another nation will change the nature of war. America will no longer need soldiers. Washington will simply press some buttons. Our military will simply send missiles or bombers to wipe out cities, utilities, and the life chances of entire peoples and regions. No combat. Only destruction from heaven wreaking havoc on earth. It will be an antiseptic war, one in which foreigners become infected while we at home remain clean."

Another brief pause. "Unless, of course—and this is my third concern—a foreign nuclear power retaliates and eliminates forty million Americans. Forty million American people, along with their dogs, cats, horses, farmland and rivers and streams and, and, and... We will all stand around shrieking in horror at these deaths. Congressman Crump will deliver speeches which bring tears to our eyes. Those forty million dead Americans will have been sacrificed. They will replace the soldiers who today serve as the scapegoats that unify our nation."

Artie surveyed the eyes of the audience one more time. "These are simply matters we in Rolling Thunder would like you to think about." He turned to Mrs. Kelly and added, "Thank you, Madam Chair, for allowing us to participate with the League of Women Voters in this public discussion."

With that, Artie remounted his Harley. After thirty seconds of engine revving, Rolling Thunder rolled out of the church yard and westward on Diamond Point Road.

CHAPTER 78

As THE ROAR of the Harleys became faint, the meeting broke up, and as attendees were heading for the cookies and coffee, the back row formed a "what-didja-think?" group. No one ventured an opinion at first.

Then Leona spoke with a tone of sarcasm. "After forty days and forty nights, the rain stopped so Noah's ark could moor safely on Mount Ararat. After forty years the children of Israel lost in the Wilderness of Sin entered the Promised Land. Now, according to Congressman Crump, if we sacrifice one million people in each of forty states then America will be on top of the world. It all sounds so biblical. Why are we not cheering?"

No one responded to Leona.

The sheriff broke the silence. "I kinda like what Rolling Thunder said." This brought some positive nods.

"What do you think about that Huron and Mohawk testimony to unity, Mohawk?" asked Leona.

"If these two squaws are representative of what's going on around here, then my suspicions of a Huron uprising are wrongheaded. I'll meander up there and talk to Misses Shields and Jenkins. I'd like to hear what they know. I just bet that Mrs. Jenkins knows my family." At that Mohawk left.

Sheriff Bolton was scratching the five o'clock shadow on his chin, the kind of scratch that carries a message: I am about to talk. "I've been thinking, Pastor Lee."

"We're all thinking," interjected Graham.

"Well, at first I thought that maybe the baby dying was due to a family struggle over custody. Perhaps that idea is one we can put on the shelf until we need it again. Now we've got to plug in an attempt to drown the prettiest pastor in the Adirondacks. No doubt these are connected."

Leona and Graham both nodded, hoping for more.

"Just who wants to see you dead, Pastor Lee? Could be Maletesto himself. But what's his motive? Are you getting too close to his operation? Whatever that operation is? And then there's that guy you met at the opera. Did you say he calls himself Magua?"

"Yes. I don't know his real name."

"Maybe he's hiding his real name. Maybe Magua wants you dead to prevent you from protecting Luciano. Maybe he tol' his Huron friends who work for Maletesto to take you out? Maybe it was the Hurons, not Maletesto. Or, all of 'm.

"It looks like the list is growing longer," commented Graham.

Leona added an item. "And we can't forget the murders of Sophia and Tikhon."

"I think I'll keep my deputies monitoring Maletesto's place until we find a lead. Can't make an arrest 'til we got a theory about who done it and why. And, of course, more evidence."

CHAPTER 79

IT WAS another one of those delightful summer Adirondack evenings. The burgers were grilled on the Weber and consumed on the parsonage porch. Buck and Hillar wrestled while Graham and Leona rocked on the porch rockers. Hillar paused and looked up. "We miss Midnight," he said.

A tear appeared in Leona's eye. Then she turned to Graham to continue a conversation already under way. The two went repeatedly over and over the facts as they had assembled them, partially whispering so that only the two of them conversed. "You know I'm jealous of Andrew," Graham confessed. "Yes, it's been a long time since you were together with him and, yes, he's married and unavailable, but Lee..."

"Why Graham, how could you be jealous?" she teased. When Leona teased in this way, Graham would fidget and look away.

A buzz announcing an incoming message prompted Leona to walk to the veranda railing and pick up her cell phone. "Amazon delivery via drone about to arrive." Leona paused to think quietly. Then she turned to her parsonage family.

"Quaz, get Buck and go into the house. Stay there until I tell you to come out. Fast!"

"Grammy, in the basement is a shotgun. Recently cleaned. Load it. Stand behind the veranda door out of sight. When I raise my right hand, come out on to the veranda and fire. Don't miss."

"What?" asked Graham.

Hillar was already on the way into the house. "Come on, Buck."

"Graham, do as I say. Quickly." Graham followed Hillar through the porch door and disappeared into the parsonage.

Leona took a place sitting on the veranda steps and looked innocent. In moments a drone with six propellers was spotted high above the church. It began a very slow descent toward the lawn between the rear of the church and the parsonage. Leona waited, as if expecting a pre-ordered package. She listened without facial expression until she heard Graham's footsteps as he positioned himself against the inside wall next to the porch door.

The drone dropped altitude slowly until it took a hovering position between Leona and the church's steeple. *Gotta wait a little longer,* Leona thought. *It's watching me.* She gradually stood upright. The drone approached. Once Leona could see clear sky behind the drone, she lifted her right arm and hollered, "Now!"

Within a second Graham was on the veranda porch just above and to Leona's left with the shotgun on his shoulder. He fired. The drone splintered into multiple pieces which fell on independent trajectories toward the ground. One large piece fell right behind the church building. But, it did not hit the ground before it exploded. Ball bearings flew. Some hit the sandstone wall of the church, so that stone chips flew in multiple directions. A couple ball bearings smacked the wooden steps of the veranda. Then, all went quiet.

"Graham," said Leona, "if I ever need someone to ride shotgun for me, you're the man!"

CHAPTER 80

THE BARBECUE COMMENCED AS PLANNED. Hillar had questions about what had just taken place, but neither Graham nor Leona answered them. Frustrated, Hillar stopped asking. Then, Hillar cleaned up the debris field. Eventually, night fell.

Leona noticed what she thought were a couple stars blinking out as she looked at the sky beyond the church steeple. She called it to Graham's attention. "I wonder," thought Graham out loud, "if that could be smoke rising."

"If so," responded Leona, "it might be on the other side of the Lake. Perhaps even in Vermont."

"The fire'd have to be pretty large for that amount of smoke," Graham speculated. "What do you say we go down to Bill Orange's boat dock and take a closer look?"

"Quaz," said Leona, "would you stay here and mind the house while Graham and I go down to lakeside? Keep Buck busy."

"Sure."

FROM THE DOCK it was clear that a fire was raging three miles east on the opposite side of Lake George. The flames were so high they lapped the sky above Long Island. Graham and Leona wasted no time starting the Orange boat and gunning the two Mercury outboards up to full speed. The all-around white light on the stern as well as the red and green sidelights were turned on for the race across the lake under the partially starry sky.

Graham and Leona passed Canoe Island on their left and later Speaker Heck Island on their right. After passing Assembly Point, they turned northward at Harris Bay and proceeded up the east side of Long Island to the site of the fire, Ripley Point. *Could it be the Maletesto mansion?* Leona quizzed herself. As they neared the fire's location, it became clear that Leona's surmise was confirmed.

"That's Maletesto's cottage complex," she exclaimed to Graham. Everything was in flames, as if every wall was burning after the roof had caved in. Other boats with spectators had arrived and were drifting about with people gawking. Sirens from arriving fire trucks were heard, coming by road, most likely from Lake George Village.

Graham maneuvered his craft until they spotted the sheriff's official boat, the only one in sight with a radar arch above the flybridge. The sheriff's boat sat in the water still fifty feet from Maletesto's dock, so close to the fire that that the heat could be felt. As they approached, Sheriff Bolton became visible, talking on both his cell phone and boat radio, evidently giving orders to boots on the ground. After being waved aboard, Graham and Leona pulled alongside and tied up to the police boat's cleats.

One deputy at the helm held the official craft steady with low engine throttle, while the sheriff breathlessly conferred and strategized and dealt out orders to various other police and firefighters. A second deputy aided the sheriff in handling the electronics. This was command central.

When a brief break opened up, Leona inserted, "Sheriff, it's the Maletesto property that's burning."

"What!" exclaimed the sheriff while turning back to get a better look. "Then this cannot be a random accident. As you can see, the fire is equal in intensity at every point. That's evidence of arson. Maybe somehow Maletesto found out you're still alive. Now he's destroying as much evidence of his operations as possible."

"What about casualties?" asked Graham. "Could Maletesto or anybody else be in that fire?"

"Dunno yet," growled the sheriff as he picked up his binoculars to survey the site once again.

The second deputy who had been communicating on the boat's radio nodded that he wanted attention. "It's one of the firefighters on the east side. Says they found three bodies. Too charred to identify yet."

"I'll bet we'll find they are Indians half dressed in tuxedos," said Leona to the group. "And I bet they did not die from smoke inhalation."

CHAPTER 81

"You were right, Lee. Three died in the Maletesto fire. All three were Amerindians. Maletesto himself was not among the dead," said Arthur Bolton.

It was the day following the fire. The sheriff had taken one of the comfortable wicker rockers at the far end of the parsonage's east veranda. Graham along with the sheriff were sipping from their coffee mugs. Hillar watched and listened to the grown-ups with rapt attention.

"So, Mohawk, what've we got?" Leona asked.

"May I speak freely?" asked the NYPD officer.

"May!?" exclaimed Leona with sarcasm. "For the sake of Constantinople, you'd better. We need to know what you know, now that it's become an increasing threat to people's lives."

"Well," began Mohawk, "we've got a number of puzzle pieces, but we don't know whether they belong to one puzzle or to a variety. Here's piece number one. There seems to be a revival of interest in Iroquois languages on the East Coast, both in the City and upstate New York. This is one of the reasons why my department asked me to get involved. When growing up, my family constantly used various Iroquois phrases and even taught me how to converse. I belong to the

People of the Flint—that means I am a Mohawk—and our language has only sixteen letters, half of which are vowels. Even if I'm not fluent, I'm familiar enough to recognize words and phrases and even motives in Mohawk speech. But that's beside the point. Because the three deaths in the Maletesto house were Indians, whether Hurons or Iroquois, we may be close to something."

"Why would anyone even notice—let alone care about—a new burst of nativism?" quizzed Graham.

"I can't answer that if that is the only question," commented Mohawk. "When I spoke yesterday to the two Indian women, they were adamant that nothing like an Indian uprising is being discussed in the Adirondack region. Virtually all the young men in both Huron and Mohawk families sign up for a term in the U.S. military before heading off to college. They think of themselves as Americans, not Native Americans. The very concept of an uprising is nonsense, they told me."

"I guess that eliminates blaming heart-stealing on the Indians," interjected the Sheriff.

"Yes, I now believe that's correct, Sheriff. So, let's go to the second puzzle piece," Mohawk continued. "Over the last year and a half, the Manhattan Opera Company has quickly become the premier opera in the world. Its protégés become stars and run off to sing elsewhere, and stars from abroad covet the opportunity to see their names on Manhattan's playbills."

"Again, Mohawk, this doesn't appear to mean a thing," pressed Graham.

Mohawk seemed to understand and even accept Graham's impatience. He went on. "Our third puzzle is this: we have a number of unsolved missing person and murder cases that share something in common. They are indirectly related to the Manhattan Opera. Grizzly. Some dismembered corpses. Body parts still missing. Some children. Some adults."

Sherriff Bolton winced. So did Hillar. Leona and Graham maintained concentrated attention. After a moment, Mohawk continued.

In one case we found a corpse with the heart removed. In another case, the corpse had been scalped. In every case I'm referring to, the victim was either a friend or family member of someone associated with the Manhattan Opera, or, curiously, a rival business associate. In two cases, star sopranos at the Met disappeared without a trace."

"Has *Last of the Mohicans* played recently in the city?" asked Leona.

"No. Not recently. It's production here at Lake George has been the first to involve Manhattan artists."

"Has J. Holmes Chapman been connected in any way with any of this?" she asked.

"Nothing points to him personally. Believe me, I've looked. In principle, he's the common denominator. But nothing by way of criminal activity yet."

"So, Mister Mohawk, once again: how does all of this in the City connect with us in Lake George?" asked Leona.

"Similar M.O.," answered Mohawk. "Chapman is here, not at Lincoln Center. It's as though the virus in New York City has spread and infected the Adirondacks."

"And the two murders?" rejoined Leona. "Sophia Korsky and Bishop Tikhon?"

"I've got puzzle pieces, Pastor Lee. Only pieces. I wish we could put these puzzles together."

CHAPTER 82

"SHERIFF," Leona said, "I recall Luciano telling me about a late-night sacrifice in which he took part. He was taken blindfolded in a boat. The sacrifice took place in a clearing on an island."

"So, what does this suggest to you, Pastor Lee?" asked the sheriff.

"Do you have drone surveillance capacity? Might you ask your drones to cover the islands with cameras, looking for that clearing? Maybe that's where will find Maletesto."

CHAPTER 83

"PASTOR LEE! I think you should take a look at this!" It was Hillar speaking. He had set himself up in a comfortable chair on the veranda with his laptop open on the circular wicker table.

Leona walked over to look at the screen. "What's up, Quaz?"

"I was searching for my game, Diablo, and look at what I found."

A YouTube video showed the countenance of a teenage boy facing the camera. His black hair was combed straight back. A thinly haired goatee hung from his chin. In his hands he held an AR-15 aimed toward the ceiling.

"I'm coming for you!" he said intensely. "You cannot escape your destiny."

The teen began to fumble for words. Then he continued with flawless grammar and no pauses. "The first palefaces who came among us spoke no English. They came in a large canoe, when my fathers had buried the tomahawk with the red men around them..."

"We were one people, and we were happy," said Leona under her breath.

The teen continued. "We were one people, and we were happy."

Hillar looked up at Leona. "How did you know he would say that?"

"Just listen, Quaz."

The young man on the screen continued. "The salt lake gave us its fish, the wood its deer, and the air its birds. We took wives who bore us children; we worshipped the Great Spirit.... The Dutch landed, and gave my people firewater.... Then they parted with their land. Foot by foot, they were driven back from the shores, until I, that am a chief and a sagamore, have never seen the sun shine but through the trees, and have never visited the graves of my fathers."

"Quaz, this is serious stuff," murmured Leona. "I wonder if this young man thinks of himself as a Mohawk. Or, maybe a Huron."

The video voice rambled on with rant after rant against the white European race. He occasionally interpolated, "I'm coming for you."

Graham had arrived to look on. What Hillar and Leona and now Graham heard sent a shudder up three spines. "I'm coming for all of you at St. John's Church. I will make of you a spectacle of Indian revenge."

"Hillar, find that guy!" exclaimed Graham.

"Yes! Right now!" added Leona. Hillar began feverishly punching computer keys. Buck's eyes seemed to reflect the tension that had overtaken the parsonage veranda. Everyone froze. Only Hillar's fingers kept moving.

"Got it," said Hillar. He pointed to a spot on a map of Warrensburg. "He's just a block north of that butcher we like," mumbled Leona. "I think we'd better get going. Not a moment to lose."

CHAPTER 84

IN ONLY SECONDS Graham was driving west on the Diamond Point Road toward Warrensburg with Leona, Hillar, and Buck aboard. Leona phoned Sheriff Bolton to report what they had learned. "Meet us there, if you can," she told the sheriff.

When the Diamond Point crew arrived at the home where the YouTube vigilante lived, the sheriff's car had just parked in front. "I think you and Buck should stay in the car, Quaz," Leona ordered.

"But, this guy's a teenager. So am I," protested Hillar. "Maybe I can be of help."

"He's got a point," said Graham.

"OK," granted Leona. "But Buck stays."

Seconds later the sheriff rang the doorbell and two disheveled persons arrived at the door. The man and woman looked both surprised and relieved to see the man in uniform on their porch. They hardly noticed the entourage, including Leona, Graham, and Hillar. A taupe-colored pug poked his head through the legs of the man and barked until shushed.

"Come in, Sheriff," invited the woman. "Is it about our son?" The entourage entered. The pug sat nearby to watch the human interchange.

"I'm afraid so," said Sheriff Bolton. "He's made a YouTube threat against St. John's Church in Diamond Point. This here's the pastor, Reverend Leona Foxx."

Leona nodded but did not speak.

The woman looked anguished. The man shook his head.

"Are you his parents?" asked Graham.

"Yes," groaned the man. "Caleb just has not been himself the last few weeks. He brings home guns. Stays in his room for days without coming out. He's begun to use foul language. Curses. We just do not know what to do."

"Caleb is his name?" asked Leona.

"Yes," said his mother.

"Let me ask something," said Leona, taking over the conversation. "What's the dog's name?"

"Minnie," answered Caleb's mother.

Leona leaned down and placed her open hand where Minnie could get a sniff. Looking up, she addressed the mother. "How does Caleb treat Minnie? Is he ever cruel to the dog?"

"Oh, no. Caleb loves Minnie. Most nights Minnie sleeps in Caleb's room."

"Do you have other pets?" pressed the pastor.

"We have a rabbit," said Caleb's father. "Out back."

"How does Caleb treat the rabbit?" asked Leona.

The couple looked at each other. She spoke. "Caleb feeds the rabbit each day. Cleans the cage. He loves the rabbit."

"Never any cruelty?" asked Leona.

The couple looked at each other again, as if to quiz one another with their eyes. "No, never," said the mother.

"Have you recently seen Caleb with a black cat?"

"No," said the couple, after looking at each other.

"Has Caleb been baptized?" Leona asked the mother.

"Oh, yes. We're a Catholic family," she responded.

"Can we see Caleb?" requested Sheriff Bolton.

"He's up in his room," answered the father. "I'll show you the way. It's upstairs."

Once upstairs the father knocked on the door. "Caleb," he hollered, "somebody's here to see you."

"Go away!" could be heard through the door.

"Caleb," shouted the sheriff, "I am Sheriff Bolton. We're coming in." At that he opened the door. There stood the seventeen-year-old in jeans, bare chest, tan leather vest, and holding the AR-15 sideways.

"Please put the gun down, son" requested the sheriff. Graham inched his way into the room and slid slowly around the room's perimeter to the left to gain triangulation.

Caleb froze. So did the sheriff. Leona, Hillar, and the parents stood still. No one moved. Except Graham, whose movements were so slow that they were unnoticeable.

"I said, put the gun down," repeated the sheriff in a slow and deliberate cadence.

"I could kill you all in only a second," growled the teen.

"Yes, I know you could," said the sheriff calmly. "That's why I want you to lay that weapon on the bed so we can talk."

"You're white. All of you are white. Even my parents are white. You should die," barked Caleb.

Leona looked puzzled. She turned to stare into the eyes of Caleb's mother. She looked back and whispered, even though all could hear her speak. "Caleb's adopted. A month ago he did a genetic test and found out he's half Huron Indian. That's when his behavior began to change."

"That's right," shouted Caleb. "And it's time for the Hurons to rise up and take back what is ours from you European thieves." He began to move the AR-15 into shooting position.

With this Graham leaped across the bed and, while still in midair, slapped his right wrist down on Caleb's forearm. This broke the teen's grip, and the gun began to fall. The sheriff sprang forward, grasped the gun's stock, and tore it from Caleb's possession. The boy now stood weaponless, facing a tense assembly in his small room.

"I believe it's time to talk, Caleb," said Leona firmly. "Sit down in your desk chair and turn off your computer." Caleb complied. Leona took a seat on Caleb's bed and discretely motioned with her hand for the parents to leave. They complied. The sheriff, Graham, and Hillar took quiet positions leaning against the wall.

"So, you think you're a Huron?" asked Leona.

"Yes."

"How do you know?"

"I have a Huron genome."

"A complete Huron genome?"

"No. But I have some Huron genes."

"Do these genes define who you are?" she pressed.

Caleb looked confused.

"Do your parents love you, Caleb?"

"Yes, of course."

"Yet, now you want to kill them because they're white. Because they're European. Is that right?"

Caleb nodded.

"And you want to kill people at Saint John's Church. Is that right too?"

Caleb nodded.

"Why St. John's, for the sake of Capetown?"

"Because the congregation at St. John's is where evil Christians that destroyed Huron practices gather—religious practices such as eating hearts."

"Who told you that?"

"A man named Magua."

"Magua? How do you know him?"

"I worked on the stage sets at the opera. I'm an artistic painter. It's a summer job. An internship, sorta. Magua was there. He's a Huron, you know."

LEONA WAS AGHAST. She recalled the moment when Magua had put his arm on the shoulder of a teen at the opera rehearsal.

Leona took a moment to collect herself. Then, she advanced with a different strategy. "Why don't you speak to me. Out loud!" Leona addressed him in a demanding voice.

"Yes, I plan to kill you and as many people at Saint John's as I can," he said in a protesting tone.

"So then, you know that I am the pastor at Saint John's?"

"Yes."

"Caleb." Leona paused. "Just when did you get this idea that I and my people at Saint John's should die? And why are you the one to pull the trigger?"

"The voice," he muttered.

"The voice?" she asked inquiringly.

"Yes, the voice. It speaks in my head."

"A voice speaks in your head. Is that what you're telling me?"

"Yes."

"Caleb, I want to know more about this voice. Do you feel like you hear it?"

"Once in a while the voice speaks. It tells me things. It tells me to do things."

"Did the voice tell you that white people are evil? Did the voice tell you to kill white people?"

"Yes."

"Did the voice tell you to target Saint John's Church?"

"Yes." It seemed that the entire room gasped.

CHAPTER 85

LEONA LOOKED AROUND, as if to count something or to find something. A moment passed. Nobody moved.

"So," she continued. "It has been your plan to come to Saint John's with your AR-15 and kill the people there. Is that right?"

"Yes." More silence followed. Caleb remained completely still. Leona stood up. Then she sat down again and leaned forward. Looking straight into Caleb's eyes she said quietly, "Caleb, I want to hear this voice. I want to speak to this voice. May I?"

"No." Caleb looked away.

"Why not?"

"It's my own private voice." Caleb refused to make eye contact.

"I don't think so, Caleb. If the voice can tell you what to do, it can converse with me too. Caleb! I want to talk directly to the voice. Not you, Caleb. The voice!"

Caleb sat still, almost in a state of rigor mortis.

"I want to talk with the voice," said Leona in a slow cadence. "Voice! I'm speaking to you. Talk to me."

Only silence followed. Slowly Caleb's face turned and soon he was looking straight into Leona's glaring eyes. His mouth quivered slightly, a physical sign that he was about to speak.

"Voice, I want to know your name!" demanded Leona.

Caleb's face broke out into a condescending smile. "Yes, you want to learn my name." It was Caleb speaking. Or was it? What everyone in the room heard was a voice almost an octave lower than Caleb's voice.

Leona sighed. Then she focused her gaze even more intently on Caleb's eyes. "I want your name," she repeated.

Caleb laughed audibly. "Yes, I know what you want. But, if I say a name, you won't know if it's the truth or not. I lie, you know."

"You lie?"

"Yes, I lie."

"Now tell me, Diabolos, are you telling me a lie when you tell me that you lie? If you tell me you lie, but it's really the truth, then it is *not* a lie. Right?"

Caleb's smile registered a shade of delight. "How would you know if I tell a lie or tell the truth? If I say I lie and it's a lie, then it's a lie."

"No. If you lie, Shaitan, and if you say you lie, then you're actually telling the truth. You cannot avoid truth, Azazel. Truth always trumps deceit." Leona studied Caleb's face while the banter ensued. She would not let go of control.

"Your name is Lucifer!" exclaimed Leona.

"No. It's not Lucifer."

"Is that the truth? Or are you lying?"

Caleb only maintained the smile, but the face muscles showed they had to keep working. The smile was an effort.

"Your name is Beelzebub!" she exclaimed.

"No. It's not Beelzebub."

Your name is Abaddon!" she added.

"No."

"It's Pazuzu."

"Yes. But that's a lie." Caleb laughed. Yet, the laugh bore a taint of anxiety. Was Leona getting closer?

"Choronzon?"

"No, of course not. Crowley was a fake."

"Well," said Leona, as if thinking. "You whisper in Caleb's thoughts. That reminds me of the *waswās*."

"You're getting cold, Pastor Lee," said Caleb.

"Asura?"

"No."

"Iblis?"

"No. I think you should just quit. You're really not much of a pastor anyhow. No Holy Spirit. You're not a person of virtue. You're overcome with shame and guilt and feelings of inadequacy. You will not be able to protect your congregation from a mass shooting. I guarantee that. You're a nothing, Reverend Lee. You might as well drop into non-existence."

Leona's posture revealed she was undaunted. "Maybe you're right, Belial. Maybe this is just a waste of time."

Caleb's body began to shrivel slightly. He folded into his chair and shrunk to only two-thirds his original size.

"Belial, I'm talking to you now," stated Leona flatly, without a tone of alarm. "Your time in Caleb's body is over."

Caleb turned to look toward his computer.

"You don't need to look at me, Belial," she said. "You can hear me clearly. In the name of Jesus Christ, the Holy One of Israel, I command you to come out of Caleb."

Caleb looked at Leona with an expression of horror. His lips were silently uttering, "Oh, no." Whatever occupied Caleb's body was terrified at what was about to happen.

"In the name of Jesus Christ, the Holy One of Israel, I send you to..." Leona paused. "I send you to outer darkness." Then, the pastor made the sign of the cross, saying, "I call on the Spirit given you at your baptism, Caleb, in the name of the Father, the Son, and the Holy Spirit, to retake possession of Caleb's soul. Amen."

At that Caleb fell to the floor in front of his chair. He quickly turned over so he was facing upward. His legs and feet flailed and kicked, sending the chair flying across the room. In only seconds, Caleb's body returned to calm. His normal size returned. He lay calmly, as if asleep.

CHAPTER 86

"I RECOMMEND you take Caleb to the hospital ER," Leona later told the boy's parents. "Phone your priest and ask him to meet you there. Sheriff Bolton will postpone filing charges for the moment. Caleb will not become the shooter he had advertised. What we need most right now is for Caleb to regain himself."

CHAPTER 87

A LUNAR ECLIPSE occurs approximately twice per year. Just before or after the total eclipse, when the Earth lines up almost directly between the sun and the moon, the sunlight reflecting on the moon is refracted through the Earth's atmosphere. Our planet's atmosphere scatters the longer blue wave lengths of light while the shorter red waves pass through. The lunar surface looks sunset-like in color. Even redder. The color of blood. It's a blood moon.

So space scientists tell us. But should we believe what our scientists tell us? Perhaps the moon actually bleeds.

CHAPTER 88

"Cut the engine," whispered Graham.

Hillar turned off the engine, while the boat continued on its previous trajectory towards the shore. Even though the frog croaking and cricket chirping made such a racket that the boat's motor could not be heard, the invading force remained as discreetly silent as possible.

Graham, already crouched on the boat's bow, leaped into the water, stood up straight, and pushed the craft onto the ribbon of sand. Gradually the bow came to rest, and Graham secured it by tying the bow rope to a sapling trunk.

Buck raced forward and jumped from the bow into the sand, taking care to avoid getting his feet wet. Leona followed. After a half bark, Graham quickly scowled out a loud, "shhhhhhh." Buck complied.

In the same loud whisper, Graham addressed Hillar. "Bring the drone. The sheriff's surveillance report tells us that the clearing is just west, perhaps only a quarter mile away."

Hillar disembarked, carrying his silver case. Graham grunted and motioned in order to communicate that the teenager should set up on the beach and send the drone on reconnaissance to locate the midnight ritual. Graham also indicated that he along with Leona would hike northward on the beach looking for the docked boats of the ritual participants. By waving his cell phone, Graham made it clear he wanted Hillar to forward his own drone data and to keep the computer-phone connection intact. And, of course, by all means remain at the boat site. "Do not approach the ritual, because it might be dangerous." Hillar gulped with a gesture of reluctant agreement.

"One more thing, Hillar," whispered Graham. "Connect with Sheriff Bolton. Share with him whatever the drone sees." In a moment, Graham and Leona were gone.

Hillar found a butt-high rock and sat himself comfortably before opening his case. He assembled the drone, opened his laptop, and sent the drone straight up into a hover. After turning on the camera he sent the drone on a slow survey in a northwest direction. On his computer screen he could make out the tree tops in an otherwise grayish green blur.

When the frog croaking and cricket chorus ceased, Hillar did not notice. He simply concentrated on the drone survey, oblivious to his surroundings. Time passed. An ominous sense that he was not alone finally took hold. Hillar looked around. He could see the water, the beach, and the darkness of the tree line. Nothing.

The reddish moonlight suddenly reflected on something, something like a pair of shining marbles. *Could it be? No, it couldn't be.* The forest beast shifted position just enough for the moonlight to reveal its shape and color. *Yes, dammit. It is, in fact, a Grey Wolf.* Even though only thirty feet away, the eyes were unmoving. They stared at the teen. *I hope my theory is right. I can't run. Gotta try to stare 'm down.*

Without moving his head, Hillar judiciously set his computer next to him on the rock. He turned his eyes on the two looking at him. *Can you see me like I can see you, Mr. Wolf? Will the moonlight help me make you squirm?*

The wolf looked away. The wolf denied eye contact. *He can see me,* Hillar remarked almost audibly. *But, breaking eye contact means he's refusing my dominance. He may be readying himself for attack. What now?*

As the wolf's eyes moved in parallel toward the ground, Hillar imagined the beast of the night was crouching for the attack. Hillar looked about for a stick or a rock to flail in defense. None seemed to be within reach. He purposely remained in a paralyzed state. The climax would commence momentarily.

But those two wolf eyes seemed stationary. Not moving. Low to the ground, but not moving. Fixed. Staring. *Could the wolf be in eye contact with someone else?*

Hillar's left ear was surprised by a new sound. It was a growl, a deep sustained low-toned snarl. The growl's resonance connoted a *basso profundo* holding a single note. In the darkness, Hillar surmised rightly that Buck and the wolf were in sustained eye contact.

More time passed. Hillar remained in his frozen state. The two wolf eyes twisted and turned upside down. This indicated the wolf was now on its back, tummy up and vulnerable. A second later, the shimmering eyes disappeared from view. The threat was over. Even though he could not see the husky, Hillar muttered, "Thanks, Buck."

CHAPTER 89

ONCE HILLAR HAD PLACED his computer again on his lap, he noticed a patch of light slowly entering the screen from above. Gradually the surveying drone revealed a location in the forest where there was light and activity. Hillar adjusted the camera to reveal more detail. His screen lit up. In a secluded meadow a party of perhaps thirty people were gathered in a circle. In the center of the circle a small fire emitted the primary light. The circumference was lit by individual candles. At twelve o'clock Hillar clearly discerned a set of two altars, one lower and one higher. Behind the higher altar at the circle's perimeter stood the obvious authority, perhaps the priest. Even to Hillar, unschooled in New Religious Movements, he could see the costume of the mythical Baphomet.

Carefully Hillar lowered the drone to get a better look. Two people lay on the lower altar which was placed between the higher altar and the camp fire. A woman was on top of a man. She was naked except for her fishnet stockings; she wore one black and one red. *Are they? Yes, they are.* With her legs straddling the man beneath, she gyrated in dramatic ecstasy while the circled chorus watched and chanted something Hillar could not make out.

Graham and Leona, who had located the boat arrival area, were watching Hillar's view from the drone on their cell phones. They concluded that the ritual location was directly west, inland, and up a small hill buried within the woods. The moonlight combined with cell screen lights made it easy to trek through the trees toward this destination.

"They're going to have guards, Graham," whispered Leona. "Let's ask Hillar to scout the perimeter before we go much further."

Graham nodded and contacted Hillar. Soon the hum of the drone signaled to Graham and Leona that reconnaissance was taking place as requested. No guards were spotted. "I think we're clear to go," Graham whispered.

The two forest sleuths approached the ceremony undetected and situated themselves where they could see clearly what was happening. The fertility priestess with the red and black hose had finished with one partner and invited a second to lie on the lower altar for his turn. He did not need to undress, because no one other than Baphomet was clothed. All were nude.

Leona thought she could make out the syllables in the chant: "Yah-lu-lay-ah." With Graham in earshot she whispered in surprise, "I think it's *alleluia* backwards."

CHAPTER 90

ALTHOUGH LEONA and Graham were close enough to hear the drum beat and the repetitious "Yah-lu-lay-ah," they were not in a position to see each individual in the ritual circle. Graham whispered to Hillar via his cell connection to pan the group and magnify each person individually. Graham and Leona then watched their cells while crouched in a thicket.

Most faces were new to the two observers. "There's J. Holmes Chapman," Leona whispered. Graham nodded as the camera panned slowly around. "Isn't that Congressman Crump?" She followed that with, "There's Lillian Serano standing next to Juliet Johns," she added.

"How can you tell, Lee? They have no clothes on."

Leona grimaced at Graham and went back to her cell screen.

"Why don't we take off our clothes and join them?" said Graham with a smirk.

"Graham, don't be ridiculous."

"I'd help you take off your clothes, if you'd like."

"Graham, shut up and get serious!" Leona focused on the next series of naked bodies until spotting Magua. "Look!" After a pause she added, "I just hope I don't see Luciano here."

As the camera pan finished its round, Graham and Leona identi-fied Karl Sogaard, but Luciano Silvestri seemed to be absent. "Whew!" said Leona.

"Oh, my God!" exclaimed Graham. "Hillar, move the camera to the right just a little."

Into the center of the screen Leona and Graham could barely make out an object hanging from a tree branch. The tree branch was high. From it hung a long rope tied to a small animal. The animal, a black cat, was held in a harness, dangling. The cat twitched, squirmed, and appeared to be hollering. It was alive. "Could it be Midnight?" asked Leona with both trepidation and gratitude.

CHAPTER 91

"I'll cut the engine," said Sheriff Bolton as the police boat neared the landing where Hillar was sitting. He was speaking to Mohawk Evans, seated in the stern.

After tying up, they found Hillar, and the teenager provided the new arrivals with an update. "I don't like it that Graham and the pastor took this one by themselves, without us and without backup," grumbled the sheriff.

"You'll have to take it up with them" muttered Hillar. "I only do what I'm told."

The sheriff and detective decided to follow the trail up the east coast of Long Island and catch up with Leona and Graham. When they arrived at the collection of moored boats, the sheriff cut them loose so that they would drift away. "This'll stop a rapid retreat," he muttered to Mohawk with a smirk.

The two then turned inland and climbed the forested hill in the direction they presumed Leona and Graham had taken. The sheriff exchanged texts with Leona, and soon thereafter they doubled the size of the party of hidden onlookers. Together they witnessed what came next.

CHAPTER 92

WHEN EUDAIMONIA HAD FINISHED her final trick, she stood up for a rigid bow and then departed to become a link in the human circle chain. The drumbeat ceased. So did the chant.

Baphomet stood tall and addressed the late-night assembly with eyes closed. "*In nomine Domini Dei nostri Satanae Luciferi Excelsi.*"

"Yah-lu-lay-ah," responded the assembly in unison.

Baphomet opened his eyes and then spoke again. "Tonight the moon has turned to blood. Do not look for a Strawberry Moon in the heavens, because the lunar blood will be dispersed right here. The blood will be dispersed on the white altar in front of me, the very altar the moon now brightens with its glow. We will consume genuine body and blood which will lead us to life-enhancing power, not some eviscerated symbols such as bread and wine. We extract the life energy of the sacrifice, consume it, own it, and become invincible servants of the Prince of Darkness, the true Lord of the human race."

"Yah-lu-lay-ah," responded the assembly again in mesmerizing unison. No one gave evidence of hearing the faint buzz of the drone's motors.

The high priest spoke once more. "Disciples of *Cultus Satanas*, our Lord and Master, the Prince of Darkness, offers us rewards for our commitment, blessings in response to our faith, pleasure as a trophy for our deeds in his service. Our Lord and Master has provided for us a Wishing Tree, a tree of life that comes out of death. For those gathered here in the dark who have already voluntarily offered their entire being—body, soul, and spirit—as their sacrifice to the Prince of Darkness, you know that your rewards have begun to materialize. Satan keeps his word. Satan renders what is due. Satan gives an eye for an eye and a tooth for a tooth. Satan renders justice."

"Yah-lu-lay-ah," responded the assembly once again.

"The moon, like the sun, shines light," Baphomet continued. "Even though the Bible calls it the lesser light, our moon provides guidance within the darkness rather than obliterating the darkness, as does the sun. Our moon is Lucifer's candle; it provides enough light for us to negotiate the paths of fulfillment within the dark labyrinth of evil. The highest form of human fulfillment is *eudaimonia*, pleasure. And the highest form of pleasure is not wealth, fame, sex, or gluttony. It is revenge. It is what so many sugarcoat by calling it *justice*. The Prince of Darkness fulfills our desire for revenge and asks only one price: eternal commitment."

"Yah-lu-lay-ah," the assembly answered with gusto.

The high priest made eye contact with numerous worshippers in the circle before speaking again. "Now, I would like to introduce one among us to give testimony to Lucifer's blessing. Magua, would you please provide the yet-to-be-initiated among us a confession of your *credo maleficium*."

At this point Magua, carrying a book in his left hand, walked slowly from his place in the circle to a spot directly in front of the lower altar. He paused. Then he began a rehearsed talk. "My name is Magua. Now, you might say, 'but that's a fictional name!' It was given by James Fennimore Cooper to the bad guy in *The Last of the Mohicans*. This is true. When I was born, my parents gave me a first and last name. But when I surrendered my soul to Satan, the true Lord of the human race, I changed my name. I have taken on the identity of

Magua. I am Magua. I am Magua in the Adirondack Opera, and I am Magua here tonight with you."

A few of those in the circle muttered, "Yah-lu-lay-ah." Not in unison.

Magua proceeded. "In the fictional story, I kill Uncas, the last of the Mohicans. Then, Uncas' father, Chingachgook, kills me. The story ends in great sadness as one Indian slays another in a never-ending sequence of bloodshed. One act of revenge leads to the next act of revenge, and so on in perpetuity. But there is hope that one final act of revenge will put an end to the sequence. That will be the act of subjugation, the complete subordination of the white race to my people, the red race. Let me read to you from Cooper's book the words of Chingachgook."

Magua opened a book he was carrying, quite obviously *The Last of the Mohicans: A Narrative of 1757*. Coughed briefly. He read with projected voice.

> The first pale-faces who came among us spoke no English. They came in a large canoe, when my fathers had buried the tomahawk with the red men around them.... We were one people, and we were happy. The salt lake gave us its fish, the wood its deer, and the air its birds. We took wives who bore us children; we worshipped the Great Spirit.... [Then] the Dutch landed and gave my people fire-water....Then they [the Native Americans] parted with their land. Foot by foot, they were driven back from the shores, until I, that am a chief and a sagamore, have never seen the sun shine but through the trees, and have never visited the graves of my fathers.

Magua paused so that the wheels of sympathy for his cause could spin in the minds of his listeners. Then he returned to his own locution, a brief crescendo. "For this colonial assault on my ancestors, I declare that my generation will take its revenge, will make just what has been unjust. It will be the final act of violence that brings redemption."

After another pregnant pause, Magua shifted his tone to a slower cadence. "What I want is justice. My ancestors were denied justice by the Dutch, the French, and the English. Today, the descendants of all of the Iroquois continue to be marginalized, rendered invisible, and consigned to non-existence by the dominant society. This three-century maltreatment of my people by European settlers will justify what I am about to do, with Satan's help."

"Yah-lu-lay-ah," said selected voices, though not all.

Silence lay over the cult like a blanket. Magua took advantage of the pause to make eye contact with nearly every individual. "Here is my plan. Satan has promised me the fulfillment of my wish, namely, to make the present generation of America suffer the indignity my people have suffered. Included in my people are not only the Hurons, my tribe, but all Amerindian nations similarly crushed by the European megalith."

"To obtain justice for my people," Magua went on, "we will need power. Power is what the Prince of Darkness offered me in exchange for my complete commitment. This power will come in a form which can destroy, to be sure; but this power will also come in a form which can persuade. It is persuasive power that I need in my pursuit of justice. It is my intention to exact justice through nuclear blackmail. You heard it right: nuclear blackmail. My compatriots and I have already secured a supply of enriched plutonium and are preparing a number of nuclear devices. We humorously call them our IEDs, improvised explosive devices, as you know. But our IEDs will be on a colossal scale. It is our plan to place these IEDs of mass destruction in strategic locations within America's large cities. Announcing this will terrify the country. No one will be able to ignore Indian power at that moment. We will take control of the national psyche first and then take control of the course of events. Nothing motivates like petrifying fear. No one has yet witnessed the level of terror we plan to unleash."

After looking around at his audience once again, Magua carried on. "We will announce publically the presence of our IEDs and demand that all Native Americans be given back their ancestors' land

and their sovereignty. Without immediate congressional agreement and full compliance with our demands, we will detonate one or more of these devices. We will destroy selected cities with advance warning, the same kind of warning given to Hiroshima and Nagasaki in 1945. We will continue the warning and detonation process until the dominant society has fallen on its knees, pleading for us to stop. Only by total capitulation can the white race forestall the apocalypse."

The faces of those in the circle were awestruck. Some began to murmur with one another. Recognizing the incredulity and anxiety this prompted, Magua resorted to words of comfort. "None of us here who have made our eternal pact with Lucifer need have any fear. Regardless of the course of events, you and I will be raptured by Satan and remain safe in our Lord's hands. The evil will happen only to those who oppose us, not to those who side with us. We will have supernatural protection. Finally, when all the radioactive dust has settled, justice will be done."

CHAPTER 93

WHILE MAGUA MADE his way back to his original location and the ritual circle reconfigured, in the thicket a vigorous whispering began to take place. "Are you two armed with weapons?" asked Sheriff Bolton.

"I carry a Glock," answered Graham. "Leona's got a Kimber .45. A one-hand cannon. We're ready for whatever comes."

Leona slowed the process of readying for an assault. She turned to Mohawk. "Mohawk, how do you feel about what Magua has just said?"

"As you can imagine," he responded, "my family and I have deep feelings about the wretched history of colonialism. But this past does not determine our future. No amount of vengeful violence will right past wrongs. Magua does not speak for me. He must be stopped, and stopped now."

"Are you connected at all with Karl Sogaard?" Leona asked Mohawk.

"Yes. In fact, I'm the one the NYPD asked to serve as Eric's contact. We never are seen together in public, but we keep each other informed."

"With Hillar's recording and our testimony of what we just

heard, we'll have everything law enforcement needs to make arrests tonight and prosecute," offered the sheriff.

"Arrests! Are you kidding?" exclaimed Graham in an excited whisper. "This'll not go down easy. If we walk in there right now, they'll release fire power on us. You don't think they would come here unarmed, do you?"

"I don't see any weaponry," muttered the sheriff.

"Believe me, it's there," added Mohawk. "If we enter the circle, bullets will fly in every direction. Many in that circle, in addition to Karl Sogaard, are as yet innocent. They've not taken out their devil's pact. They might get hurt. A direct assault is out of the question."

"I must add another concern," interjected Leona. "We are dealing here with evil. It's radical evil, because violence is being planned in the name of evil, in the name of Satan. But, as you could hear in Magua's speech, it's also garden-variety evil. It's violence with justification. Magua deludes himself; he thinks nuking millions of people is justified; he thinks his violence will redeem America. This is a lie. But, here's the big problem: we can't fight evil with more evil."

"What are you saying, Pastor?" demanded the sheriff with consternation on his face.

"I'm saying that if we rush into the circle with guns blazing, we'll only add bloodshed to bloodshed. Even if we arrest or kill this cult's leadership, we will only have piled evil on top of evil."

"Well, how the hell do you expect to take them out? Are you going to just hug and kiss them all into surrendering? Come on, Pastor, get real! You're the Bible person. If you got a sword, you die by the sword. Am I not right?"

"The sword kills. The sword does not stop the killing," she responded.

It appeared clear that the four in the thicket would not immediately agree on an assault strategy. Nevertheless, the sheriff, with tacit approval from his comrades in arms, used his cell phone to call for additional backup.

CHAPTER 94

Baphomet nodded to his left. Two burly men marched a naked and recalcitrant woman into the circle and stood her behind the smaller altar but in front of the larger altar. Leona observed that J. Holmes Chapman registered not only surprise but an agonized fear on his face. *Will Chapman faint?* Leona turned to Graham: "You gotta Google something and fast. Look up Helen Chapman, wife of the owner of the Manhattan Opera. Get a picture on your screen. See if this sacrificial victim is her."

"It's time for the *Missa Solemnis Satanis*," announced Baphomet. The high priest rearranged a number of items on the high altar, displaying a large ritual knife along with a cup and paten. Then in a commanding voice he addressed the assembly. "Do you renounce belief in any god other than Satan? Do you renounce belief in Yahweh, Allah, Zeus, Odin, Shiva, Shakti, Shang Ti, and in any of their prophets, including Moses, Zoroaster, Mohammed, Shankara, Confucius, and Laozi?"

"We renounce them. *Rege Satanus!*" responded the circle in concert.

"Do you renounce faith in Jesus Christ, in the forgiveness of sins, and the promise of everlasting life in God's saving grace?"

"We renounce them. *Rege Satanus!*" Hearing this so upset Leona that she covered her ears.

"Do you renounce trust in God's Holy Spirit, the giver of life and distributor of divine grace?"

"We renounce them. *Rege Satanus!*"

"Do you devote your heart, mind, and soul to the service of Satan? Do you promise to obey Satan's representatives here on Earth, especially the High Priest of *Cultus Satanas*, regardless of what you are ordered? Do you commit your actions to destroy what others have built, to demolish peace and promote war, to dissolve unity and sow disunity, to replace order with chaos, to undercut virtue with vice, to replace compassion with disinterest, to undermine meaning with meaninglessness, and whenever possible to drop what exists into non-existence? If so, then answer: we are committed."

"We are committed. *Rege Satanus!*"

Having completed the creedal portion of the liturgy, the high priest spoke more informally. "As we turn now to the *Missa Solemnis Satanis* proper, let me say something to those here who are not yet fully initiated. The *Missa Solemnis Satanis* is the ritual which turns reality upside down. It buries divine being and exalts nonbeing. It turns universal life into a power possessed only by ourselves. It trusts in Satan's reward for our devotion by energizing our deepest wish to become godlike. *Homo similis Deo haud nascitur, sed fit*—that is, a human being is not born Godlike but becomes like him at the whim of the Prince of Darkness. We have just gotten God out of the way with our litany of renunciations. We turn now to the sacrifice, the sacrifice of body and blood through which the power of universal life becomes our own empowerment. *Rege Satanas!*"

"*Rege Satanus!*" shouted the already initiated within the circle.

"*Ave Satanas!*" shouted the high priest.

"*Rege Satanus!*" responded the initiated as some of the uninitiated joined in the antiphony.

"*Ave Satanas!*" shouted the high priest with increased volume.

"*Rege Satanus!*" repeated the entire group.

"*Ave Satanas!*" shouted the high priest still louder.

"*Rege Satanus!*" echoed through the forest, ricocheted off the rocks, and drifted in muffled form out to the waters. It was a triumphant liturgical moment.

CHAPTER 95

"Yes, it is indeed Chapman's wife," mouthed Graham to his three companions. "She's the one standing just under the hanging black cat. Her name is Helen Chapman. Now, we have a real situation on our hands!"

"It is time for the living sacrifice to be placed on the altar," the high priest announced.

The two guards attempted to force Helen toward the high altar. She resisted, screaming, "No! No! No!"

Helen threw her elbows recklessly, hoping to catch a jaw or rib. Her flailing was in vain. The two brutes successfully lifted her writhing body up and stretched her out on top of the altar. They quickly tied her hands and feet, securing her on her back with naked femininity upward and in everybody's vision. She screamed. One of the thugs covered her mouth with duct tape, silencing the human lamb about to be slain.

Baphomet slowly lifted the ceremonial knife high above his head. He held it. Leona, Graham, Sheriff Bolton, and Mohawk rustled and readied their side arms. Then the high priest slowly lowered the knife to chin level and spoke: "Mister J. Holmes Chapman, please come forward."

All eyes turned on the Manhattan Opera owner. Clearly weak-kneed and in anguish, Chapman was holding on to the shoulder of Sogaard, who happened to be standing next to him. The two thugs walked deliberately over to Chapman and escorted him via the elbows to a position between the two altars, facing both his wife and Baphomet.

"Is it your desire, J. Holmes Chapman, to give your soul to Satan, for Satan to possess your soul for all eternity, and to reward you with the fulfillment of your wishes within this temporal life?" asked the high priest.

"Yes," Chapman muttered. Then, Chapman began to stammer out loud. When he had regained some of his composure, he exclaimed, "But, this is not part of our deal! I did not agree to this! I thought you were going to use some invisible or supernatural or clandestine means for eliminating Helen. Not this public event. Not with my participation. I hired you!"

Helen, already in torment, turned to look at her husband. It seemed to dawn on her that what was happening was the product of her spouse's design. Her face registered a new level of distress. *"Holmes! Holmes! No! No! No!"* she screamed to herself through the duct tape.

"Will you take this knife and cut out this woman's heart?" asked Baphomet, holding the blade where Chapman could grab it.

"This is not what we agreed to!" he screamed. "You said all it would take would be a verbal curse. I can't get personally involved. I offered you my soul, but I thought you'd take care of this for me, without me."

"This is the moment, Mister Chapman," the high priest said, "wherein the everlasting contract with the Devil is signed and sealed. This is the moment when the body and blood of this woman will be eaten and drunk by you and the rest of us, endowing us with powers supernatural in strength. This is the moment that seals the deal, that commits Satan to you as you have committed yourself to Satan. Now,

I ask you, cut out the heart of this sacrifice so that we all may eat and drink."

"But..."

"No *buts*, Mister Chapman. Helen, your wife, is an adulteress. Her death is what she deserves. Her death will also empower us."

"But you lied to me!" argued Chapman.

"Mister Chapman, you should know by now that the Devil is the Father of the Lie. Because you have made this commitment, you will become a Son of the Lie. You will benefit from the lie."

Helen's wide-open eyes expressed abject terror. Chapman reached toward the priest. He slowly grasped the knife. He nervously began an upward movement.

In the thicket also there was terror. Leona whispered so the other three could hear: "Yes, I'd love for the Holy Spirit to zap Chapman with radical repentance. But just in case the Holy Spirit waits too long, I plan on trusting my Kimber." She pressed an eight-bullet clip into the handle. "Sheriff and Mohawk, spread around to the right. Graham, to the left. When you hear my shot, leap into the circle's center. I will just have to sin boldly."

"Keep your shot high," said Graham. "You don't want it to go through Chapman into his wife."

"I got you," she said while looking forward without blinking.

The group silently and with alacrity took their positions. The drum began to beat and the liturgical circle started chanting *yah-lu-lay-ah*. Leona fixed her eyes on Chapman, watching every movement, no matter how slight. Helen's husband held the knife high, waiting for Baphomet's command to commence.

Leona exhaled. Then inhaled. Her mind took total control of her body. With a steadiness that even Gibraltar would envy, she aimed her Kimber at a spot in the back of Chapman's head. If the bullet penetrated and exited, it would fly off into the woods without hitting a secondary target.

She squeezed the trigger. A single carefully aimed shot. With a pop, blood oozed on the back of Chapman's skull. Gradually, his body slumped. The knife fell from his hands. His eyes closed. He dropped to the ground.

Immediately, Bolton and Evans leaped into the circle's center and placed themselves back to back facing everybody. Graham entered from a third direction. Leona remained concealed in the thicket. When the circle realized that the worship agenda had been interrupted, they turned to run.

"You are all under arrest," hollered Sheriff Bolton. It was too late to stop the panic and the egress of the worshippers. They scampered still naked in different directions. None stopped to honor the police command. Despite the threat, no one holding a gun fired an additional shot.

Baphomet shed portions of his costume and ran northward. Magua ran to the west and down the hill, with Karl Sogaard on his tail. All three of these escaped into the darkness of the forest. Graham, Arthur, and Mohawk lowered their weapons into a relaxed position, looked at each other, and began to chuckle.

"We untied their boats," snickered the sheriff.

"That means they'll be swimming home," added Graham smiling.

After Leona emerged from the thicket, she and the sheriff approached the altars. Indeed, Chapman was dead. Leona's well-aimed bullet was responsible. They freed Helen. Leona immediately offered Helen the discarded tunic shed by Baphomet to wear. The two women comforted one another with an embrace.

"Oh! Midnight!" exclaimed Leona. Then she ran to the tree holding the cat. She lowered the branch. Yes, indeed, the cat was her forlorn and terrified black treasure. Mutual joy at reunion immediately trumped the previous moment of terror.

CHAPTER 96

"Have you ever had any contact with *Cultus Satanis*?" Leona asked Reverend Stephen Korsky.

Leona and Stephen were sitting on the east veranda of the Saint John's parsonage with the usual retinue, Sheriff Bolton, Detective Evans, and Graham. Karl Sogaard had joined them. Hillar had served them all coffee but was instructed by Leona not to linger. Korsky's face was solemn. It betrayed anguish, remorse, even dread.

"No, never," said Korsky. Silence followed.

"So...just how *did* you kill your wife, Stephen?" asked Leona, as she turned and slightly tilted her head to fix her stare at Korsky with a potency that was fierce even for Leona.

"How dare you ask such a question!" Korsky bellowed. "You ask me here for coffee, and you have the gall to accuse me? How dare you!!"

No one else spoke. Korsky fidgeted in his chair, slammed down his coffee mug, then stood up, firmly planting his feet on the floor of the porch. "How dare you!"

He glared at each person with a powerful intensity, making chilly eye contact that sent a shiver through everybody. Korsky held his ground for a full minute. As the emotion welled up in his body, he suddenly began to sob.

"I used a tire iron. I hit her in the head."

Korsky sat back down with the full weight of his body, continuing to sob, holding his bowed head in his hands. "I can't believe I did such a thing...but I did."

"And the bishop?" pressed Leona.

"Same way. Same tire iron." Korsky's voice was barely above a whisper.

"What was the meaning of cutting that cross into Sophia's back? Why did you dress Bishop Tikhon in his stole and then defile the stole?" she asked.

"Because of all this talk about Satanists. I thought symbol defilement would throw suspicion their way. After all, a couple more murders wouldn't make much of a difference."

"Telling us all this now? How..." asked Sheriff Bolton, hesitant, but Korsky interrupted.

"Perhaps it's obvious. I am a priest, after all. I'm overwhelmed with guilt. I can't believe my own behavior, my motivation, my sin. I snuffed out the life of my dear wife. She was an angel. Why did I do that? And the bishop! He was a genuinely holy man. I can't live with myself anymore."

The previous silence of disbelief softened to mix with a tinge of compassion as all eyes fixed on the weeping priest.

"You told me that you believed it was God's will that you become bishop," said Leona. "Do you still believe this?"

"No. I lied to myself. I wanted to see myself as bishop, as somebody really important. I confused my own petty pride with divine destiny. Oh, how could I have done all of this?"

More silence.

Leona broke the silence again. "Did you make a contract with the Devil?"

"No. Absolutely not. I know what you said about shedding innocent blood, Leona. That is exactly what I did. I thought it was justified because I was doing God's will. I was clearing the path to become bishop. I was helping God out. Oh, how could I be so evil?" Korsky put his face in his hands.

"Sometimes evil is out there, in our enemy or in the Devil. And sometimes evil is in here," said the sheriff, patting his chest. "It splits the heart in two. It divides us. It fractures us. It destroys us from within."

Heads nodded. Korsky's head nodded too.

"Perhaps it's time," said the sheriff, rising. Korsky stood up and put out his hands for cuffing. All rose from their chairs.

LEONA SMILED through her glum expression. "I'll visit you in jail tomorrow. Would you like me to bring the Sacrament?"

"Ordinarily, we Orthodox don't commune with the heterodox. You Lutherans are heterodox, you know," he said with a slight smile. "But, yes, bring the bread and wine for communion. I will definitely need it."

CHAPTER 97

By ONE THIRTY in the afternoon, the Saint John's Church parking lot was already full. Numerous arriving cars drove through an opening in the fence and parked here and there on the large lawn. A line of news vans roofed with conspicuous aerials were parked outside the hedge flanking Diamond Point Road. The clergy were gathering in the sacristy at the church's rear, donning their albs and stoles in preparation for the two o'clock worship service. The moment of altar reconsecration was approaching.

Ray Santucci walked among the clergy with the master order of worship on a clipboard, checking with each regarding their intonation key and other details. "Luciano is here, Pastor Lee," said Santucci.

"Oh, I'm so glad," she responded. "Did he agree to sing the Lord's Prayer?"

"Yep. We're all set."

The old church was filled with flowers, mostly white, conveying a sense of purity and new life. Vases of lilies encircled the altar, and each pew was tied with blue and white ribbons securing large white mums. The fragrance of the lilies permeated every corner of the sanctuary.

Eventually the clergy took their assigned seats in the chancel, while Santucci and Silvestri sat behind the organ. To Sheriff Bolton's right sat Caleb and his parents. To his left sat Shelly Wennes.

At precisely two o'clock, Brenda Beale stood up, greeted everyone, and introduced the Pastor of St. John's, Leona Foxx.

Leona entered the sanctuary from the sacristy to the left of the chancel. Leona was holding back tears as best she could. She was filled with hope and inspiration as she looked out over the standing-room-only crowd. She positioned herself on the front chancel step to address the sanctuary overflowing with congregants, dignitaries, reporters, and curious guests.

"Welcome to Saint John's Community Church. All of you. This is an important moment in the life of our congregation and in the larger community that surrounds Lake George. Before we begin the liturgy, I should bring you up-to-date on recent events."

Worshippers and the press gave Reverend Leona Foxx rapt attention. She spoke. "As you undoubtedly know, the altar here in this sanctuary was defiled during a midnight ritual performed by uninvited guests. We have since found out that those who perpetrated this sacrilege belong to an international organization known as *Cultus Satanas*. This organization operated the Wishing Tree in Lake George Village until shut down by authorities last week."

Leona took a moment to survey the nave and make mental notes regarding those in attendance. "This defilement took the form of a ritual murder, a version of the ancient black mass in which the disciples of Satan literally consume human flesh and blood. This black sacrament included the murder of an innocent child, a child not yet identified. Some mother and father somewhere have lost their beloved child in an unspeakable atrocity. We can only grieve and share our grief in prayer for the loss of this precious little one.

"Each one of us in this room should periodically examine our souls with the spyware of our faith and defragment our consciences. Here is the virus to look for: whenever, wherever, under any and all circumstances, when you hear the call to shed innocent blood then you must recognize that this is the call of Satan. Whether figuratively or literally, in daily gossip or political rhetoric, violence against innocence is the sign of citizenship in the kingdom of darkness. Don't answer that call!

"Now, for the news. *The Last of the Mohicans* at the Adirondack Opera has closed. It was a success, if you can call good attendance a success. The owner of the Manhattan Opera, J. Holmes Chapman, is deceased. His wife, Helen, is worshipping here with us this afternoon. I would like to say personally, I hope that Helen and I might develop a friendship now that these horrific events are history."

Helen's eyes and Leona's met in confirmation of growing warmth between them. Leona continued to speak to the assembly. "It turns out that both the FBI and the NYPD had been investigating *Cultus Satanas*. Its international leader, Renard Maletesto, has gone missing. A manhunt continues. The individual known as Magua, both in the opera and in real life, has been apprehended by Detective Evans and a government agent who will remain nameless. Mister Evans is sitting today in the front pew, alongside that nameless colleague in the FBI. Magua is now behind bars awaiting trial for terrorism.

"I think those of us assembled here should be proud of the work of our own Sheriff of Warren County, Arthur Bolton, who spearheaded the investigation and resolution of this enigmatic case. Sheriff, would you kindly stand?"

Once the applause had subsided, Leona slowly raised her right hand to make the sign of the cross and announced, "we open our worship in the name of the Father, the Son, and the Holy Spirit. Amen."

The liturgy progressed with ease and fluidity, the music effortlessly uniting the congregation. Luciano Silvestri offered a solo, Albert Hay Malotte's setting of the Lord's Prayer. Just prior to the Lord's Supper, Leona invited the clergy to join her at the altar. She invited everyone in the pews to place one hand on a shoulder in front and the other hand on a shoulder next to them. Soon, everyone present was in physical contact with at least two other people.

Leona lit a single candle situated in the middle of the altar, on the very spot little Sarai had died. Then, in a loud voice, she said: "I rededicate this altar to the one and true God, the holy one, our creator, redeemer, and sanctifier. And I hereby rename Sarai, Sarah. 'sarah' connotes triumph, victory for God's people. In God's eyes this little princess is a blessing, not a curse." The pastor followed with a voiced prayer:

O Master, Lord our God, we beseech you who are merciful and understanding of our own sinfulness: hearken to the prayer of your servants gathered here today. Your holy altar and this sanctuary have been defiled by sacrilege and your eternal light has been temporarily overcome by darkness. Redeem this place just as you have redeemed this world. Draw light out of darkness, life out of death, faith out of doubt, compassion out of passion, and communion out of competition. For you are our sanctification, and to you do we send up glory to the Father, and to the Son, and to the Holy Spirit, now and ever and unto the ages of ages. Amen.

CHAPTER 98

Following worship, Leona invited all in attendance to immediately join her at the parsonage for coffee, tea, and cookies. She slipped out the sacristy door so she could greet everyone as they arrived at the manse veranda.

Members of the press sought individual interviews with Leona, the principal figure of the day, but she courteously agreed to take them only after the group's dispersal. So the reporters interviewed random worshippers to get their man-on-the-street takes.

In the midst of the hubbub, Leona found herself standing next to Luciano Silvestri. Midnight was quietly purring in her left arm while her right hand held a coffee cup. She spoke. "Luciano, your rendition of the Lord's Prayer this afternoon was magnificent. I know this has been hard for you. But I'm genuinely grateful. When you sang a few moments ago, *Thine is the kingdom, and the power, and the glory*, it was in honor of the true God of grace. I had goose bumps, Luciano."

The soloist lifted his cup to take a sip, an action that bought him a reflective moment. "You know that church people are hypocrites, Pastor, don't you?"

"Well, yes, many are, but hypocrisy is not exclusive to Christians, you know. Almost all humans, at some time or other, exhibit false virtue whether they are Christians or not. Many people live most of their lives as hypocrites, never knowing how sanctimonious they are," Leona retorted with a slight frustration in her voice, tired of hearing this over-used stereotype. At the same time, she realized this accusation was central to the satanic rhetoric. She made the statement anyway.

"The Satanists are not hypocrites. They're really good people. The Manhattan Opera coven even operates a charity program. They gather clothes for the homeless. They raise money to buy medicines to fight malaria and AIDS in Africa. This is more than many churches do. Most importantly, they fight for justice on behalf of the poor against the rich."

"Luciano," Leona responded slowly. "I think you have a compassionate heart. Do you feel it's important to give clothes to the homeless, medicine to those who need it, and justice to the poor?"

"Of course, I do."

"Think about what you're saying right now, Luciano. Do you truly think that churches do nothing for the poor and homeless, and only the coven does? The coven recruiters are appealing to these compassionate motivations in you. If a Satanist would come up to you and say, 'let's go out and sin,' you'd say 'no,' right?"

Luciano nodded affirmatively.

"So, these coven recruiters know how to talk to you, how to persuade you. But, Luciano, it's all a lie. The Devil is the Father of Lies, and the Devil's disciples lie too. Just say 'no'!"

"Pastor, it's so hard. I really want what Lilian Serano and Juliet Johns have. I really really really want this." He paused, then placed his coffee cup on the table. "I've got to go now. Thanks for trying to help, Pastor Lee." At that he turned to walk toward his car.

"Wait just a moment," insisted Leona. She dropped the cat and ran into the parsonage. A moment later she returned carrying a ceramic cross. She handed it to Luciano. "Would you take this as a gift?"

"Sure," he said, with a mixture of reluctance and gratitude. "Thanks."

"Please keep this cross. When you're alone, put it where you can see it. Then pray. This cross will remind you that God loves you, even when you're having a bad day."

"Okay. I'll do just that. Good-bye." Luciano walked toward his car.

"One more thing," Lee hollered. Luciano turned to listen. "I hope I never see your name on an opera play bill."